THE ONES WE KEEP

THE ONES WE KEEP

BOBBIE JEAN HUFF

Published by Sourcebooks Landmark, an imprint of Sourcebooks
P.O. Box 4410, Naperville, Illinois 60567-4410
(630) 961-3900
sourcebooks.com

Library of Congress Cataloging-in-Publication Data

Names: Huff, Bobbie Jean, author.
Title: The ones we keep / Bobbie Jean Huff.
Other titles: Children's corner
Description: Naperville, Illinois : Sourcebooks Landmark, [2021]
Identifiers: LCCN 2020056402 (print) | LCCN 2020056403 (ebook) | (trade paperback) | (epub)
Classification: LCC PS3608.U349664 C48 2021 (print) | LCC PS3608.U349664 (ebook) | DDC 813/.6--dc23
LC record available at https://lccn.loc.gov/2020056402
LC ebook record available at https://lccn.loc.gov/2020056403

Printed and bound in Canada.
MBP 10 9 8 7 6 5 4 3 2 1

for Tony

prologue

2002

It's threatening rain, but she never minds about the weather. Mostly she walks just before dinner, but today, because Alex is bringing his daughter for her lesson, Olivia decides to go earlier. Grabbing an umbrella, she lets herself out the door and sets off as she usually does—walking, walking—faster and faster.

I have three children, she says out loud. *Three children.* She repeats the phrase over and over, the beat taken up by her feet pounding the hard earth—one, two, three. The woods are silent, as they often are on hot summer afternoons. All she can hear are her footsteps and the murmur of waves lapping against the rocky shore. She rounds one bend and then another, until the path narrows and she reaches *the* bend, where she stops, gazing across the lake to the resort on the opposite shore. Today there's no one in sight.

The rumble of thunder that began when she left home is getting louder. A bird along the shoreline gives a plaintive cry.

Olivia doesn't linger; she never stays long. It's enough that she comes every day, as she has for years. It's enough. After a final look at the deserted dock, the motionless trees and dark water, she turns back.

PART ONE

one

1971

To begin, there's the heat. The heat of New Jersey in August, the heat of the car, the heat of restless children packed in the back.

"When will we be there?"

"I'm hungry."

"Mom! He's looking at me!"

Olivia sits behind the wheel of their blue Valiant, her straight, black hair blowing over the back of her seat where it will, she knows, get a tug from Andrew.

"Let me know when you want me to drive," Harry says, sliding his favorite Janis Joplin cassette into the tape deck.

"I'm fine. Relax. Take a nap." She doesn't mind driving. She's barely left New Jersey since Brian was born, and that was—wow!—nine whole years ago.

Outside Albany they stop at a roadside café for lunch. At his own table sits a cigar store Indian in full regalia. Andrew spots him, and even though he recently turned four, he begins to scream. Which means that Olivia has to hold *him* rather than Rory, who frets at the injustice. Only Brian manages to behave himself, eating his fries one by one, instead of by the handful, and drinking, not blowing, through his straw.

Harry takes the wheel after lunch, and an hour later they begin their ascent into the mountains, which are wreathed in mist. The air has cooled; the children have fallen asleep. *Too bad,* Olivia thinks mournfully as the peaks emerge suddenly from the fog and then disappear just as quickly. They'll be up until all hours.

She slides back her seat and closes her eyes. Now that Harry has been made partner, life is about to change. By Christmas they'll be living in the New York brownstone they closed on earlier this week, with space for Olivia's mother's grand piano—in storage these past ten years—and a room on the third floor for an au pair.

She envisions striding along Bleecker Street on Christmas Eve, past the grocery stores with their trees piled on the sidewalk, past Faicco's (*only in New York, a store that sells only pork!*), past the cheese shops and pastry shops and other amenities that she left behind after Juilliard. *No one should be required to live in New Jersey,* Harry's brother, James, has always said from his apartment on East Forty-Third, where from his toilet seat he can just make out a sliver of the UN building. Olivia is inclined to agree.

"We're here," Harry says, and Olivia opens her eyes.

They're traveling along a broad gravel drive. To their right is the lake and, around a sharp curve, a three-story timber building:

the main lodge. Behind it, a manicured lawn extends to the base of a hill, dotted with eight or ten cabins.

An elderly man in a white uniform appears and guides them into a parking space beyond the boathouse. He speaks into a walkie-talkie, and within seconds they are joined by two young men who relieve them of their luggage and usher them to their quarters—a four-room cabin plus bath.

Once inside, Brian spots the bunk beds and stakes his claim. "I guess I should have the top, since I'm the oldest," he says while placing his dinosaur bag on top of the pillow, at which point Andrew bursts into tears and Rory shouts, "Cookie! Cookie!"

"I feel like an impostor," Olivia says to Harry after she's given Rory an animal cracker and settled him in the playpen that's been set up in the living room. "I'm afraid to go to sleep, in case this is all a dream."

Harry hands her a glass of wine from the bottle that was left for them in the tiny fridge. "Get used to it," he says, rolling up his sleeves to run a bath for Brian and Andrew. "This is just the beginning."

She sinks into one of the two sofas that flank the stone fireplace and looks around the room. Logs on the hearth, a basket of kindling in the corner, a built-in bookcase along one wall. From the sofa she can see that, along with the usual vacation mysteries and sci-fi, there are a number of recent novels. She smiles at the thought of evenings spent beside the fire reading.

Through the diamond-paned windows she can see the birch trees that surround the cabin, with their graceful branches and peeling, silvery trunks, and it occurs to her that she is—perhaps for the first time in her life—completely happy. If she were granted three wishes, she wouldn't be able to come up with one. Except, perhaps, that her mother had lived to see her now, happily married after all, and with three lovely boys.

"More! More!" Rory shouts from the playpen. Olivia pulls three more animal crackers from her bag and passes them over, feeling only slightly guilty. Each cracker will buy her precisely two minutes of quiet. She knows; she's counted out the seconds.

Closing her eyes, she visualizes her mother's face, not as it was just before she died but further back in time—long after she had been widowed, but before she'd lost her looks to alcohol. During the period of Olivia's engagement to Harry.

She had almost refused the present her mother had offered, the Constable that had been in her family for generations. "This isn't for your living room wall," Eleanor had said. "You can find something at Bloomingdale's for that. This goes straight into the bank until you need to sell it. *If* you need to sell it." She paused. "Consider it your security. Your ticket out."

She held out the painting, which she hadn't even bothered to wrap. Olivia was tempted to bang her over the head with it. Instead, she asked coldly, "My ticket out of what?"

But Eleanor refused the bait. After lighting a cigarette, she added, "I'll send you a check later in the week to cover the insurance."

Her mother was angry at her daughter's impending marriage, that much was clear. Olivia wasn't sure if her objection had to do with her choice of groom—or if it was because she assumed the marriage was the reason for Olivia's revised career plan. "I've decided to teach music," Olivia had informed her days before. "Not perform it."

What Olivia failed to mention was that, the previous week, her piano teacher had stated quite matter-of-factly (as Olivia's dreams of Carnegie Hall hit the ground) that although she was technically adequate, she lacked passion.

"You don't soar," he'd said simply. Olivia wondered why after four long years of study she was hearing this for the first time. If she hadn't felt so humiliated, she might have been able to tell her mother, who had pinned her hopes on an illustrious career for her daughter.

Nonetheless, Olivia knew instantly what her teacher's comment implied. Only a tiny minority of graduates became star soloists like Itzhak Perlman or Van Cliburn. If there was to be any performance in her life after graduation, it would undoubtedly be with a local orchestra or, God forbid, as an accompanist to popular community theater productions like *The Sound of Music* or *Fiddler on the Roof*. They were always advertising for amateur musicians.

This moment—with her mother holding out her generous gift—might have been the time to admit all of this. But she couldn't, she just couldn't. Instead she took the Constable and said, with a sweep of her hand, "Could you please not smoke in my house." And after carefully leaning the painting against the wall, she changed the subject. "Why don't you like Harry?"

Eleanor thought for a moment.

"Harry's an architect," she finally said. "An artist. He's driven to design buildings and other spaces. *Driven.* You can hear the passion in his voice when he talks about it. I can't see that he will make you happy. Men like that—" She shrugged, allowing Olivia to fill in the blank.

"You criticize me for not being driven, and Harry for being exactly that! Anyway, I don't need anyone else to make me happy." Which wasn't strictly true.

Eleanor switched gears, inflicting more pain: "Those who can't do, teach."

Contrary to her mother's wishes, Olivia hung the gilt-framed painting in her bedroom. Now the first thing she sees each morning is the boy leaning over the wall with his fishing pole, the trees that meet in an arch above the canal, the rambling red-roofed houses, the man with his pole in the stern of a boat, a patch of gray sky. All of it in muted colors, like a Japanese painting, but luminescent nonetheless. *Beautiful,* Olivia thinks when she wakes, wondering how her mother, in getting it so right, had managed to get it so wrong.

"Shall we go down to supper?" Harry asks, pulling Olivia out of her trance. He's holding a stack of resort brochures. "It says here that Saturday night is pizza night."

"The kids'll love that."

The next morning Olivia and Harry and the boys change into bathing suits and walk down to the lake. A lifeguard is seated in a raised wooden chair at the edge of the dock. Behind him an older couple apply sunscreen to each other's back. When they've finished, they descend the wooden ladder that's attached to the dock and back slowly into the water. Olivia hands out beach towels and, pulling two kiddy inner tubes from her carryall, passes them to Harry, who removes one of the plastic plugs, takes a deep breath, and blows.

The shallow area is between the water's edge and the dock. Olivia holds Rory out so that his little feet dangle in the cold water. He screams and twists his body to get away.

"Look, Rory," Olivia says, laughing. "See Mommy do it." With one hand she splashes water on her own legs. Then she bends him forward, and, after a moment's hesitation, he begins to splash his hands and chortle in ecstasy.

Behind her, Harry is fastening Brian into the box swing hanging from a branch of a large tree that's bent over the water. When he's done, he pulls Brian back as far as he can, then lets him go to sail out over the lake. Each time he returns, Harry gives him a push.

Andrew, whom Harry has promised can go next, is seated cross-legged in the shallows, pouring water from one pail to another while he waits his turn.

Harry comes over to Olivia. "I can do that," he says, reaching for Rory. "I'll take it from here. Why don't you go for a swim or spread your towel out and catch some rays?"

Needing no further persuasion, she grabs her towel and takes it to the dock, where she spreads it out and, not bothering to put sunscreen on her face, lies down and closes her eyes. The sound of the waves lapping against the shore, the murmur of the old couple in the water, Andrew exclaiming over something he's found, all combine to induce a feeling of tranquility. Why can't it always be like this?

She must have fallen asleep, because the next thing she knows Harry is running his hand over her head.

"It's almost noon."

She sits up and blinks. Thrown over his father's shoulder, Rory sleeps. Brian and Andrew, wrapped in dripping towels, loom over her.

"Come on, Mom."

"Yeah, Mom. C'mon."

Over lunch Harry says, "I thought I might teach Brian to play tennis this afternoon."

Olivia reaches for a napkin and dunks it in her glass of water before wiping macaroni and cheese off Rory's face. "That's good. He could use some time away from his brothers."

But back in the cabin, Andrew begins to fuss. "Why can't I go? I can play tennis!"

"You can help me get Rory down for a nap," Olivia says. "If you help me with Rory, I'll help you color."

An hour later they're seated on the floor of the living room, a coloring book between them. When she's finished with Cinderella's ball gown, Olivia sits back to observe this child who always seems to get lost in the general cacophony of family life. He's too young for Brian and too old for Rory. Until now, she's never really noticed how focused and methodical he can be, carefully replacing each crayon, right side up, in the box before removing the next one. He even manages to stay within the lines. As he concentrates, his tongue pokes out the side of his mouth and he scrunches his eyes and forehead into a frown, which makes him appear more like a gnome than a child of four.

His personality is still a mystery. He seems almost unformed, compared with his brothers. But this afternoon has shown Olivia that he blooms when he's given some one-on-one time. How could it have taken her four years to figure that out?

With Rory and Brian, love came easily. Not so with Andrew. Olivia suspects this was because he was born six weeks early. Seconds after his birth and without her even being allowed to hold him, he was whisked away to the NICU on another floor. Despite her protests, she wasn't allowed to see him for two whole days. By the time he was finally placed in her arms, she'd convinced herself that he'd died and they were afraid to tell her. Even after she was persuaded otherwise, she couldn't help but feel that he belonged not to her but to someone else—some other woman, a stranger who'd decided she didn't want her baby after all.

But she loves Andrew now, of course she does. Her attachment to him just took a bit longer than it did with the others. People who claim to love all their children equally are merely lying to themselves. Each child is different. Rory is an easygoing, laid-back boy who doesn't demand much, other than that he be fed on time and allowed plenty of sleep. Brian is much more solitary, not often willing to share his feelings. As heavily defended, Harry once observed, as his mother. And Olivia has to admit that it's true. When she was a child she would never allow herself to show her feelings for anything or anybody, convinced as she was that the object of her desire would be denied her, merely because she desired it.

When did that start? she wonders, passing Andrew a green crayon for the leaves, at the same time recalling the first big upsetting thing that had happened to her, when she was six. They still lived in England; her mother was pregnant and convinced it was a boy. Each morning at breakfast Eleanor would take Olivia's hand and let her feel how the baby was growing. "He's yours," she would whisper in her ear. "Your own little brother." And Olivia believed her. One day Eleanor bought Olivia a baby doll and a small toy carriage, and as they walked together to the shops, Eleanor showed Olivia how to gently tip the carriage onto its back wheels and up over the curb so her baby doll wouldn't get hurt. "Soon you'll be pushing your little brother," she would say.

When Eleanor went into the hospital, Olivia stayed with her grandmother. "Did my baby come yet?" she'd ask her granny every day, but her grandmother always seemed to want to talk about something else. After what seemed like a long time, Olivia's father came to take her home. When Olivia asked, "Did my baby come yet?" he replied, "There is no baby, Liv. The baby died."

At home, Olivia bolted from the car and ran into the house and upstairs to her parents' bedroom. Eleanor was lying on her side, facing the window. As she'd done every day for months,

Olivia reached over to touch her mother's stomach, but to her shock, Eleanor slapped it away. Then she turned to face her daughter and said, "It's expectations that get you into trouble, Olivia. Remember that. No expectations, no disappointment."

"Look, Mom!" Andrews says, pulling Olivia from her reverie. He points to the cloud he'd just very carefully colored purple. "There's lightning in there. You can't see it, but it's there! There's going to be a storm. See? See?"

Olivia points to the horse-drawn carriage Cinderella will presumably be getting into and asks, "What color should we make that?"

"Gold!" He reaches for a yellow crayon.

"Of course!"

When she was pregnant with Brian, she thought she was prepared for motherhood—for stopping work for two months, for feeding another person from her own body, for constantly having to wipe a dirty bottom, for not getting enough time for herself, and for never, ever getting enough sleep. What she wasn't prepared for was the love. Often the joy she feels when she's with her children is so intense it's almost painful, and, fearing that misfortune will rain down upon her and her family because of it, she turns away from them.

After dinner Olivia takes the children to the dock while Harry wanders over to the tennis court in the hope of lining up some games for the days ahead. The sun has disappeared behind a mountain; a nearly full moon hangs in the sky. Olivia sits on the dock in the half-light with Rory in her lap, his hand gripping a clump of Indian paintbrush he'd picked on the way down from the cabin, while Brian and Andrew attempt to skip pebbles across the water.

"Look, Mom, look!" Andrew says after he's thrown a stone in the water, not understanding how to make it skip but thinking that he has. Olivia is too preoccupied to compliment him. Rory has been straining to be off her lap, and she knows he'd be in the water in a flash if she let him go. She manages to distract him by pointing to a water-skier gliding behind a speedboat, its captain shouting back loud commands.

After a few moments, a woman of about Olivia's age and two little girls appear on the dock.

"All boys?" the woman asks, raising an eyebrow and smiling.

"Not for lack of trying!" Olivia shoots back. She fishes with one hand into her diaper bag for Rory's sippy cup.

"Your first time here?"

Olivia nods. Brian is still skipping stones, but Andrew has dropped his pebbles on the ground and is examining his left thumb, which she has been encouraging him not to suck.

"It's a great place. We drive all the way from Nebraska. Every single year."

Andrew's thumb makes its way into his mouth, and Rory's eyes are closing. Bedtime. She would like to chat with the woman, but there'll be plenty of time for that in the coming days. She stands and hoists Rory over her shoulder. His shorts are damp.

"Are there any other children here?" she asks as she reaches for Andrew's hand. "I promised them lots of friends."

"It's only ours, at the moment. It's still early in the season. After Saturday three large families are coming. Or so I'm told. Enjoy the peace and quiet while you can."

That night the children, exhausted from two swims in one day and an excess of ice cream after dinner, fall into bed early—even Brian, who often reads until late. Olivia follows shortly with an Agatha Christie she found on the bookshelf. But after a few moments her attention flags. She's tired. Too many characters have been gathered together in the drawing room; she can't keep track of them all.

When Harry comes in, she's nearly asleep. "Are you okay?" he says, hopping on one foot so he can remove the sock from the other.

"Just sleepy. Why?"

"You've seemed a little tense lately. I just wondered—" He shrugs.

"Harry, we have three children and a big move ahead of us. There's so much to think about, is it any wonder that I'm a little wound up?"

"Of course. Of course." He tosses his shirt on a chair and unzips his pants. "Anyhow, I was thinking that you might like to go off on your own tomorrow morning. Maybe explore the town. The brochure shows a quilt shop there, and a couple of craft places and a silversmith. That kind of thing."

Olivia is silent for a moment. He slides in beside her and turns off the light. Finally, she says, "Thank you."

"For what?"

"For agreeing to babysit for a few hours."

"For Chrissakes! It's not called babysitting when it's your own kids! Anyway, they offer childcare here, remember? Lots of activities for the kids. A small farm, in fact. There's pigs, even. You could go to town, and I could play tennis."

She smiles, considering, before she says, "I didn't come here to shop. What I'd really like to do is go for a hike. By myself. Those brochures you keep looking at show some trails that lead out of here. If I could get an early start—"

"Of course."

He reaches his arm over and pulls her close. "Liv," he whispers. He kisses her shoulder and then her back. She opens her eyes and watches him, watches the contours of his body, washed of color in the moonlight that's shining through the window. She feels his warmth as he moves above her. "Liv," he says again, groaning.

At midnight she's still awake, listening to the unfamiliar noises: the rustle of a breeze through the trees, a boat on the lake, its motor idling, and someone in a nearby cabin muttering loudly in his sleep.

"Harry," she whispers, but there's no response. Her thoughts circle back to New York. Maybe she'll find some friends there. Or at least *a* friend. As an only child, having arrived from England at the age of thirteen, with funny clothes and a funny accent, she had learned to be alone, but she often missed being part of a gang, especially when the girls in her class paired up and she was left on the sidelines, wishing she had the courage to share her intimate secrets—if only she had some. Her mother said if she weren't so intense, she'd have tons of friends, instead of just the one, Fran, the girl a year behind Olivia who lived next door. But as her father had always said, she had her music.

"Harry," she repeats, a little louder this time. Nothing. She turns on her side, away from the moonlight. Once they get to New York, she'll advertise for students. And maybe she'll look for a music group to play with. A chamber ensemble, perhaps, or a small orchestra. The good thing about Harry's promotion is that while his hours may increase, he won't be on the road so much. For the first time since they were married, they'll be able to make plans, with the reasonable expectation that…

Something makes an eerie laughing noise out over the lake, the sound echoing back to shore. A child in the next room kicks the wall. The earth falls away beneath her.

"It was a loon," says Harry, cutting into a waffle.

Olivia reaches for a napkin. "A loon! I thought it was a hyena. Don't hyenas laugh?"

"There *are* no hyenas in Vermont!"

They're in the dining room finishing breakfast. Harry looks at his watch. He's managed to line up two games, one with an old duffer who, rumor has it, had been a pro in his youth, the other with an accountant from Cleveland.

Despite her late night, Olivia had awakened early, slipped on her bathing suit, and gone down to the dock. The water was frigid, and she swam quickly out to the middle of the lake. When she swung back around, she could barely see through the mist, which lay thick along the ground, obscuring the dock, the trunks of the pine trees, and the first floor of the main lodge. Now, as she spoons cottage cheese into Rory's mouth, she's glad to see the sun pouring through the windows. After breakfast she's going for that hike. She wipes the baby's mouth with her napkin and, looking up, sees a young girl approaching the table.

"I'm Carla," the girl says, holding out her hand. "I'm told you need a sitter for the morning." She smiles at the boys. "Hey, guys. Would you like to see the ponies?"

With unaccustomed boldness, Andrew asks, "Can I ride them?"

"Of course! There's a pony in the barn, just for you. Are you finished with that waffle?" And she whisks the napkin out of Andrew's T-shirt, tosses it on the table, and reaches for Rory, who is too surprised to object.

Carla says to Olivia, "There's a packed lunch on the mantelpiece in your living room. Oh, and a map. There's no possible way you can get lost, as long as you keep to one of the three marked trails."

Harry looks at his watch and says, "I've got to dash. Enjoy your walk."

Olivia watches him depart, followed by Carla and the children, who in their excitement about the ponies seem to have forgotten their mother. Then, after a useless attempt to wipe jam from the arm of Rory's high chair, she walks back up the path to the cabin, which she spends a few moments tidying.

Rory has his own small bedroom, with a plain wooden dresser and a crib with balloons painted on its sides. Olivia picks his giraffe up off the floor and places it beside his pillow, where he can rub his nose against its neck. She smooths his yellow quilt. She can smell him; if she were led into the room blindfolded, she'd know it belonged to Rory. She's slightly hurt that he let her go so easily. He's never done that before. A tiny worry flickers at the back of Olivia's mind, but she banishes it. Worry will not be the price she will pay for happiness today.

In the older boys' room, red bunk beds and dressers line two walls. Along the third is a stack of shelves filled with paint sets and crayons and books and blocks and a box filled with colored pencils. Beneath the window are two small chairs and a table.

She pulls the coverlet over Andrew's bed and tucks his Mickey Mouse pajamas beneath his pillow, then stoops to retrieve the small square of fuzzy purple velvet he insists on carrying with him everywhere, one of the many pieces she cut from the much larger blanket he became attached to before his first birthday. She lays it across his pillow. He'll outgrow it; they all do. He just needs time. No eighteen-year-old carries around a small, fuzzy piece of material.

Brian's bed is unmade, his pajama bottoms thrown across the top railing. Before she leaves the room, she raises the shades. Then she goes into the master bedroom, where she grabs a sun hat and pulls a sweater from the closet. Tying its sleeves around her waist, she retrieves her promised lunch from the living room. The clock on the wall says it's just past ten. She tucks the lunch into her backpack and slides her arms through the straps. Then, consulting the map, she chooses the trail that appears to be the longest but least arduous of the three.

A moment later she's passed through the camp and reached the beginning of the trail, which she calculates will take her about two and a half hours. The mist has burned away, and the air is crisp and clean. She looks out over the lake. It's still, except for the motion of the water insects sculling its surface in the glittering light and one small boat containing an elderly fisherman hunched over his pole.

Two minutes later the resort is out of sight. Ahead, the trail wanders gently uphill, and Olivia's glad she's chosen the easier path. She doesn't feel energetic enough to tackle even the smallest of mountains today. An elderly couple—the same man and woman she noticed yesterday on the dock—smile as they pass, and farther along the trail a young man in cutoffs, tapping the ground in front of him with a stout stick, barks "Hello." At this end of the lake, the pines have given way to smaller trees and scrub, and through them she can see a clearing carpeted in wildflowers. *Daisies and buttercups and chicory,* Olivia rhymes off, and the lovely lavender fireweed, which, someone once explained, grows on the spot where forests and houses have burned. Nature's compensation, Olivia figures.

After a while the path takes a turn around a heavy stump bearing a metal triangular sign marked 7. She consults the map—she's come nearly halfway. The brush here is thick, the path narrow, and she frequently has to duck beneath the low-growing limbs of the conifers or push the branches from her face. The sun grows stronger as Olivia walks. It's becoming hot, and she's getting hungry. She wipes her face with her bandanna and peers through the scrubby brush to the lake. A short descent will put her on the wide, flat boulder she can see jutting out into the water. She makes her way down and out onto it, then shrugs off her pack and removes her lunch. After gobbling her sandwiches and drinking the iced tea, she crumples the wax paper and tucks it into the thermos. Then, drowsy from food and the heat, she lies back on the warm, flat rock and closes her eyes.

———

When she wakes, she sees that the sun has shifted to the mountain side of the trail. Olivia looks at her watch. It's after two thirty. She should have been back ages ago. Harry will be worried. She grabs her hat and, scrambling to her feet, slides her arms into her pack and climbs back up the embankment to the trail.

For the next three-quarters of an hour she keeps up a brisk pace. Finally, after passing marker number 13, she sees signs of civilization: a frame house, unpainted, a couple of outbuildings, and a little farther on, the rusted-out skeleton of a pickup truck. A few minutes later the trail takes a jog around an outcropping of rock, and just ahead—the relief of it!—is the driveway to the resort.

Walking toward her are two young girls, one of them bending toward her cupped hand. And then, as Olivia watches, a police cruiser pulls out of the resort driveway and turns onto the town road.

Of course. She's hours late. The police will have been notified. She begins to run, her pack swaying heavily from one shoulder to the other. When she is within a few yards of the girls, her toe hits a rock and she stumbles to the ground.

A patter of footsteps, and then a voice: "Are you okay?"

She's winded. She pulls one arm out of her pack and looks up. The girls are standing over her. The taller, in a flowered skirt and white T-shirt, is holding a lit joint in one hand and reaching out to Olivia with the other.

"The police!" Olivia gasps. Her right elbow hurts, and the palm of one hand is studded with gravel.

"Oh, that's just Homer," the girl says. "He doesn't mind, just as long as it isn't more than a couple of joints." She pauses for a moment. "He's been at the resort." She passes the joint to her friend, a pale, slight girl—a child, really—wearing threadbare shorts and a red baseball cap. "There was a drowning."

"At the resort?" Olivia swallows.

The girl nods. "Yeah. A little boy from New Jersey, Randy said. That's my boyfriend. He mows the lawns there." She waggles her fingers for the joint, saying, "Tracy!"

"Really sad," her friend says.

The girl in the skirt takes a long toke, holds it in, and while exhaling gasps, "Are you okay? Can we get some help?"

Olivia doesn't respond. The light falling through the trees has begun to shimmer. She blinks.

"Can you get up?"

They want to be on their way, smoking up without interference from her.

"I'm fine," Olivia says, struggling to her feet. "Thank you."

The girl in the flowery skirt looks at her friend and shrugs. "Well," she says. And then, to Olivia, "See you."

Olivia watches them depart, hears them snicker. A jay lights on a branch of the tree beside her, squawking angrily.

"Who?" she says to the jay, or to no one. "Which one?"

Her voice echoes back. The jay tilts its head, as if trying to understand, and, failing, gives up and swoops through the trees.

She turns and looks up the gravel drive. The pines at the spot where it curves around obscure all but the tip of the timber building, the main lodge where she and Harry and the boys had gathered for pizza that first night.

She has to go back. She has to walk up that driveway. She has to find out. She has to...

She tries, but her legs fail her. Both, it seems, are paralyzed. She takes a breath and tries again—and then again. Nothing. She can't move. *Walk*, she tells herself. She can feel the ticktock of her heart speed up, as if her future is rushing toward her and she is running out of time to change it, to undo whatever happened, to put her back on that rock beside the stream, that cabin where earlier she had smoothed Rory's quilt and replaced Andrew's purple blanket, that car where she had driven with her family two days before, that house in New Jersey where she had lived, innocent...

Walk. After several more attempts, she realizes that she can no more walk up that driveway than she can burst through the door of a burning building or hurl herself into the central vent of a volcano.

She looks back at the girls, who are disappearing into the distance, and shouts, "Wait!"

They turn.

"Is there a bus station? In town?"

"It's a few miles from here. But once you get there, it's just past the fire station. On Davenport Road."

For a moment Olivia remains there, on the path, so still that a chipmunk dares to dart in front of her, disappearing into a tangle of rotting branches that protrude from a deadfall lying beside the road. "Who was it?" she asks again, so quietly now that if anyone had been standing beside her, they wouldn't have heard. They wouldn't have even known she was speaking.

Seconds, hours later she glances back up at the sky, which is blue, still, but with a dull edging of gray. The color of the sky in her painting. The Constable.

She pulls on her backpack and begins to walk. When she passes the resort driveway, she doesn't falter.

No, she says—to herself, and to the universe—as she walks. *No. Do not scream. Do not cry. There will be time for that. For now, just wait.*

She walks for fifteen, twenty minutes without seeing a soul. But before the gravel road gives way to pavement, she catches sight of a young man just ahead who's wearing yellow ear protectors. He's standing by the side of the road pulling the starter cord of a chain saw in and out, in and out. Nothing happens. Finally, he disappears with it back into the bush. Olivia stops walking and waits. The chain saw chokes and sputters. "Fuck," the man shouts, which seems to do the trick, because she finally hears the chain saw's whine and, a moment after that, the sound of a limb crashing to the ground.

What if she were to walk over? He's just a few yards away, in among the trees. She could be there, waiting quietly, on the other side of the tree where he just felled it. What's to stop her?

She sinks to the ground. Leaning back against the trunk of a tree, she thinks, *I can't, I can't,* and finally she weeps, holding her palms against her face to keep her head from exploding. She sobs until she is weak with exhaustion. A car goes by and doesn't stop, and then another. Not too long from now it will be dusk, and then dark. She has to move. She has to keep walking. A distant dog barks steadily for a moment, stops, then starts again.

Maybe someone will see her; maybe they will stop and offer help. Perhaps they will even, somehow, save her. That's what she needs—it's the only thing she needs. To be saved.

She remains on the ground, her face wet with tears, her nose steadily running. Lying back in the dirt, she wipes her cheeks and her nose with the back of her hand. Even though she has stopped crying, there are little choking noises coming from within her chest. She gazes up at the sky, trying to breathe normally. A plane, high overhead, silently passes behind a cloud and reappears on the other side. A couple of broad-winged birds circle, making screeching noises. They must see something; there must be something in the bush that is tempting them, something nearby, some dead rotting piece of…

No, Olivia says again, hoping that if she says it often enough the universe will change its mind and return things as they were. It was such a short time ago—surely it wouldn't be difficult. She once read an article about time, which isn't, as she'd thought, linear but instead circles back on itself. Wouldn't it then be possible that she could one day find herself back at home with her family, making dinner or playing the piano or reading to her children—all three of them—completely unaware of the disaster that had struck one summer afternoon and torn her family's life in two?

The bus station, she thinks. *I must get to the bus station.*

She slowly rises to her feet, as steadily as she can. *The bus station. Don't think about Harry, don't think about the boys. Think about the bus.*

She's back on the road, which is straight now, and at the end of it, when it turns into Davenport Road, will be the bus station. That's what the girl said, the girl with the baseball cap and the alabaster skin and dark, almost black hair. *Think about that girl.*

"I am walking," Olivia says and begins to count her steps. One, two, three, four. But here it comes again, building up in her chest. How many sobs are allotted to each person during a lifetime?

Five, six, seven, eight.

Think about something else. Think about anything. Think about your mother.

She says the word mother, and suddenly she's back at Eleanor's funeral, sitting in the church hall surrounded by her mother's so-called friends, who, with their white handkerchiefs and tears, hadn't actually been part of her life for years, friends who had in fact dropped her because she drank too much. Too many vodka tonics, the only thing that alleviated her sorrow after her husband—Olivia's father—had gone.

What number is she at now? Never mind; she'll start again. One, two, three, four.

Up ahead is a smattering of buildings and cars, and a few people walking along the sidewalk. She must be nearly there. Brian suddenly pops into her mind. Wasn't there a movie called *Brian's Song*? Or was it *Somebody Else's Song*? James Caan played him in whatever the movie was called. Or was it that other actor she has always mixed up with James Caan, that short one with the gravelly voice? Harry would know; he remembers things like that.

She's so tired, she would like to drop back to the ground and sleep. She doesn't need a bed, just a horizontal surface. Up ahead there's a man coming out of the Grand Union. He walks to his car, but before he unlocks the door, he turns to look at Olivia. Why is he staring at her? She's just walking along the road, like anyone else. He should mind his own business.

She must have walked miles by now. Her feet are blistered, which is good. She'll focus on them. The blisters. They're a blessing.

But there, crossing the street and walking toward her, is a cop. "Do you need some help?" he asks Olivia, but she walks around and past him. She could have said "No, thanks," but she chose not to. There is nothing he can do for her—even if he is a cop. He should mind his own business, too.

One, two, three, four, and there, finally ahead of her, is a large, concrete building. It must be the bus station. That's what she wanted, isn't it? That's what she intended. But why? *Why the bus station?* She can't remember. She starts to cry again. *Go back,* Olivia says to herself. *Go back, starting with the cop, and you'll figure it out.*

So, the cop. And before that, the blisters on her feet. Then the man coming out of the Grand Union. And before that, the gravelly voiced actor, followed by *Brian's Song* and *Somebody Else's Song*. Was that the correct order? Those last two should be reversed, but no matter. Then Brian, of course, and then—vodka tonics? And her mother's funeral, with the handkerchief ladies and their tears. The broad-winged birds, circling overhead. The airplane behind its cloud. The chain-saw guy.

The blue jay. *No.*

Hang on. She's nearly there.

The girl with the alabaster skin and the baseball cap, Olivia thinks in a rush, even though she doesn't want to. Even though she wants, most awfully, not to. And then the other girl with the floral skirt and the joint between her fingers.

And? Before that?

No.

The sign on the front of the building says, simply, Bus Station. She likes that. Nothing more is needed, and nothing less. And here's the door, and people are coming out through it. She doesn't even have to push it open.

two

1971

He hadn't wanted to be left with that babysitter after breakfast, even though he pretended not to mind. She was too jolly when there wasn't any reason to be. She didn't know them, had never met them, but when his parents left, she acted as if they were all best friends—Carla, Brian, Andrew, and Rory.

She'd taken them down to the lake to the spot she called "The Shallows." The water there wasn't more than a foot deep unless you walked out really far, which you couldn't actually do because of the orange rope strung between two buoys that had a sign on it saying You Are Not Permitted Past This Point.

Brian was insulted. He had learned to swim when he was six and had no interest in paddling and splashing with Rory and Andrew. He'd have loved to go around to the other side of the boathouse where there was a dock he could jump off—the dock his mother had taken them out on the night before. Beside the walkway to that dock was a big tree with a knotted rope tied to it.

You could grab on to that rope and swing out over the water. He so much wanted to try it out. It would have been a lot more fun than that swing his father had attached him to the previous day.

But he and Andrew removed their shorts as instructed—they had bathing suits on underneath—and Carla took Rory's off as well. And there in The Shallows they played, with the buckets and spades and silly-looking inflated animals Carla had brought with her, while she sat cross-legged in her jeans at the edge of the water, getting her bottom wet. Beside her sat Rory, laughing and patting the surface of the water, hard, so that it splashed his brothers' faces.

After a long while there was a whistle and Carla said it was time to go. The waterfront would be closed, she said, until after lunch. Instead of returning to the cabin, she made good on her earlier promise and walked them over to the miniature farm behind the main lodge. There was a small red barn that stood in the middle of a muddy ring, and the whole thing was surrounded by a white fence. Carla, with Rory slung over her hip, ushered Andrew and Brian through the gate, up the path, and into the barn. A teenage boy, sitting on a bench between the two pony stalls, was smoking a cigarette. He stood up and greeted Carla with a kiss.

"So who's riding the pony today?" the boy asked, and Andrew jumped up and screamed, "Me, me, me, me!"

"How about you?" Carla asked Brian, who shook his head. The pony being led out of the stall was hardly bigger than his friend Ben's German shepherd. He'd feel pretty silly perched on its back. Now if there was a real horse on offer...

The boy lifted Andrew into the air and placed him on the saddle and, holding him fast, slid his feet into tiny stirrups and secured the rest of him with leather straps. Then he guided him out into the field and proceeded to walk him in circles around the ring.

Brian, already regretting his decision, watched from the gate. He would have loved, after all, to be sitting on the animal, provided he didn't have to be led around like a baby. He liked the way the pony smelled. It was a combination of grass and sun and something he remembered from way back, before he was even in school. The smell of the inside of a robin's egg, that's what it was. He'd found it between the branches of a hedge.

Andrew, whooping it up in the small saddle, was clearly having the time of his life, while Carla, still holding Rory, accompanied the pony boy round and round. Brian scowled and scuffed the toes of his shoes, one by one, in the dirt. He felt like an outsider. He *was* an outsider. Whatever their intentions, they had made him feel like a bad sport.

After a while another whistle blew, and the boy led the pony, with Andrew still mounted on it, back to the tiny barn.

"Lunchtime," Carla said, pushing open the gate. "Your parents will be in the dining room."

But when they arrived, only their father was at the table. Carla got Rory seated in the high chair he had used at breakfast, and Harry passed the two older boys plates of sandwiches. "Where's Mom?" Brian asked.

Harry tied a napkin around Rory's neck. "She'll be back soon. She's taking an extra long walk today."

He turned toward Carla. "I have another game at one. Are you free to stay with them in the cabin if my wife hasn't returned? Rory needs his nap."

Carla hesitated. "Sure. But I was supposed to get together with my friend this afternoon. Would it be all right if he came up to the cabin? We could look after the kids together."

Before Harry left for his game, the boys and Carla went back up the hill to the cabin. Carla lifted a protesting Rory into his crib with his blanket and closed the door. She turned to Andrew and Brian and said, "You boys can play in your room for a while. When Rory wakes up, we'll go back down to the water."

Andrew said, "I want to go now. *Now!*"

Carla produced a bag of chocolate-covered marshmallows from her pack and, waving it in front of them, said, "If you stay quietly in your room until Rory wakes up, you and Brian can share this whole bag of marshmallows. Then we'll go down to the water."

Andrew sat on the lower bunk, twirling his purple blanket between his thumb and forefinger. Brian climbed the ladder to the top bunk and, lying flat, stared up at the ceiling, which like the rest of the cabin was made of unfinished wooden boards. A little black spider was crawling across one of those boards. Brian gritted his teeth and tried, unsuccessfully, to think about chocolate-covered marshmallows. Instead, he thought about the spider. What was to stop it, only inches from his head, from letting out its silken cord and dropping onto his face?

He shut his eyes, tight, so he wouldn't have to see it. After a long while he fell asleep. When he woke, it was to the sound of the bedroom door being thrown open. Carla came into the room, and behind her was the boy from the little farm, the pony boy. He was scowling.

"Where's Andrew?" Carla asked.

three

1971

Inside the bus station she catches sight of herself in a wall of mirrored glass. The rubber band she had used to hold back her hair for the hike has fallen off, and clumps of wet, unbrushed strands hang around her shoulders. She's hot and bright red, and rivulets of sweat are running down her neck. No wonder the people she passed on the sidewalk had stared.

At the ticket counter she joins a short line. When it's her turn she shrugs off her backpack and, while the lady at the ticket counter waits, tapping her fingers on the counter, Olivia unzips the various pockets until she locates her wallet. It contains only two fives and one lone credit card.

"Can I help you?" A clipped, impatient voice. The woman is glaring at her.

"Can you just hold on a sec?"

"Where do you want to go?"

"I thought—"

"Portland," the woman barks. "Bangor, Albany, Woodstock, Middlebury, New York City."

Why can't she think?

But New York, of course. That was the plan.

Her ticket finally in hand, she studies the board. There's a full two hours to wait. Arrival time: four in the morning. Taking a seat at the back of the waiting room, as far from the door as she can get, she closes her eyes and dozes off.

She comes to when she's jostled by a man settling into the seat beside her. The station is filling with people. A few are standing in front of a television screen that's mounted high on the wall, and everyone's eyes are riveted. What are they watching? Olivia holds her breath. Has it got something to do with what happened earlier today, just a few miles from here?

"*Apollo 15*," the man beside her says. The screen is filled with clouds, advancing and receding and advancing again, and then, in the distance, a tiny black speck, getting larger and larger. The camera recording the historic moment jerks this way and that. Suddenly the speck becomes two parachutes that open, and the moment after that the whole station claps as what the narrator calls the command module falls into the water.

"Three parachutes were meant to open," Olivia's seatmate says. "But there are only two."

"—appears to be all right," the narrator is saying in excited tones, "—hasn't turned over."

Was it supposed to turn over so the astronauts could extricate themselves? Olivia watches, spellbound, as the module bobs up and down. How ironic if, after the flight all the way to the moon and back, the astronauts, supposedly safe now on their own planet, were to perish as the world watched.

Her eyes fill with tears. *If I am to do this,* she tells herself, *I must numb myself. That is my task, my only task: to numb myself while I wait.*

"They're fine," says the man beside her, holding out a tissue.

Wait for what?

"They're safe. Wouldn't it be funny if—" But she's stopped listening to him. When a voice over the loudspeaker announces the Middlebury bus, he reaches for his bag and gets up.

"You take care of yourself," he says. A few minutes later, buses to Bennington and to Manchester, New Hampshire, are called. Olivia consults her watch. It's nearly four thirty.

She hasn't had anything to eat since the sandwich she'd had on that rock. In a corner of the terminal is a coffee bar with a few small tables. She walks over and orders a Coke and a bowl of tomato soup. Pulling her credit card from the side pocket of her backpack, she offers it to the woman behind the register.

"Plastic for $1.08?"

She looks helplessly at the woman, who accepts the card and runs it. Olivia's hesitant to let the two fives go. Ten dollars cash leaves very little margin for error, at least until she gets home, where, under her jewelry box, the one Harry gave her when he asked her to marry him—*Oh, pray that it's still there*—is the five hundred dollars they keep for emergencies. Still, without a plan, she has no idea how much money she will need and when, and the credit card is risky. She could be traced. Even now, she thinks, glancing at the entrance to the station, as if someone might burst through the door looking for the lady who just ordered a bowl of tomato soup.

She carries the tray to a table under the window. Through it she can see an old man seated on a bench. He has something in a paper bag, which he drops in bits onto the pavement, and greedy pigeons peck it up. When he's finished, he crumples the bag and tosses it on the ground. Then he yawns and, reaching into his pocket, pulls out a cigarette. He bends forward to light it, inhales deeply, leans back against the bench, and gazes over at the station.

Olivia draws back, not wanting to be seen watching. Instead she sits, letting her soup grow cold, as people move in and out of the waiting room before boarding their buses. When the bus to New York City is called, she's the first on, choosing a window seat at the very back. The driver swings into his seat and maneuvers the bus into the road with a screech of metal.

It begins to rain, softly at first, then harder. Water streams down the windows, blurring the tiny towns they pass through, each with its white painted church and town square. It's as if the artist, upon completing his work, had taken his thumb and drawn it across the scene, rubbing it back and forth until what was left wasn't the thing itself but the suggestion of it.

By the time they pull onto the highway, the rain is teeming down, flooding the road and the green fields, pouring off the branches of trees. Olivia stares through the window until it grows dark and the cars speeding toward them on the other side of the median are replaced by the reflection of a stranger in a sun hat.

Perhaps there is a place where you can run from your family and friends with impunity—a strange and wonderful place where the point isn't to love and be loved so hard that, if something happens, you can die of the wounds that love has inflicted. The point, Olivia thinks as she begins to nod off, is something quite different, although at the moment she can't imagine what it might be.

At Woodstock she's awakened by a tall young man in a raincoat taking the seat beside her. It's nearly two thirty in the morning. She smiles briefly, then closes her eyes again and finds herself being swallowed by a whirling blackness until she, too, is whirling, whirling, away from the day and everything that has happened. When the bus finally pulls into Port Authority, her cheeks are wet. She's been crying again but has no memory of it. She glances at her seatmate, who is studying her face. She holds his eyes for a moment, then reaches under the seat for her backpack. When the doors open the young man steps into the aisle, allowing her to proceed.

"Is there someone meeting you?" he asks, and when she doesn't respond, he says, "Take care of yourself, hear?" echoing the words of the man in the bus station.

The heat rushes to envelop her as she steps off the bus and into the station: New York City in August. Fatigue assails her as she makes her way up the escalator and takes her place in the line that snakes out of the door of the ladies' room. Once inside, she notices two women, each with a shopping cart overflowing with plastic bags and tattered blankets. One of the two is squatting beside her cart in the corner at the end of a bank of toilets, fanning herself with the torn-out section of a magazine. The other is at one of the sinks splashing water into her armpits.

After using the toilet, Olivia takes her own place beside the woman at the sinks. Pulling a comb from her backpack, she drags it through her hair, knotting it in a roll at the back. Then she washes her face with cold water and blots it with a paper towel. She's feeling slightly light-headed, from heat or hunger or just plain fatigue.

The woman beside her buttons her shirt, then wheels her cart back to the corner opposite where the other woman is squatting. Are they friends? It doesn't appear that way, although they are of similar age and equally decrepit. Olivia remembers reading about them recently, the women who inhabit that bathroom. The article said there was no official attempt to oust them. Olivia was surprised to read that, and glad. She can't imagine what their lives must be like, other than the obvious—that they each must have left a situation more untenable than the Port Authority ladies' room.

At a bakery on the main concourse she picks at a bagel and downs a cup of lukewarm coffee. Then she joins the line to buy a ticket for a bus she barely has time to catch. A little more than an hour later she's pulling up to the house in a cab. Leaving the backpack, she asks the cabbie to wait, she won't be long.

It's eight thirty in the morning by the time she stumbles up the walkway to the front door, where she removes a key from beneath a pot of wilting geraniums. But before inserting it in the lock she stops, imagining for a moment that they are all there, in their beds, asleep. It is, oddly, an easy thing to believe.

Turning the key, she pushes open the door and goes straight upstairs. Without even glancing into her children's bedrooms, she enters her own. And there it is, hanging on the wall opposite the bed. The boy leaning over the wall. The trees. The red-roofed houses. The man in the boat. The water and the gray sky.

She lifts the picture from the bottom to judge its weight. It's surprisingly light. Removing it carefully from the wall, she carries it down to the kitchen, where she places it on the counter while she rummages in the cabinet for paper bags and scissors and tape. When her task is complete, she carries the wrapped painting to the front hallway and sets it beside the door.

Then she returns upstairs and, barely allowing herself to breathe, enters each of her children's rooms. In Brian's she grabs his Cub Scout hat from the top of his dresser. From Andrew's room she takes a small piece of his purple fuzzy blanket. And from Rory's little bed, his nylon bear, the one he wouldn't stop screaming for when he spied it on a shelf in Kresge's. She runs her hand over his pillow. Perhaps she will curl up in his bed, just for a minute. She draws the quilt back and pulls it over herself.

When, exactly, had it happened? While she was walking along the path through the trees, thinking about how happy she was, how her life seemed, all of a sudden, to have achieved perfection—or the closest thing to it? Did it happen when she was eating her sandwiches, drinking her cold tea? Or lying asleep on the flat rock beneath the sun, as if she hadn't a care in the world, as if she alone had been singled out—by God or fate or good fortune—for a future untouched by grief or blame or loss?

And how? How had it happened? Was he—her nameless, dead child—left alone in the cabin? Did he slip out the door and walk by himself to the lake? Was he in the water with the other children, playing with the plastic toys and attended to by a lifeguard who in a split second—while he bent to scratch his ankle, perhaps, or turned to greet the pretty girl he was hooking up with after work—failed to notice when a small boy slipped beneath the surface of the water and didn't come up?

If some god—or evil force—had chosen that particular ending for her son, he couldn't have accomplished it more brilliantly. Olivia thinks about the various components that needed to be assembled in order to achieve the goal, to deprive a child of his life. There was the timing of her own walk, which was of course dependent on the weather. There were the choices, by the resort, of that particular babysitter and that particular lifeguard. There was the timing of the tennis match between Harry and the accountant from Cleveland—and Olivia could only imagine his story. Perhaps he could only play at ten because his wife was wanting him to accompany her to the little tea shop in town where she'd spotted, the previous day, the most precious china dog…

She stares up at the ceiling. If she stays here long enough, if she remains in this bed and in this house, she will eventually find out what happened—and who it happened to. She remembers her Sunday school teacher saying once, "You're only given what you can bear." At the time, Olivia had believed it. But now she knows how wrong her teacher was. Sometimes you are given more than you can bear—and if you are, can you be faulted for taking the only course of action that you can see? For trying to save yourself, the only way you know how?

Couldn't a tragic death be so life-wrenching, so cataclysmic, that the manifestations of ordinary grief—if any grief could be called ordinary—are unavailable or impossible?

In the street a car door slams, and, a moment after that, the doorbell rings. *The cabbie*, Olivia thinks, and, throwing the quilt aside, she opens a window and shouts down. Then she goes back to her own room, where she pulls a large suitcase from the closet, and after filling it with as many of her clothes as she can, she stuffs in the three items belonging to her children. She feels beneath the jewelry box on her dresser and finds—with relief—five one-hundred-dollar bills. Moments later she's back in the cab. As the cabbie pulls out of the driveway and proceeds down the street, Olivia closes her eyes tight, to keep herself from looking back at her receding life.

Back at Port Authority the crowds stream around her. *Move.* Someone elbows her impatiently in the shoulder. *Move!* She's standing, frozen, in the huge hall of a major transportation hub with a pack on her back, a suitcase in one hand, and in the other, a painting by one of the most famous English artists of all time. And she has no clue what to do next.

Her brain is addled with heat and hunger and lack of sleep. But of course, she remembers it now. The Metropolitan Museum of Art. That was the point of retrieving the painting. But her immediate concern is—or should be—finding a place to stay. Somewhere to wash, somewhere to change her clothes. A place to sleep. She can't go to the Met looking like this; they wouldn't let her in the door.

She takes a seat on a bench beside a man with snow-white hair tied back in a ponytail while she tries to plan her course of action. When he gets up to leave, she picks up the month-old *Village Voice* he's left behind. On the front is a picture of Jim Morrison, who had died in a bathtub in Paris of a heroin overdose. She flicks through the pages. At the back of the paper are the rentals. One jumps out at her, a studio in the West Village for $120 a month. She can afford that, she's sure of it, because of the painting. If it's still available.

She casts the paper aside. *One step at a time,* she tells herself, mother and child at the same time. She needn't figure all of this out now. She might not be able to commit to an apartment, but a night in a hotel—just the one night? She can manage that. She stands, adjusts her pack, picks up the suitcase and painting, and goes back outside, where she flags a cab and asks to be taken to a hotel—any hotel. Moments later she's deposited on the street in front of the Chelsea, where, weighed down by her possessions and exhausted, she struggles into the lobby.

There's a room on the fourth floor. "Home of the famous," the concierge says as he hands over the key to her room. Did she know that? She did not. She's to be sharing a balcony with Dylan Thomas, he says—or would be, of course, if he hadn't... He fails to finish the sentence. Perhaps he's been told not to use the word "died" when addressing the clientele.

A bellboy reaches for the painting, which Olivia relinquishes only because she's too tired to explain her reluctance. *That will probably be the most expensive item you ever carry in your lifetime,* she thinks as she follows him. In the elevator on the way up, and then along the long corridor, the man keeps up a steady monologue. She only half listens, catching names that might have impressed the old Olivia but that hold no interest for the new. The Grateful Dead in the room beneath Olivia's. Down the hall, Sid Vicious and his girlfriend, whom he stabbed in the bathroom. Janis Joplin and Leonard Cohen, sharing a room only because Cohen failed to locate Brigitte Bardot, with whom he'd had an assignation, and Janis couldn't find Kris Kristofferson, ditto. The bellboy is well versed in these details. Probably bored with them by now. But, Olivia thinks, it's probably a selling point to offer the room where Dylan Thomas, his best days behind him, lay in bed drinking himself to death. "And death shall have no dominion," she recalls, from one of his more famous poems. But death obviously did.

The room is small but adequate, with a double bed, a chest of drawers, and a desk. A TV stands in the corner. Olivia covers it with a towel. She won't listen to the news or watch TV, nor will she buy a newspaper—not for a long time. She knows that, realistically, the city—with its shootings, drugs, fires, gangs, break-ins, and what have yous—couldn't care less about minor incidents that occur in small, bucolic towns hours away. Still, she won't take the chance.

In the bathroom she washes her face and combs her hair. Then she goes out in search of food. There's a Spanish restaurant below the lobby, where she orders paella to take back to her room, consuming it cross-legged on her bed while perusing a pamphlet about the services the Chelsea has to offer.

It's noon by the time she unpacks her few possessions and places them in a drawer. Then she lies down on top of the bedspread and, clutching the Scout hat, the teddy bear, and the purple blanket in her arms, she falls asleep.

One day goes by, then another, then two more before Olivia gathers up the courage to bring the painting to the Met. She spends most of those days in bed, venturing out only to scrounge for food to bring back to her room. Each morning she buys two packets of Twinkies and a large coffee from the deli up the block; every evening she eats paella from the same restaurant below the lobby.

On the fourth day she wakes early. The sky is gray and it's

drizzling, and although last night she'd decided that this would be the day, she has serious doubts. If she had covered the painting with plastic there'd be no problem, but what if the paper wrapping soaked through? There'd be justice in that, she decides, though not sure exactly how or why.

One step, she thinks, the phrase now shortened to an easily repeated mantra. *One step. One step.*

It helps.

She ventures out into the street. The sky is clearing. She buys her Twinkies and coffee, brings them back to her room, and, before climbing back into bed to eat and drink, removes the painting from the closet and lays it across the top of the chest of drawers. Loosening the tape, she draws the paper back.

As a child, she'd wondered about the boy. Who was he? What did he do when he finally caught his fish—bring it home for his mother to cook for dinner? She'd imagined him seated on a bench around a bare wooden table with five or ten siblings as their mother carried the fish to the table. His father wasn't present—perhaps he was dead or gone to sea. The family bowed their heads in prayer before...

She loves the picture and will miss it. But it has always reminded her of how angry she had been at her mother for insinuating that it could offer her a way out of a tricky situation.

After all, her mother was right.

She pulls the paper back over the picture and flattens the tape. Then, recognizing the moment, she abandons the Twinkies and coffee on the bedside table and leaves the room with the painting.

Outside, she balks at the idea of spending her money on a cab, but really, who takes an authentic John Constable on the number 6 train? A crazy lady, that's who.

After the Met, the cabbie drops her at the deli, where she buys a sandwich. Then she walks around the block to the park. It's nearly two; the lunch crowd has dissipated, and the few benches near the entrance of the park are empty. The heat that had earlier been blown away by the rain has returned. Puddles of water steam beside the walkways. Olivia selects a bench, unwraps her sandwich, and eats it quickly.

Away from the museum, she's left with an array of confusing impressions. Pity, in the eyes of the young woman she had been led to by the uniformed man in the atrium. Obvious skepticism, from the older woman that first woman had summoned. And then disbelief, after Olivia removed the wrapping from the painting, having been instructed that only she could do that. Suddenly there were more people in the room, men this time.

Almost as if Olivia weren't there, they talked among themselves. One person kept remarking on the sky in the painting, which was just a small patch, not even blue, but a muddy gray, with a few yellowish clouds off to one side. Someone else mentioned a financial slowdown in September. And the response from someone else: "But it's not September yet, is it?"

Finally, one of the men turned to Olivia and said, "How did you come by this?"

"It was my mother's. Her mother—my grandmother—bought it from—"

"Do you remember when?"

She shook her head. "I don't. I don't remember. It always seemed to be there, hanging in—" She had been about to say "the living room" but was sure he wouldn't care about that.

"I don't remember," she repeated.

Someone mentioned the word "authentication," and the process was explained to Olivia. The museum had to send a letter to the appropriate agency in the presumed country of origin, and if they didn't hear back within forty-five days that there was some kind of problem—

"Problem?"

One of the men said patiently, "A problem with authentication."

"But—"

The young woman chimed in, "It's standard procedure. There are fakers who are so good—"

"*Original* fakers," the older woman interrupted, making air quotes around the word "original."

"—that you can only spot it with an X-ray. That's because an original faker can't rid himself of his own personal style."

"It's not a fake," Olivia stated flatly, but of course everyone pretended not to hear.

"How long will it take?" she asked as everyone stood. The meeting was obviously over.

The young man, who had been silent until then, said, "Forty-five days, tops. Or maybe earlier, depending. That would be—let me see—sometime in early October."

Before leaving the Met, she entered the gift shop and bought a small box of botanical note cards and a pen. As she headed for the park, she tried to construct in her head the letter she would send to Harry.

Early October! Olivia thinks now as she crumbles her sandwich wrapper and tosses it into a trash can. An unfathomably long period of time, considering she has no place to go and nothing to do.

She unwraps the box of note cards, removes the first one, and sits, thinking. After a moment she looks up. A drunken or drugged young man has staggered over to take a seat on the bench opposite. The guy is staring at her and shaking his head slowly from side to side, as if she had asked him the reason for her existence and he was trying to convey to her that there was none. Olivia stares back hard until he is cowed. He gets up from his bench and lurches off.

What should I say? she wonders. *What can I say that will ease this, other than the truth, which will certainly not ease anything for anybody.* Still, the truth is all she has, and so she must say it. She uncaps the pen, finally, and writes, "I am sorry. I have gone away and I won't be back. Please do not try to find me. I'm sorry." She inserts the card into its envelope and thinks. Is this all she can come up with, after eleven years of marriage, three children, and a whole lot of love? There must be more. There must be a better, kinder explanation. She removes the card from its envelope and sits with it. After a while, she gives up and writes, at the bottom of the card, "Love, Olivia," puts the card back in, and seals the envelope.

She leans back and closes her eyes. The thrum of a bass from someone's car makes an alternating rushing and receding noise, and as it does, *they* suddenly appear, the boys in the back seat, she and Harry in the front, winding their way through the Green Mountains at dusk, as they did only a few nights before. She blinks and they're still there, a phosphene and she knows it, but still. She looks hard at them, knowing it will probably be her last look.

four

1971

Brian is seated on the couch in the living room when Harry arrives home from work. He hears the key turn, the door open, and the usual few steps to the hall closet where his father drops his briefcase and calls out a predictable "Hello?" with a rising final syllable, as if his remaining family might have disappeared since he left that morning.

Toni and Rory are in the kitchen, Rory screaming "Up!" as he always does when he catches sight of his father coming into the room. Toni's making dinner.

Or, at least, Brian assumes she's making dinner. He stays out of the kitchen and away from Toni as much as possible, but he can smell garlic and onions and meat frying. It's manicotti, probably, or maybe lasagna. Toni only does a few dishes, and they're always Italian.

Brian considers, then rejects turning on the television. That will only draw his father's attention to the fact that, yes, Brian is still avoiding being in the same room as Toni, which pretty well means he's avoiding all human contact—at least at home—since his dad and Rory invariably gravitate to wherever Toni is. She's only been their housekeeper a few weeks, and already she's been accepted as part of the family.

It's as if, when his mother vacated her space, Toni stepped in to fill it—Toni with her tiny red dresses and long, pointy fingernails and heels so high Brian is amazed she manages to stay aloft. And to make things worse, his father installed her in Andrew's room, which now smells of hair spray and jasmine incense. And Shalimar, the very same perfume his mother wore. *How could she?*

On one side of the fireplace is the piano. The music stand still holds the last piece Brian had learned, the last piece his mother had taught him. He hasn't touched the piano since that day, and he has no intention of going near it again. He knows that if he ever hears that piece again, something inside him will probably burst.

Still, he insists the music remain there and doesn't allow Toni to touch it when she's dusting. It's the one thing that hasn't changed since that day, the one piece of evidence—the only piece of evidence—that he once had a mother who loved him enough to shout from the kitchen, "F-sharp, buddy!" when he hit an F-natural by mistake.

He can hear the voices in the kitchen now: Harry's deep baritone, Toni's light laugh, and Rory's hungry whimpers. Sometimes, when he presses his palms lightly against his ears, he can imagine it's his parents talking, his mother beside the stove stirring something—not Italian—while his father, having poured himself a Scotch, perches on the step stool to talk about his day in the city.

That scene is one of the many that made up what was once an ordinary day. Brian wishes he could turn back the clock. Instead, he had taken it for granted. If he ever woke up and found that the whole thing—his brother's death and his mother's disappearance—had been a dream, he'd never take anything—not even the tiniest or most boring of moments—for granted again. Not in his whole life.

His father finally comes into the room. "Hey, Brian," he says, and Brian can tell from his tone of voice how worried his father is about him.

If only Brian could, somehow, help. If only he could force his dad's attention on something that didn't make him seem so sad and anxious, some minor, fixable problem, perhaps, that could permit him to smile the way he used to when he came home from work.

"Hey, Dad," Brian responds.

"Dinner in ten."

"I'm not hungry."

Harry stands beside the sofa, his hands in his pockets, regarding his son. "You can't not eat."

"I hate her food."

Rory, wearing only a yellow T-shirt, runs into the room screaming, "Dada! Me up!"

Harry grabs him and deposits him on the sofa beside Brian,

then turns on the TV. Rory falls silent at the sight of a straw-hatted farmer with a pitchfork being chased off a cliff by a contingent of angry mice.

"Toni's going out tonight," Harry says. "I thought maybe we could make hot fudge sundaes. Play a few games of Hearts." He raises his eyebrows at Brian.

"That sounds good, Dad. Let me know when she's gone."

In an exasperated voice, Harry says, "*Her* name is Toni."

Brian leaves his brother on the couch sucking his thumb and goes upstairs. The first door off the hallway is his parents' large bedroom. His father usually keeps the door locked now, but Brian often checks it, and sometimes he finds it open. This morning his father must have forgotten to lock it, because the door is standing slightly ajar. Brian quietly lets himself in.

The bed is, as it's been since his mother's departure, neatly made, the white bedspread pulled up tight to just below the pillows, the comforter folded across the bottom. Brian bends over the pillow and inhales deeply. He can still smell his mother's lavender night cream, though he expects that will fade. Across the top of the pillow lies one long black hair. He won't remove it.

He stands beside the bed listening to the ticking of the gold clock on his mother's nightstand. Beside the clock is the book she was presumably reading before they left for Vermont, John Updike's *Rabbit Run*. Opposite the bed is the spot where the painting had hung. Brian used to come in on weekend mornings when his mother was still in bed and stare at it. His mother said it was painted over one hundred years ago, but the boy with the fishing pole could have been any one of Brian's friends. He wonders, every time he sees the gap in the wall, why his mother took the painting. She knew how much Brian liked it.

His parents each had their own closet, and Brian opens his mother's. Hanging on the inside of the door are the many scarves she liked to wear, long frothy things that, when wrapped around her neck, floated behind her back. Brian catches one up in his palm, a narrow band of cloth patterned with alternating lines of pink and purple flowers. He presses it to his face. It smells of nothing more than clean silk. There is a hook for Olivia's three belts, all present and accounted for, and the peg she hung her headbands on. Brian's favorite is an inch-wide loop of elastic onto which are sewn tiny blue and white beads. Olivia wore it stretched around her forehead, and, with her straight black hair, she resembled a princess.

She didn't take her headbands with her when she came for the painting, and some of her clothes still remain in the closet. As far as Brian can tell, she abandoned most of her possessions. He can't conceive of doing such a thing. When he thinks about her, which is all the time, he imagines her in an empty room somewhere, anywhere in the world, with nothing but an old painting to show for her former life.

Before he leaves the room he notices the window seat. The long cushion his dad removed when they got home from Vermont is still on the floor, and on top of it lie a pillow and his father's army surplus sleeping bag. Brian wonders, as he always does when he comes into the room, why his father has never returned to the bed.

He closes the door and crosses the hall to his own room. It's perfectly neat. Before, it had been a mess, a major point of contention between him and his mother. The day after Andrew's funeral, Brian tidied it. Now there's no clutter, no mess anywhere, nothing out of place. On the bedside table is a lamp, a box of Kleenex—its edges perfectly aligned with the table corner—and a pristine Superman comic book underneath the Kleenex, read every night and then replaced. On the other side of the room below the window, the top of the small wooden desk is bare. The quilt that Olivia stitched together one winter, of blue and white patches—blue because it's Brian's favorite color—lies folded into a tight rectangle at the bottom of the bed.

His mother would be proud of him.

He removes his shoes and, placing them side by side beneath the bedside table, lies down. On the ceiling above him his mother had, a lifetime ago, painted, freehand, one hundred gold five-pointed stars. He remembers the day she did it and smiles.

He can recall everything that happened that day, up until the moment Carla and the pony boy burst into his bedroom. But for some reason, everything from that point on is fuzzy and kind of mixed up, like a dream. Some things he thinks happened maybe didn't, and vice versa.

He has questions, but he doesn't have the heart—or the courage—to ask his father. Or maybe he's just afraid of the answers he might receive. Did Andrew try to wake him before he left the room? How did his brother leave the cabin without anyone knowing, and what were Carla and the pony boy doing when he pushed open the door and went outside? Where was his mother when Carla and the pony boy and Brian and Rory and their dad went down to the dock, where Andrew, surrounded by a small crowd of people, lay flat on his back, staring up at the sky? When Carla was crouched beside the boathouse sobbing quietly, was Rory still in her lap, or had his dad taken him from her? When the police arrived, why did they keep asking questions, the same questions, over and over again? Did anyone supply them with the answers? And who was it—when Brian had his hands over his eyes—who kept repeating, "Does the mother know? Does the mother know? *Where is the mother?*"

Of course, that's what *he* wants to know, too. *Where is his mother?* He asked his father only once, when they were driving home from Vermont, and his father had just replied, "No one knows yet, Bri."

"Is she dead?" he asked, because he thought she must be. Either that, or she'd fallen ill somewhere—or gotten hurt. She'd have never left them if she was still alive.

His father looked at him, then, even though they were speeding down the I-95 in traffic. Brian was terrified—not of the traffic, but of his father's possible response.

"No," his dad said, quite emphatically. "She's definitely not dead!"

As they entered Montclair, Brian couldn't help wondering whether his mother would be home when they got there. He couldn't imagine her not being *somewhere* in the house. Maybe she was in the kitchen, making dinner. He was hungry. He hoped it was hamburgers.

But when they went inside, the house was silent, in a way it had never been when his mother was there. His father came into the room and settled Rory in his high chair. He opened the fridge, stood in front of it for a long minute, and then sighed. When he turned around, Brian could see the tears in his eyes.

That was when Brian got it, finally. She was gone.

Every time Brian thinks of it, he's aware that things might have turned out differently if he hadn't fallen asleep that day. And that he wouldn't have fallen asleep if he hadn't closed his eyes. And that he wouldn't have closed his eyes if it hadn't been for that spider; he would have read his book instead, the one he'd brought with him to the resort, the one his mother had given to him about the children who went through the wardrobe and ended up in a magical kingdom.

Whatever the answers to his questions are, he knows he can't change a thing, can't go back and make things right. But maybe he'll at least be able to understand what it was that happened that day—which means he just might be able to stop lying awake every night wondering how it was that in the space of five short hours on a beautiful sunny summer day in Vermont, surrounded by every person in the world he loved and who loved him, his whole world could so thoroughly be smashed to pieces.

Harry appears at his bedroom door. "Toni's gone for the night, and Rory's in bed. It's just you and me, buddy."

Brian sits up. "What about dinner?"

"I made you grilled cheese and bacon."

In the kitchen he perches on a stool to eat his sandwich while his father does the dishes. The radio's on. A woman with a British accent is talking about a man who had hijacked a plane and parachuted out into a thunderstorm with the $200,000 ransom money he'd collected.

"They'll catch him." Harry squeezes more detergent into the sink. "They always catch them." He puts the bottle back on the windowsill.

"Dad?"

"Yup."

"Are you sure we can't go to New York?"

Harry turns to face his son and says, slowly, "I did explain, didn't I, that I thought that moving would mean too many changes all at once? For all of us?" He reaches for the colander, but before he turns back to the sink he says, "Anyway, your mother's the one who really wanted to move. I was okay with whatever." He pauses, then says, "We're happy here, aren't we? We're okay, right?"

There's a silence as Brian pulls bacon from his sandwich and places it carefully on the table beside his plate. "I'm a vegetarian now," he says.

"Okay." Harry turns on the faucet and runs water through the colander. "And, oh, by the way, what's going on with Ben these days? I haven't seen him around lately."

Brian licks his fingers and says, "Nothing. He's fine. We're working on our bird project together."

"That's good." Harry scrapes the inside of a pot. "Why don't I get you and Ben some tickets to see that magician who's coming to the high school next month? It might be fun."

"Maybe," Brian says, but, suddenly recalling the conversation he'd heard between his father and Toni the other night, he reddens. Toni had said, "I put a note from Brian's teacher on the counter. She says he needs help with his bird project. Apparently there's an odd number of students in the class this year, and he's without a partner."

Harry lets the water out of the sink and says, "Time for those sundaes." He pulls a bottle of Brown Cow from the cabinet and squirts a dollop of it into a small pot, which he places on the stove to heat. Brian gets the ice cream and maraschino cherries from the fridge. The only tricky moment comes when Brian says, "The whipped cream! We haven't got any whipped cream."

"Oh yes, we do," Harry says. "I saw some the other day on the top shelf."

Brian opens the fridge and pushes aside a large jar of mayonnaise. At the back is an unopened can of Reddi-wip.

It hits both of them at the same time: Olivia must have bought that Reddi-wip before she left, for some dessert she'd intended to make but never got around to.

Harry takes the can from Brian, who pretends he can't see the tears in his father's eyes. He yanks off the tab and shakes the can back and forth. "We'll just have a tiny bit each," he says. Squirting a small amount over each mound of ice cream and chocolate, he passes Brian his bowl and says, "If we go easy on it, this can will last a long time."

five

1971

By the time the note and check arrive at the North Port guesthouse where Olivia has been staying, she has almost lost hope. The sheer relief at depositing the money into her newly opened account is almost palpable. She imagined, before going into the bank, that she might be questioned about the enormously large sum, but if there was nothing else she learned during her short period in Vermont, it was that Vermonters mind their own business. The teller, after a slight fuss about Olivia's retaking her maiden name without the requisite documents, had a tight smile on her face, but she said nothing.

She leaves the bank and wanders across the street to a real estate office, photos of large clapboard houses papering its front window. She goes inside. Except for an older man who's sitting in a corner typing quickly with one finger, the office is empty. She walks over to his desk and waits. After what seems to be an eternity, he looks up and, appearing neither surprised nor apologetic, asks how he can help.

His name is Ed, he says, offering no last name. He motions her to a seat at the empty desk beside him, and, as she recites her few requirements (house on the lake not too far from North Port, within one to two miles of the resort), he appears mildly bored, drumming his fingers lightly on his desk. When she has finished he looks up, his brow furrowed, as if waiting for her to go on. But what more does he want? She's said all there is to say. Losing patience, she tosses the card with her guesthouse phone number on it into the wastebasket beside his desk and walks out of the building.

The day is freakishly hot for mid-September. For weeks Vermont has been caught up in a heat wave similar to midsummer Jersey boilers. The trees along the roadside are coated with dust; the sun beats down on the road, turning the pavement to melted tar. If Olivia were to close her eyes, she could easily imagine herself back in New Jersey, perhaps in Camden or even Trenton, with its summer smells of car exhaust and stink bugs and overflowing garbage cans left outside too long.

Turning the corner, she sees a Grand Union and, going inside, buys a carton of milk and a Hershey's Bar, which she devours quickly on the way out. She's lost weight in the past month; her clothes are hanging off her. On the way to the bank she'd caught sight of her reflection in a store window and, for a moment, failed to recognize herself. No wonder Ed didn't take her seriously. She resembles one of those unhoused women in the Port Authority ladies' room.

Fifteen minutes later she reaches the guesthouse, panting

slightly. The heat has exhausted her. Tears prick her eyes as she steps onto the porch, where several elderly women doze in wicker rockers. She has no idea what to do next. She will ask her landlady for a referral to another real estate office, if there happens to be more than one in the area, which is unlikely. But here she is now, her landlady, holding open the front door. Someone called Ed has just called. He will be picking her up in an hour to show her a property.

What the hell! She climbs the steps to her tiny, unventilated room at the top of the house. She's sure Ed had never listened to, much less taken in, what she told him. He'll probably show her a Victorian monstrosity in the middle of town, or a bungalow in one of those drab developments nowhere near the lake, much less the resort. Does it really matter, anyhow?

The feeling of loss and the yearning she has to remain in the area are what's keeping her going. But oh, the irony. Two months before, had she found herself alone in a stifling boardinghouse, she'd happily have left the place and the town and the whole godforsaken state, where the real estate agents are only marginally brighter than the metal Santas that, even in the summer, dot the roadside, pointing the way to Santa's Land.

Ed arrives exactly on time. Olivia instructs him to drive to the part of the lake that faces the resort. The trees have that bleached look they get before they start to turn. Nearly autumn here in the North Country, she thinks, closing her eyes and remembering other, happier autumns. Ed turns onto a dirt road, and a half mile up he slows the car and comes to a stop.

She opens her eyes. They are beside a lake. *The* lake. Across it is the resort. Olivia's heart picks up its pace. So he was listening, after all. Lighting a cigarette, he says, "If you want to get out and look around, I don't mind waiting a few minutes."

She pushes open the door and crosses the road. Visible through a break in a stand of dusty poplars and a few feet down an embankment is a small, sandy inlet. She scrambles down, then removes her sandals and steps out onto it. Cupping her eyes against the sun, she looks across the water. Just opposite is the main lodge and, to the left of it, the boathouse. On the other side of the boathouse is the dock. That must be the place where…

Whatever she does, she must not fall apart—not now, not here, and not in front of Ed the real estate agent.

She climbs back up the bank and, swallowing hard, gets back in the car. Without speaking, she catches Ed's eye and nods. Tossing his cigarette butt out the window, he turns on the ignition and they continue up the road. After a mile the road forks. Ed follows it to the left, and in another moment they are parked on a gravel turnaround beneath the trees. Ahead of them stand two white wooden buildings, side by side. The smaller one with the tiny belfry and frosted glass windows is—or was—a church.

"When you come to a fork in the road, take it," quips Ed predictably. He gets out of the car, and Olivia follows him up the path to the narrow porch of the larger building. Producing a key from a circle of twenty or thirty, he inserts it in the lock and pushes open the door.

It's basically one large room, with windows running along

the back, one small bathroom, and two very tiny rooms, closets almost, off the entryway. Stacks of desks covered in a thick layer of dust have been shoved into one corner, and on the spaces between three large windows, wooden chairs hang from pegs.

"A schoolhouse," Olivia says and walks over to a window. "It was a schoolhouse." What once would have been a lawn is now a tangle of thistle and chickweed, but there are some good sturdy maples along the perimeter of the property and, beyond them, a small forest of balsam and pine. Better yet, there isn't another house in sight.

She takes in the space. The floorboards are grimy and scarred, the walls gouged here and there. But replastering—if she were so inclined—and a coat of paint would fix that. The room is on the large side, well lit by its wall of windows.

"How much?" she asks, turning from the window. Ed, looking quite as bored as he had earlier, is examining his fingernails.

"How much?" she repeats.

He names a price that seems absurdly low.

"I'll take it. I'd like to move in tonight."

"Whoa!" He's obviously surprised. "There's a procedure you have to follow. First you make a formal offer to the town—a legal offer. It's the town of North Port that's selling. Then they hold a meeting to consider whatever it is you're offering. This process usually takes several weeks." He pauses, patting the pocket of his shirt and pulling out his cigarettes. Then he taps the pack against the side of one finger. "After that, they get back to you." Striking a match, he inhales deeply, then adds, unnecessarily, "These things take time."

Olivia says, "I'm offering full price. And my offer will expire at six o'clock tonight." And she walks past him and out the door.

They drive back to his office in silence. Olivia remains in the car while he phones whoever it is he thinks might allow her to bypass the formalities. Pulling her notepad and pen from her purse, she draws two columns, labeling them Things to Buy and Things to Do. When Ed finally appears, he has a small smile on his face.

"The paperwork won't be ready for a week, but yes, they'll let you move in tonight—provided you write a check for 20 percent. I'm guessing you don't have a car?"

"You guess right."

He offers to drop her back at the guesthouse to pack while he goes back to the office to write up the contract of sale.

"I don't have much stuff."

"No bed, then?"

She shakes her head.

"Not an air mattress, even? I think there's one in my basement—"

"I have a sleeping bag. It'll do for a while."

He drops her off. When he returns, they drive to the Grand Union, where she buys soap and a pocketknife and a broom and some groceries. It's nearly seven when they arrive back at the schoolhouse. Olivia refuses his offer to help her in with her few possessions. Wordless—but shaking his head—he unhooks the key from his chain and solemnly hands it over. Then he gets back in his car and drives away.

She drops everything, including her groceries, on the floor of the entryway. There's a mirror on the wall, and after examining her gaunt reflection in its wavy glass, she speaks to it, out loud: *I am a woman with three children.* The face in the mirror fails to respond.

She goes out the back door. There is plenty of room for a garden here, once she's cleared it, and lots of light and good dark earth. She makes a mental note to buy a spade, a fork, and some other gardening tools. She will make a start tomorrow, to prepare the soil for next spring's planting.

Between the church and the schoolhouse are a few overgrown shrubs. On its other side, and partly surrounded by an iron fence, is a small cemetery. Pulling apart two branches with her hands, Olivia steps through. There are perhaps forty or fifty graves here, some marked with monuments, many by nothing more than a simple cross. Within ten minutes she has read the inscriptions on all of them.

Most of the graves are those of soldiers who died in the Civil War, but there's one that marks the burial ground of seven (*seven!*) children of the Ward family. It stands beneath an oak tree, a lichen-encrusted obelisk engraved with the names and dates of each child. The three girls and four boys died within five years of one another. They were, in order of their deaths: Mabel, John, Ezra, Frances, Tom, Matthew, and Nancy. Olivia says each name slowly, out loud, trying to absorb the incredible fact that she is standing over what must be seven little bodies in seven little graves.

Finally, she turns back. The sun is setting, streaking the windows of her new home red. Inside she unpacks, placing her few possessions in the cubbyholes along the end wall, where the schoolchildren must once have kept their pencils and readers. When she's finished, she slices a piece of warm cheddar with her pocketknife and, chewing slowly, wanders through the place, taking stock. There are things she needs to buy, things she can't do without. Not many—a single bed, a small table, a comfortable chair. Mousetraps, she notes, are required. Soon she will need a woodstove. But there is electricity, and running water in the tiny bathroom.

It will do, she tells herself, as she unrolls her sleeping bag on the floor of the small room adjacent to the vestibule and begins to undress. It isn't much, but it will do.

six

1971

She's never lived alone. After high school she went straight to Juilliard, and at the end of her final year she married Harry. From time to time, when contemplating a future by herself, she has imagined a quiet, undemanding existence—the flip side of her actual life, during which she often has trouble finding the time to read a book or learn a whole piano sonata. Now she'll have all the time in the world. She'll be able to do anything she wants.

But that's just it, she thinks, as she wakes on that first morning in the schoolhouse, her back sore from the hours spent on the bare wooden floor. Apart from that one thing—the only thing she *cannot* have—there's nothing that she wants.

In the bathroom on the other side of the vestibule she splashes cold water on her face. Then she puts on the clothes she wore the day before and goes into the area in the corner of the main room that must once have been used as a small kitchen. On the counter is the remainder of the cheddar she'd eaten, and standing beside the window, she finishes it. The sun is up, but its rays haven't yet penetrated the treed back of the property, which is still in shadow, or the tangle of rugosa in the corner, its orange rosehips still clinging to their stems.

She drinks from a carton of orange juice, then takes pen and paper from her purse and goes outside. Two steps lead from the small porch to the ground, and she perches on the top one. On the paper she writes "kitchen sink." Beneath that, "stove." Then "fridge." For all of that, she will need to call someone—a plumber, obviously, for the sink, which could sit beneath the window on the bathroom-wall side of the room, between the fridge and stove. That way she'll be able to see outside when she's doing the dishes.

She has to find an appliance store, quickly. Only problem is, she has no phone and no car. "Car," she writes at the bottom, then crosses it off and writes it at the top, above "kitchen sink."

She goes back inside. Her head is muddled, probably from the bad sleep she had last night—and perhaps from the situation she finds herself in. She looks at her watch. It's ten to seven. She goes into the bedroom and lies back down on her sleeping bag. In ten minutes, Rory will be hollering from his crib for Harry, who will bring him back to fall asleep in their bed—Harry's bed. A few minutes after that, Harry will leave Rory to wake Andrew and Brian. At seven forty-five Harry will have had his toast and the boys will be sitting at the table, eating their cereal. Rory likes Rice Krispies, because of the noise it makes in his mouth. Brian likes Cheerios. And Andrew—he loves that disgusting chocolaty marshmallowy stuff, dry in his bowl.

Olivia closes her eyes. That's not how it will be today. That's not how it will ever be. Today there will be only two boys at the breakfast table. Instead of three bowls of cereal, two.

A ray of sunlight slants through the window, touching Olivia's forehead. She opens her eyes. The sun is fully up, the sky an empty, cerulean blue. It promises to be a beautiful day. *If I hadn't gone for that hike,* she thinks, *I wouldn't have lost one of my children. My child died because of me.* She says that out loud: *My child died because of me.* Then she pulls the sleeping bag over her head and, for the first time since that day at the lake, begins to scream.

That afternoon she sets out for town. It's as hot as it was the day before, and barely cooler on the shady side of the street. The odor of grease turns her stomach as she passes two burger places, both surrounded by pickup trucks. Beyond them is a furniture store, a large hardware store, and a place that sells only foam, for mattresses. Then there are two malls, none particularly busy, and finally, on the other side of the road, an automobile showroom. She pushes open the door and a half hour later drives off the lot in a rented black Camaro, with a promise from Gerry (a yellow smiley face stuck to his shirt pocket) that she will be able to pick up her VW Beetle a few days later.

She then heads to the appliance store on the other side of town and selects, in quick succession, stove, fridge, and sink.

Back at the schoolhouse, she resists the lure of the sleeping bag, instead pulling from a box the cleaning materials she'd purchased the previous evening. On her hands and knees with a bottle of Mr. Clean and a bucket, rhythmically scrubbing each floorboard, she recalls the bank teller's tight smile. In a small community like this, Olivia can imagine what might be said: *Did you hear about that crazy lady who lived in Gertie's boardinghouse and deposited a huge check in the bank?* Or: *She bought the old schoolhouse and moved in that very same night, even though there was nothing there but those old desks and chairs. Ed said she didn't even have a bed.* Or: *She might wear a wedding band on her finger, but that doesn't fool me. She's obviously on her own. Probably divorced, or a you-know-what.*

Olivia examines her gold band. She'd taken it off precisely three times since she was married, at the end of each of her pregnancies, when her hands swelled.

It slides off easily now. She shoves it into her jeans pocket and wipes the floor dry with newspaper. Then she stands up, empties the soapy water into the toilet, and goes outside, letting the door slam behind her. A crow, perched on the lower branch of a maple tree, shrieks and flies off.

Birds like shiny objects, she thinks, and taking the ring from her pocket, she slides it partway up the recently vacated branch, where it dangles in the sun, a now meaningless, glittering object.

That evening she walks to the same part of the lake Ed had driven her to the previous evening from where, dropping onto the sand, she could see the resort. It takes her just under twenty-five minutes. There's not a soul in sight. The lifeguard's chair has been overturned on the dock, and rubber tires have been stacked beside the boathouse, which is obviously closed up; Olivia can see the heavy chain hanging from its lock. The camp rowboat, usually tied to the dock, is gone. But of course, it's out of season now. The staff will have closed up and left shortly after the remaining families had gone home. But the place, at this distance, is basically as she remembers it. It wouldn't surprise her if someone were to run down the path to the dock and dive into the lake.

For some reason, her father has been in and out of her mind all day. Funny, because she can barely remember him. He died just after she started high school. He had jumped off the Fifty-Ninth Street Bridge and was discovered a week later, having drifted down the East River to Hunters Point, where he eventually got tangled up in the net of an illegal fisherman.

Told it was an accident, Olivia only learned the truth about her father's suicide weeks later when a boy in her class asked, "Why did your dad off himself?" Instead of denying it, Olivia told him to get lost; her father had died from a fall. But even as she said it, Olivia knew that what the boy had said was true, and when she confronted her mother later, Eleanor admitted it.

"Why?" Olivia asked, expecting to be told he'd had cancer or lost all their money. But "He was sad" was all Eleanor had offered. And then, looking her daughter in the eye: "Selfish and sad."

And even though Olivia was barely fifteen, she knew what her mother said couldn't possibly be right. Selfishness didn't enter into it. You had to be in unspeakable pain to end your life, and as she thinks about this now, looking across the lake, she knows that what she did was the near equivalent of her father's act. It was just another way of ending her life, and perhaps a more painful one, because even though she remembers her inability to walk back to the resort, how her feet wouldn't take her up the driveway, she knows she will always live with the guilt of her treacherous abandonment. A worthy punishment. She can never go back.

A few feet away a squirrel scampers up a tree, making her jump. A school of fish dart by; she watches their lovely silvery forms as they undulate their way to another part the lake. She wonders if they are going home, or whether the whole lake is their home.

She takes one last look at the lake. Maybe if she stares hard enough and long enough, she will be able to see herself and the boys as they were the night she brought them down to the dock, holding Rory in her arms while the two older boys skipped stones across the lake. Who's to say whether that can happen or not? There are things that go on in this universe that even the best minds are unable to understand or explain.

After a while, she scrambles back up the embankment and walks home. *I have three children,* she thinks and then says out loud.

She sits outside late one night with a mug of coffee. The heat wave has abated; it finally feels like autumn. The new stove is in, along with the fridge and kitchen sink. A brand-new hot water tank stands in the corner beside the bedroom door, and hot water gushes from kitchen and bathroom taps.

How do you uncreate a life?

On the surface, it doesn't seem that difficult. Because the geography is different, most of the old cues don't exist, or at least not the physical ones—except, that is, for the items she'd grabbed when she went back to the house to fetch the Constable. She has them now in the drawer beside her bed. She will leave them there until—well, until she no longer has to. If that day ever comes. Meanwhile, she won't look at them. They're just objects, after all.

But aside from the few clothes she brought with her, there's nothing to remind her of her old life—no people to care for, and no evidence that the ones she had cared for ever existed. All of the furniture and most of the other objects she's since collected—as few as they are—she's purchased new or secondhand.

The mental cues, though, are what bring her to her knees. Consisting, in her former life, of those small increments of time to which she had never placed any significance, they are those seemingly mundane moments that occur between other, presumably more important, day-defining events. It's those moments that undermine her efforts to move forward.

In her old life, they had often occurred in late afternoon, when she was by herself and outdoors, perhaps retrieving the cushions from the lawn chairs before a storm, or making a quick trip by herself to the shop around the corner while Harry and the boys were inside and not in need of anything from her. Unpinned, then, to the familiar, she would be struck by the fragility of her existence.

"Entre chien et loup," she once heard it called. That hour between dog and wolf. Here in Vermont she finds she hasn't left it behind. It often occurs when her dinner is in the oven and she has nothing particular to do.

The hour between dog and wolf. When she first heard it, she assumed it was a maxim meant to warn you against taking your happiness for granted. Now she knows it's more than that. The wolf can be tricked, he can be temporarily diverted or delayed, but however safe you believe you are, you have to know that he's always waiting to pounce.

Within weeks, she's acquired most of what she imagines she will ever need. Although the money she received for the Constable was unimaginably large, she has opted for frugality as a way of life. You can never anticipate what might come along down the road.

Nevertheless, the future is something she has gotten very good at *not* contemplating. Her only option is to exist—if exist she must, and she's not convinced that she must—in the here and now. No looking backward, no looking forward.

Somewhere along the line she lost or misplaced her watch, and she decides not to purchase another. She has no events to attend, no appointments to keep, no friends to meet. Nor will she succumb to a TV. She needs no reminders that the world she has so recently been a part of will continue to turn, blithely unaware of her griefs or concerns. She won't buy a calendar, not even at Christmas as she has always done, making an early December event of selecting the most sophisticated one she could find at MoMA, as she imagined the reactions of her friends coming upon it in her kitchen, pinned to the wall over the stainless-steel coffee maker that resembled the engine of a small European sports car.

When she first arrived at the schoolhouse, she ate her meals seated in one of those small desks with the connected chair, a piece of furniture so low to the ground that once in, she found it difficult to extricate herself from it. She set it beneath one of the windows that looked out onto the little cemetery. By early November, when the light had dwindled, she found herself staring out into the black night as she ate her solitary supper. That was too depressing, and she moved the desk to the space beside the fridge, positioning it so that it faced into the center of the room, below the overhead light.

If only they could see her now, she thinks one morning, imagining the long-ago students, somehow able to see, a hundred years into the future, an escapee mother in jeans and a sweatshirt crammed into one of their desks, eating toast and jam. It's absurd—she will have to go out and buy something.

But can you purchase a table and just one chair? Surely you can, but it would seem weird and pathetic. It has to be four chairs or, at the very least, two. The next day she drives to a secondhand furniture store and arrives back home with a dinette set: a square white-chrome-and-Formica table flecked with gold, and four matching chairs.

In mid-November she purchases a wood-burning stove. It snows the day the installer arrives—the first storm of the season. When she opens the door, he says, stamping snow from his boots, "And not a day too soon." He removes his gloves and, stretching out a large hand, introduces himself as Hans.

She holds open the door as he wheels the stove into the house on a dolly. She offers coffee, and he drinks it as he works, talking steadily and seemingly requiring no response to the few questions he asks.

He came to America from Holland as a small boy, thirty years before. "Just before the war." He reaches for a metal tool. "My parents called it the New World, as if, somehow, the old one had worn out." He glances briefly at Olivia. "Which in view of what was to come, I guess it had."

He extricates a tube of sealant from the pocket of his work apron and sets it on the windowsill. "My father works in a greenhouse. It was his trade in Holland, and it's his trade now." He fits the first piece of metal pipe into the hole in the ceiling. "He likes plants."

"Tulips," Olivia says, then cringes at the stereotype.

"Hmm." He steadies the pipe in one hand while applying epoxy with the other. "That and some other kinds." Smoothing his finger around the pipe, he says, "Where are you from? People think New York. City, that is, I guess from the way you speak."

"They're not far off." *Rumor mill confirmed.* "New Jersey."

"Ah." His movements are quick and graceful. Olivia stands beside the refrigerator watching, intrigued by his patience at the fiddly parts of the task.

He has a wife and five children, he mentions as he's finishing up. When Olivia hears this, she finds herself close to tears.

"My wife works at the library in the evenings." He picks up his tools and sets them beside the door. "Lara," he says.

"There's a library here? In North Port? Where is it?"

"Behind St. John's." He replaces some of his tools in the loops hanging from his carpenter's belt. When he's finished, he stands by the counter and writes up the bill. Handing it to her, he says, "You'll want a library card. There aren't any bookstores between here and Burlington." He pauses. "That is, if you read."

"I read."

After she hands him a check, he lights her first fire—pointing out exactly how much newspaper to crumple up in the firebox (*too little and the kindling won't catch, too much and it will smother*)—and how to cross the sticks, one over the other, to allow for proper air flow.

When he leaves, she curls up in an armchair. The fire crackles in the stove. Occasionally she feeds it another piece of wood. When it gets dark, she doesn't bother drawing the blinds, instead remaining in her chair, listening to the sputter of the logs, which emphasizes the silence she lives with every day.

Her thoughts are drawn back home. *Home.* When will she start thinking of Vermont as her home? She half expected, when she first came, that she would spend less and less time thinking of her family, but instead she finds herself thinking about them almost constantly. At any given moment, wherever she is, whatever she is doing, they are never away. She wonders whether it will remain the same over the course of her lifetime—however long that is.

After a while the fire dies down and the room grows cold. She fetches her bathrobe from the bedroom and, bringing it back to her chair, wraps it around her shoulders. She hasn't had any human contact in such a long time. She hasn't even read a book. She thinks about what Hans said about the library. Maybe she'll check it out.

Finally, she goes to the bedroom. Before she draws the curtains she looks out. The snow has continued to fall, steady and hard. She stands for a long while, watching it coat the lawn and the branches of the trees and the tops of the cemetery markers. Eventually, she gets into bed and reaches to turn out the light. Before she goes to sleep, she thinks about the white world she will face in the morning. But when she dreams, it's of Hans's slender fingers, his strong brown arms, his tranquil countenance, and the way he speaks, in such matter-of-fact tones, as if she were a normal woman who had moved into this tiny house in this isolated area for no other reason than that she'd discovered it when she vacationed here, decided she loved it, and decided to stay.

Over the next week the firewood Hans left for her dwindles to a few sticks, and she realizes she'll have to go for more. Perhaps she'll stop in at the library as well.

Late one afternoon, she drives into town. Wreaths of pine branches bolted to the telephone poles on Main Street are threaded with white lights, and ten spruce trees lining each side of the canal that bisects the town are lit and decorated. Shoppers, alone or with children, call out to one another. Above the din, Bing Crosby's signature song is blasted through the fire station sound system.

Her first Christmas by herself. As she parks the car she thinks about the dreams she's been having lately of past Christmases with her family—like the time Brian pulled the six-foot pine over on himself, and when Harry heard the shout and raced into the living room, he found the tree lying across the floor pulsing up and down as an unseen Brian laughed. And the Christmas two years ago when Olivia was huge with Rory, and Harry worked away in the kitchen, producing as good a Christmas dinner as she'd ever made. And last Christmas Eve, when Andrew wandered through the house after the party she and Harry had thrown, drinking the remainder of the eggnog people left in their glass cups and almost passing out.

Those dreams seemed more real to her than the day she faces when she finally wakes, and she realizes that her only hope of not lapsing into depression is to spring out of bed and throw herself into whatever tasks she has set herself the day before, however mundane. It's difficult to lapse into depression when you're scrubbing a floor or painting a wall. The hardest thing of all is to try not to remember.

An oxymoron, she thinks.

She elbows her way through the crowds rushing along the North Port sidewalks. No one smiles, no one nods. She might as well be invisible, as she buttons the top of her jacket against the cold wind. A few dry flakes of snow drift by.

The library is an unremarkable brick building with floor-to-ceiling windows, very modern, very out of place among the white colonials that predominate in the center of town. Olivia stands before it and takes a breath, then climbs the steps and pushes open the heavy wooden door.

Inside the entrance is a narrow hallway that opens out to a large space. "Community Room" reads the placard above the fireplace, in which a fire now blazes. A leather sofa and a couple of armchairs are positioned around it, and seated on the sofa are two exhausted-looking mothers, chatting above the noise of the three young children on the floor in front of them who, obviously not tempted by the stack of Dr. Seuss books placed beside them, are whining for ice cream.

Neither woman looks up as Olivia scans the shelves. Nonfiction, travel, news and fashion magazines, and a shelf of tattered *National Geographics*. Beside them is a line of ancient-looking gardening books. Olivia pulls one out: *Practical Gardening and Food Production*. She flips through black-and-white photos of men in plaid knickerbockers pushing large rollers over what, hopefully, became a lawn. Back in 1937 anyway, she thinks, as she notes the publication date.

She will have her garden, too. She's already contemplated it in her evenings before the fire. Next summer she will plant peas, squash, lettuce, and bush beans. Perhaps some flowers, just a few, although something within her resists the notion of planting something only for her pleasure.

Spring seems a long way off, but it's only three months; she's already put more months than that behind her. Three months until spring, and in six months it will be summer—and that will mark a year.

She replaces the book and goes through to the main room at the back. The books there are more encouraging. There are a couple of shelves labeled New Fiction and, beneath them, a line of mysteries. The opposite wall is dedicated to biographies. In the center of the room is a desk, and behind it stands a woman shuffling through a pile of magazines.

Olivia takes a novel from a shelf—a recent Anne Tyler she's not yet had the chance to read. Then she scans the biographies. A book catches her eye, an antiquated-looking book with a faded title and worn, whitened corners. *Merry Hall* by Beverley Nichols. She opens it and, scanning the first few pages, smiles. It's written with that particular brand of self-deprecating humor only the British have mastered. She brings both books to the desk and asks to take out a card. The woman smiles and holds out her hand.

"Welcome to town. Elaine Foss. You're new here, right?"

Olivia nods. She fills out a form, and Elaine then types the information into a machine, which spits out a card that reads Olivia Enright. Borrower #2412. As she turns to leave, Olivia notices a bulletin board on the wall beside the door to the restroom. It's plastered with restaurant flyers and community notices and pleas for part-time jobs and photos of lost dogs and cats and one lone canary (probably frozen by now). In the top corner of the board is a card with the words, scrawled in bold black marker, PIANO FOR SALE. The bottom of the card is cut into vertical strips, with a phone number printed on each.

She hesitates for only a second before she tears off a strip. As she places it in her purse, Elaine Foss comes over.

"Do you play?"

"I do. I *did*, that is. Not in a while, though. I'm not even sure I'm in the market for—" She casts her eye at the notice board as her voice dwindles away. *Go away, Elaine Foss,* she says silently. *Go back to your desk.*

But instead of going away, Elaine says, "That piano belonged to a friend of mine who moved away last year. Sam was the only piano teacher for miles around. She moved to Poughkeepsie to take care of her sister. Such a shame."

Olivia is silent.

"Do you teach?" Elaine asks. "We need a teacher here, badly. My niece, she's really good. Sam taught her. But she's heading for Eastman. My niece, that is, not Sam. Sam studied at Eastman as well..."

"No," Olivia interrupts, hoping to stem the flow of words. "I don't teach. I just like to play." She zips up her purse and turns to go. When she reaches the door she hesitates, then turns around again.

"But thank you anyway," she says to Elaine, who is still standing beside the bulletin board, looking slightly puzzled.

She almost makes it home before she realizes she's forgotten the firewood. She backtracks, then takes the turnoff to the farm Hans had directed her to. A sign in front of a dilapidated barn reads CORDWOOD FOR SALE. PLEASE HONK.

A moment later a teenage boy appears. Olivia rolls down her window.

"Not much room in there," he says. "But that's okay. We can deliver. Cordwood, right? How much do you need?"

"You mean, how many pieces of wood?"

"Cords. Or face cords. Whatever."

Olivia stares.

"You must be the lady in the schoolhouse, right?"

Does it show?

When she gets home, she calls about the piano. It's an upright, she's told by the friend of Sam's, who sounds eager to have it removed from her place. "On the old side, but I'm told the tone's still good. Nice and bright."

They agree on a price, and Olivia arranges for it to be delivered the next morning, at the same time realizing how irresponsible it is to buy a piano, or any musical instrument, without first trying it. Before she goes to bed she moves her dinette set into the middle of the room, making a space for the piano, which will go in the corner beside one of the back windows.

First thing the next morning it arrives on the back of a pickup. Two men honk and hop out, and within five minutes the piano is removed from its plastic shroud and placed where Olivia has indicated. When they've gone, it stands against the wall, looking as if it's always been there.

She lifts the lid. The keys—the color of old ivory, because they *are* old ivory—are dusty. She goes to the sink, dampens a cloth and, bringing it back, carefully wipes them, so gently that they don't make a sound. She's not yet ready to hear the instrument speak. But several times during the day she returns to it—lifting the lid, gazing at it, closing it back up.

After dinner she feeds the fire with the wood that had been delivered that afternoon. Then she makes tea and brings it back into the living room, where, seated in her armchair, she drinks it as she watches the blue-tipped flames through the glass doors. Across the room the piano waits.

Olivia thinks about the pieces she's enjoyed playing in recent years. There was Schumann's *Fantasiestücke*, in particular, the one in A-flat called "Soaring," but she prefers to call it by its proper name, "Aufschwung." There was the Bach suite, the one in D Minor, trickier than it sounded, but then all of the suites sound easier than they actually are. That's the beauty of Bach. There was a Mozart piano concerto, her favorite one in D, but of course there's no orchestra to play it with. She mastered it in the spring and had been keeping her fingers crossed that she might find an amateur orchestra in New York she could play it with.

Stop, she tells herself.

Then there was "Doctor Gradus ad Parnassum" from Debussy's *Children's Corner*. It's meant to be played fast, and she can play it that way, but what she loves is to play it slowly, almost like a dirge—or a lullaby. She was teaching it to Brian when she left…

Stop.

She finally makes herself get up and go over to the piano. After a moment she takes a seat on the stool Sam's friend threw in with the purchase.

She lifts her hands and places them on the keys.

Da-da-Di-da, she begins, tentatively. The Debussy. *Da-da-Di-da.*

She removes her hands from the keys. It was a mistake, a huge mistake. She never should have bought the thing. She'll call Sam's friend first thing in the morning, have the two guys come back for it. It doesn't matter about the money; she'll return it for free. She'll pay to get rid of it. She doesn't want to play it, and she doesn't want to hear it. She wants it out of her house.

She closes the lid. Then she goes into her little bedroom and, without even removing her clothes, climbs beneath the sheets and closes her eyes.

PART TWO

seven

1981

By the time Harry and Toni get married, Brian has been out of the house—except for Thanksgiving and Christmas—for almost nine months. He really has no desire to come back from Princeton for the ceremony; it's nothing less than a sham. His dad and Toni have been sleeping together for seven years. No, make that eight, he thinks, as he pulls from his closet shirt after shirt, examining each for stains or frayed collars. When he has selected one and put it on, he stands before the mirror beside his roommate's bed, examining the crop of zits that has colonized his chin. If he can manage to refrain from picking them, they'll disappear—but definitely not in time for the wedding. He'll try to remember to buy some acne cream tomorrow, before the ceremony.

His packed bag stands beside the door, ready to go, but he isn't. This is the first twenty-four-hour period he and Louise will have been separated since they met in January. Even though it has been four months, he still can't believe his good fortune that someone—a girl, so beautiful and smart and easygoing—would even bother trying to get to know him, Brian, who had never even had a date, much less a real girlfriend.

He glances at his roommate's bed, unmade, as usual, and stinking of beer and tobacco after last night's party. Overflowing ashtrays sit on top of the grubby sheets. If it weren't for Louise, Brian would almost look forward to getting out of the dorm and Princeton—it's only for one night, after all—even though it promises to be a bore.

He's doing it for Rory.

He looks through the leaded-glass window above his bed. The quad is deserted. Dusk on a Friday night in May. Soon it will come alive with students heading out for the eating clubs, or back to the library. Before he met Louise, he was one of those students—the ones who returned to the library.

There was a moment last month when he told Louise about the wedding, and she asked, "Am I invited?" But he hadn't told his father about her, and he doesn't plan to. At least not yet. He mumbled something about "just for family," and she changed the subject. She doesn't mind. She never minds about anything; that's what he likes about her. He minds about everything.

He removes his jacket from its hanger and swings it over his shoulder. Then he grabs his bag and lets himself out of the room.

"Where ya going, Somerville?" Shaefer, in jockey shorts and a bare, hairy chest, peers out from his darkened lair at the end of the hall.

"My father's wedding."

"Well, well. Better late than never, they always say."

He descends the two flights of stairs and pushes open the heavy door. As he crosses the quad and walks up the path to catch the Dinky train to the Princeton Junction station, his thoughts skip ahead—past the inevitable drink with his father tonight, past the wedding and the reception—and back to Louise. Sunday morning she'll meet him at his dorm with her dog, Buster, and they'll walk the half mile or so to her family's house on the other side of campus.

But before they do that, they'll spend an hour in bed making love. He'll tell her—just a little—about the wedding; she won't press him for details. And then, wrapped together, they'll fall asleep until Buster, tied to the closet doorknob, remarks that it's time to get on with his day.

The Dinky is late in and late out, and by the time it arrives at the main station he has less than a minute to board his train. He walks through until he finds a car that's empty. Picking a seat at the back, he hoists his bag onto the seat beside him, removing his psychology textbook from one zipped pocket and an apple from another. The door at the front of the car opens, and a student from Brian's English class comes through—the annoying kid who constantly complains that their edition of *The Canterbury Tales* is whitewashed, that in the original, Chaucer used words like *cunt* and *fart*. He nods at Brian and walks past. Behind him are two elderly ladies in similar floral dresses who take the pair of seats just across from Brian. He groans inwardly. Who does that, in a near-empty train? The ladies chatter loudly. Brian hears "my purple crepe," "I'm telling you," and "wasn't but two days cold by the time..."

He opens his book. His psych exam is a week away and he hasn't kept up, can't seem to focus on the material. When he was accepted into Princeton, his father had asked him what he wanted to study. Brian answered, automatically, "Psychology." Automatically, because as far back as he can remember, he's always wanted to be a psychologist, someone who can help people with the problem he's diagnosed in himself: loneliness.

Now he's not so sure about his career choice. There's only one chapter in the psych book, the one at the end, that covers the human mind, and it's nothing but a teaser for those who are eager to delve more deeply into the topic. The rest of the book is about rats and monkeys and labyrinths and salivating dogs. Brian had thought, when he registered for the course, that he would come to understand such concepts as the unconscious, the subconscious, and the Oedipus complex—topics that had been addressed briefly in his last semester of high school. If he understood those things, he reasoned, it would go a long way toward explaining his mother's behavior.

He isn't doing well in most of his other courses either. They aren't particularly difficult, but as soon as the professors begin to speak, his mind wanders off to the plot of a movie he's seen, to a sweater at the U-Store he likes, or, more commonly, to Louise.

The train screeches to a halt, and the lights flicker out. New Brunswick. The Chaucer expert exits the train. One of the ladies across the aisle reaches into her huge purse and pulls out a Milky Way, which she unwraps, breaks in half, and offers to her companion.

Brian looks out the window. As the train leaves the station and picks up speed, he can make out, in the dim light, telephone poles and large trees, and, a moment later, the outlines of several huge apartment complexes. Building after building, all full of people, thousands of them stacked one above the other. He polishes his apple on his jacket and takes a bite. If he were to knock on any one of those countless doors and ask a question, just a simple question—*How did you get to where you are now?*—to whoever answered, the explanation would probably reflect a complete lack of insight. Which is why he studies psychology. If he can understand how he got to where he is now, he might be able to determine where he wants to go. Who he wants to become.

If, for example, he were asked, "Why Princeton?" instead of Berkeley or Brown, where he had also been accepted, he would probably respond that while all three had great undergrad programs, Princeton had the most beautiful campus. Which is true, but he also knows there was a deeper, half-hidden truth behind his choice. Olivia, his mother, grew up in Princeton. She lived in a large stone house on Elm Road, the daughter of parents who died before he was born. Once or twice a week he finds himself biking by the house—a movie star and his family are said to live there now, part-time—and if no one is around, he brings his bike to a halt and stands on the pavement and stares.

He's looking for answers, although that's not what he tells himself. He imagines the young Olivia upstairs in the nursery, or peering through the window of the glass conservatory that juts away from the side of the house. Or sitting in a low branch of the oak tree in the back, her straight black hair—Brian knows that hair from the few photographs that exist of her, and also because his is just like it—blowing behind her in the breeze.

Somewhere in the depths of his consciousness, and even though he knows it's silly, he believes that if he stands there long enough, if he stares hard enough, he'll be able to see his mother going about her day. And maybe then he will understand the decision she made when he was nine years old.

Of course, he'll think then, getting on his bike and pedaling away, finally able to get on with his life. To let her go.

Now I get it. No problem.

It's dark by the time the train arrives at the station, and the interior lights flash on and off as it slows. Looking out the window, he can see his father standing alone on the platform, his hands in his pockets. Although it's a warm evening, Harry is wearing a sports jacket over his usual white shirt.

The train comes to a halt, and Brian, transfixed, continues to stare at his father, who is no more than three feet away. Harry's face appears yellow in the harsh station light. He seems to be looking in at Brian, but because the car lights are out, Brian isn't sure whether he can see inside. Above his father's upper lip, beads of moisture glisten; his hair is damp-looking, as if he just stepped from the shower. The expression on his face is bleak.

The lights suddenly flicker back on. For a brief moment Brian notices what appears to be a look of panic in his father's eyes. Then, seeing his son, he smiles and raises his hand.

"Toni's staying with her mother tonight," Harry says, although Brian hadn't asked.

They're sitting in the backyard on loungers, which are backlit by the fairy lights his father has strung along the bushes. Between them is a cooler packed with melting ice and bottles of Heineken. Dinner happened an hour ago, leftover pot roast Toni cooked over the weekend. Rory is in the living room watching TV.

Brian raises his eyebrows, hoping to convey interest, even though it's too dark for his father to read the expression on his face. He takes a bottle from the cooler, and his father passes him the opener.

"She's superstitious," Harry says. "Going all out for that 'something old, something new' thing. Et cetera."

Brian has no idea what he's talking about. Since he arrived home, Harry has been speaking almost nonstop. This is unusual; he's never been talkative. In fact, Brian can remember long periods when his father was near silent.

Most of those periods revolved around Toni. One night, in her second or third year with them, she suddenly packed her bags and left. It was summer, and instead of trying to find a local babysitter, Harry took a leave of absence from his firm. The whole month of July and part of August he stayed indoors, watching cartoon after cartoon with his sons and sending out for pizza every night. He barely spoke. Laundry piled up in the bedrooms; clumps of dust drifted across the floor. One morning Brian woke early to the sound of Toni singing in the kitchen. When he came downstairs she said casually, "What do you want on your pancakes, syrup or jam?" His father had already gone to work. No explanation was ever offered, and the incident was never mentioned again.

Another time, when Brian was in high school, Toni got sick. For weeks she spent most of her time in the bathroom; she was exhausted and feverish and her shins were covered in shiny, purple bumps. Her parents came and took her away. Brian remembers her mother leading Toni, in a nightgown and coat, out of the house and into a waiting taxi. During the month she was gone, the same scene was repeated: cartoons in the family room, pizza boxes piled on the kitchen counter. His father, noncommunicative.

The only other occasion Brian remembers Harry being so silent was when Andrew drowned and his mother disappeared.

"Your brother's in a school play next weekend," Harry says, reaching for another beer. "He's been rehearsing every day." He holds out his hand for the opener. "It's not a big part—in fact, he's playing the family dog. But he's having fun. We thought you might like to come back for it."

Brian registers the "we." That's a first. "I don't know, Dad. I'm pretty busy. Exams are coming up."

"Well, I can understand that. But here's another possible plan. I thought we might rent a place in Beach Haven for a couple of weeks, after you get back this summer. It might be nice for you to spend a little more time with your brother."

Brian tips his head back and swallows, all at once, the second half of his beer. Then he sets the bottle on the grass. There's a cool breeze, but he feels his neck and head get hot, like it always does when he's feeling cornered.

"I've been meaning to mention it, Dad, but there hasn't exactly been a lot of time. I've got a job near Princeton. A summer job, taking tickets on the turnpike. It starts the week after exams and goes until Labor Day."

"That's great, son. But the thing is—" He stops.

"What, Dad? What is it?"

Harry sits up and swats at an insect. Then he repeats, "The thing is, your brother's been having a hard time lately."

Brian waits.

"You know, he started middle school in the fall, which meant the addition of some new kids in his class. And, well, he's doing fine at school. As usual. He's extremely smart, plus he works hard. But on the playground it can get a little tough."

Brian hasn't seen his brother in months, but at dinner he didn't notice anything different. "What do you mean, Dad? What kind of tough?"

"Well, nothing physical; I don't mean that. But he's being

teased. Last week one of the boys—apparently there was a group of them—asked him why he didn't have a mother."

"And?" Why is it always so difficult to pry information from his father?

"And he said he told them he had Toni. At which point they all laughed and began chanting, 'Toni, Toni,' and one of them asked if he knew that I paid Toni to take care of him."

God, Brian thinks. *Kids can be such jerks.* "And? What did he say?"

"I don't know. But when he got home he asked me if it was true, if I paid Toni. And I told him that she does a lot of work for us, so yes. But it didn't mean she doesn't love him."

Brian considers. "He's always seemed happy. So well adjusted. Not like..." He stops as he thinks about himself at that age—full of hate, mostly at himself. But he doesn't want to open that can of worms.

The door to the house in back opens, and the elderly man who lives there limps slowly down the steps, his dachshund on a leash in front of him. Whistling lightly through his teeth, he leads the animal to a clump of bushes along the side of the house, where the dog squats.

"He *is* happy and well adjusted," Harry says. "But that doesn't mean he's not sensitive. It doesn't mean he wasn't affected by your mother's absence, even though he was a little guy. And it doesn't mean he's not affected now. That kind of thing—" He shrugs.

They watch as the man in back limps up the steps and, with his dog, disappears back into the house.

As long as they are talking, Brian decides to ask the question he's always wondered, the question he used to ask but hasn't in a long time. He takes a breath, then says, "Dad?"

"Yes, son."

"I have a question."

"Go on."

"Have you heard from her?"

"From who?"

"My mother. Has she ever gotten in touch? Do you know where she is?"

If Brian had held his breath before his father spoke, he probably would have expired.

Finally, Harry says, "No, son. I have no idea."

It's the same answer he gave years ago, when Brian first asked. It's the same answer he's given every time Brian has asked, although at some point Brian stopped asking. Now Brian asks, "Do you know *anything*?"

From down the street a screen door bangs and a woman shouts out, "Here, kitty-kitty-kitty."

Harry rotates his bottle in one hand before he brings it to his lips. *He's stalling for time,* Brian thinks, watching him take a long swallow. His father sets the bottle down and says, simply, "She didn't want to be found."

And for the first time, he tells Brian about the missing person report he filed when they returned to New Jersey.

"When I told the police she'd taken a lot of her clothes and other possessions, they said it meant she'd obviously gone willingly. And that there was really nothing they could do."

"And you let it go at that," Brian says. It's not a question.

"Everyone has the right to disappear," Harry says. "That's what they told me. It's the law. Privacy and all that. They said they'd accept the report anyway, but they might have just said that to placate me."

"And you let it go at that," Brian repeats.

His father clasps his hands together and lowers his head, almost as if he's praying. But Brian waits, and he won't stop waiting until Harry says something that makes sense, something that will explain what he's been wanting to know since he was nine.

Finally, Harry looks up. "I received a letter. From your mother, a week or so after Andrew's funeral. It was postmarked New York City."

Brian waits.

"She wrote that she was sorry. That's what she said, that's all she said—that she was sorry and that she wouldn't be back." He takes a deep breath. "She told me not to get in touch with her."

"But why?" Brian suddenly finds himself close to tears. "Why did she leave? Why didn't she want us to find her?"

Harry smiles slightly. "I've thought about that. I've thought about it for a long time, and the only answer I can come up with is that she either felt guilty for leaving you boys to go on her hike, so guilty that she couldn't face coming back—or when she discovered that one of you had drowned, she decided she didn't want to know which one. She couldn't face knowing." He shrugs. "Or both. It could have been both. People are complicated. They don't always act like you think they're going to act." He pauses. "Sometimes, when something terrible happens, people make bad decisions. And sometimes they just shut down."

"She *knew* one of us had drowned?"

Brian looks up at the house. Rory's bedroom, on the second floor, is faintly lit by his night-light. Brian's own room—he supposes he still thinks of it as that—is across the hall. He hasn't gone up there yet, but he imagines that it's as he left it the day he started at Princeton: Beatles posters on the walls, his childhood books lined up alphabetically on the shelf above his desk, and the quilt his mother sewed for him, neatly folded at the bottom of his bed. Down the hall is his father's bedroom. As of tomorrow, his father and Toni's room. Officially, finally.

"The day Andrew died," Harry says, "there were two girls. They'd met your mother on the road leading back to the resort soon after it happened, and they told her the news about Andrew, but they didn't mention his name. They didn't know it. All they said was that there had been a death at the resort, a drowning of a little boy from New Jersey. And they said your mother asked them the way to the bus station."

Brian raises his eyes. He can see the cup of the Big Dipper, the only constellation he can recognize, between the tip of the blue spruce and the chimney of his father's house. And to the right of that, the scrap of a new white moon.

"The police went to the bus station. They were told by the ticket seller that a woman of your mother's description had bought a ticket to New York."

Without looking down, without meeting his father's eyes, Brian says, "So you never even tried to find her?"

He could have left off the word even.

"No. I never did."

"Why not?" Brian pleads, making one last undignified stab at understanding. Tonight has seemed to him to be the final opportunity for answers, even though he now knows there aren't any. Tomorrow—after almost ten years—the chapter will be truly closed. If Olivia by some miracle returned, she would find herself neatly replaced by another woman, in her kitchen and in her husband's bed.

"I thought it would be unkind." Harry swats at a mosquito on his arm and then one on his forehead. "She didn't want to be found."

They get up from their chairs. Something rustles in the rhododendron—a bird, disturbed by their approach, or maybe a toad. Brian reaches for the back door to allow his father to pass, but before they go inside Harry turns to look his son squarely in the eyes and says, "Believe me, Brian. I loved your mother. I loved her more than you will ever know."

"I'll try to make it home next weekend," Brian says when they are inside the house. "I'll try to come home for Rory's play."

"Why didn't you want to be best man?" Rory asks. They're seated at a booth in a downtown luncheonette, drinking Coke and coffee and sharing a plate of fries.

After the ceremony, photographs were taken outside the church. Harry's side of the family was short on numbers: just his sister Ellen, who came with her latest husband; his brother James, who brought his roommate, Daniel; and an old aunt of Harry's who flew up from D.C.

But Toni's family more than made up for the lack of Somervilles. Mother, five sisters, three brothers, countless aunts and uncles and cousins, all of them talking at once, the minute the bride and groom came back down the aisle.

Brian had backed away from yet another family grouping until he reached the cover of the high hedge that bordered the church cemetery. He needed a break from all those people. An opportune moment came when Rory discovered his brother sitting on a gravestone and smoking a cigarette.

"You smoke!" he said, shocked, and, grabbing Brian by the arm, he complained that he was thirsty, he needed a soda and couldn't wait a whole hour until the reception.

"Why didn't you?" repeats Rory, twisting in his seat as he waits for his Coke refill. "Why didn't you want to be Dad's best man?"

"I thought Uncle James should do it," Brian explains. "He came all this way. Dad was just asking me to be polite."

"He was not! I heard him telling Toni."

Brian winces. "I wouldn't have liked it," he says. "All those people looking at me. And all those pictures. No thanks."

"*I* would have done it," his brother says. "I like it when people look at me." He takes a long glug of Coke. "Did Dad tell you about my play?"

"He mentioned it."

"Are you coming?"

Despite what Harry said last night, Brian can't see anything wrong with Rory. He appears far more normal than Brian was at his age—which isn't really saying much, considering. He has always tried to put his finger on what Rory has that he himself lacks, and as the waitress comes with his coffee refill, the answer flashes across his mind. Rory says what he feels. He's only eleven, and he asks for what he wants. For some reason, Brian has never quite mastered that trick. How can such a way of being seem so simple for one person yet so complicated for another?

"I'm not sure," Brian says. "I'll have to see. I've got exams starting in a week, but I'll try to be there."

Rory bites off the tip of his straw paper and blows it across the table. "Exams!" he says, frowning. "They're just the same as tests. We have a social studies test every Friday. And a spelling test every Tuesday. It's no big deal. I like them!"

"We should go soon," Brian says, eyeing the clock above the counter. "The reception officially began fifteen minutes ago."

"Toni wants us to rent a house in Beach Haven in August," Rory says after guzzling the rest of his second Coke. "And Dad said yes! Do you remember that house on Florida Avenue that had the secret passageway? Remember the time Toni couldn't find us because we were hiding in there and she called the police? Ha, ha, ha."

"You couldn't possibly remember that," Brian says, smiling. "You were hardly two years old. You must have been told it."

"I remember it! I remember everything!"

Their waitress, who had been in the grade behind Brian's, hands him the check. "I hope you're not getting uppity," she says, smiling. "I know all about you Princeton men."

Brian hands her some bills, and she wiggles Rory's ears back and forth, then disappears back behind the counter.

"Do you remember Mom?" Brian asks, returning to the topic as they leave the restaurant.

"I remember a *lady*," Rory says. "I don't know if it was Mom."

"What did she look like?"

"I don't remember the *look* of her."

On their way back to the inn where the celebration of their father's new life has begun, Brian says, "Did you ever wonder what happened?"

Rory picks up a stick and starts swinging it. "To who?"

"To Mom!"

As they walk, his brother taps a traffic sign, and then a couple of trees, and, finally, each post in the low picket fence that surrounds the inn. "Toni said maybe she died."

Brian feels as if he's been struck. What does Toni know about it? She never even met Mom. Mom's not dead! For a moment he's tempted to tell his brother what his father told him the previous evening, that somewhere out there was a woman who had once loved them all. But he decides not to. Rory is too young to understand, and besides, who really knows all the facts? Not him. Not his father. And certainly not Toni.

Instead he says, "She's not dead."

"I don't care if she is. I hope she is. Because if she isn't dead, it means she left us. No mother ever does that." Rory throws down his stick and turns to his brother with a scowl. "Anyway, how would you know? She could have fallen down a well or something, like Jonathan's Aunt Ruth. Remember? They didn't find her for years, and when they did find her, her body was blue, they said, and there was this awful—"

"Boys? There you are! Your father's been looking for you. Come in and have some champagne, Brian."

Toni, stepping out onto the inn's front porch, has changed from her wedding gown into a rose-colored dress that falls in light folds to just above her knees. Rory takes one look at her and runs up the steps. From behind, in his dark suit, shiny black leather shoes, and new, slicked-back haircut, he looks like a little man.

"Can I have champagne, too, Toni? Can I? Can I?"

"Ma is making popovers for brunch," Louise says.

It's Sunday, the day after the wedding. They're walking through the campus with Buster, who, having been tied up for the past hour, is straining to be off the leash. Because it has been raining steadily since Brian arrived back in the middle of the night, the campus walkways are sodden, and Louise has to restrain Buster from hurling himself into the puddles.

When she arrived at his dorm in the early morning, Brian was still asleep. He was dreaming that the phone had rung, and when he picked it up a familiar voice said, *Brian, I'm surprised at you. I always felt that of the three, you were the most sensible.*

When he tried to defend himself—against what, or to whom, he has no idea—there was a click on the line, and it went dead.

After the dream he drifted back to sleep and didn't hear the buzzer. Louise had had to shout his name from the quad below. When she entered his room, laughing, he pulled her toward him. Her head smelled delicious, of soap and maple leaves and dog.

"Popovers with syrup?" Brian asks as they approach the broad stone steps that lead up to the archway.

"Of course."

As he predicted, she doesn't question him about the wedding. Instead, she tells him about the game of Scrabble she played with her father and sisters the night before and won.

"Bet you don't know what 'ai' means," she says, twisting her red scarf to the front of her neck so that its tails fall between her breasts. "That was my winning word."

"*Ai*," Brian says. "Let me think. Could it possibly be a *three-toed sloth?*"

Louise shrieks and runs up the steps through the archway and back down the other side, disappearing from Brian's view. He chases her over toward Nassau Street, then down Library Place. When they reach the house, they go around the back, where Louise's father is slumped in an Adirondack chair beneath a tree. He's in his pajamas and robe; sections of the *New York Times* litter the lawn. There's a coffee mug in one hand and an unlit cigarette in another, and when he sees Brian he scowls—but it's only a mock scowl—and groans. "Finally. *She* wouldn't let me eat until you got here. As if the whole complicated process of salivation, peristalsis, and the release of digestive hormones can't be accomplished except in the presence of others of the species, doing precisely the same thing. Did you know, Brian, that there are no mammals for whom eating is a social act? Other than us humans, of course." He corrects himself. "We humans."

"Dad!" Louise says, flinging her arms around her father. "Is Ma inside?"

Mr. Kirkland reaches into his bathrobe pocket for a book of matches. "What do I know?" he says to his daughter. "I never know what your mother does. Nobody around here tells me a thing."

Louise, holding on to Buster's leash, takes off for the back door.

"Hit it over the head," Mr. Kirkland says, confusing Brian. *Hit what over the head?* "Drag it to the fire, then dig in." He reaches into his other pocket and pulls out part of a croissant, which he tosses to Brian.

"Couldn't be simpler."

Brian laughs, but he hasn't the faintest idea what Mr. Kirkland is referring to. He often has no idea what anyone in the family is referring to. But it doesn't matter. It seems, oddly, to add to his enjoyment.

"I snatched it from the bread box. Don't tell." He motions Brian into the other chair and, with his cigarette, indicates the discarded sections of newspaper.

But Brian doesn't eat the croissant or read the paper. He's learned that it doesn't matter if he does exactly what he wants here; in fact, in this house, that's the only thing that's expected of him.

He leans back in his chair. Through his half-closed eyes he can see the waving shadow of a tree branch as it plays across the sun. The lilac beside the house is in bloom, and the odor of it provokes the memory of images from his past: an empty rocking chair, moving slightly, as if it had just been abandoned, a gold-framed picture hanging on a wall, and, from somewhere close by, the last few bars of a Bach fugue.

"Hey, zit-face!" The image vanishes and Brian opens his eyes. Louise's fourteen-year-old sister, Rose, is staring down at him and frowning. "Brunch," she says. Then, "Come on, Dad." She turns and runs back toward the house, where her sister, Maggie, is bouncing a tennis ball on the walkway leading to the kitchen.

Zit-face, thinks Brian, happily, as he takes his place at the table. At the same time, he marvels that he isn't offended. He's never known people who refuse to make allowances for him, people so determined to overlook the fact that he's different. If he didn't know any better, he'd believe they don't even notice.

The atmosphere in this house isn't shrouded in the miasma of false cheer. That's one of the reasons he comes every Sunday. It's why he took the train back right after the reception yesterday, even though he knew that by doing so, he had probably offended his father and his new bride.

Louise's mother, in a loose purple dress, smiles at Brian and holds out her hand for his plate, on which she places two large popovers. Rose passes him the bowl of butter. Maggie, waylaying the jam, reaches her finger into the jar and hooks out a strawberry, which she deposits on the tip of her tongue. Then she passes the jar to Brian.

Beside him, Louise places her hand on his thigh and gives it a squeeze, while her father, at the end of the table, says, "Interesting, this new nuclear fusion thing. It was in the paper the other day. It'll save the world, they said, and here we are today and they're saying the whole thing is bogus."

"Here we go," Rose says, rolling her eyes.

"More coffee?" Louise's mother asks, holding the pot toward Brian.

He can't help smiling as he bites into his popover. Sunday brunch, the highlight of his week. He holds out his cup to be filled and listens to Maggie's story about the new girl in her class.

"She wears these long skirts. Every single day."

"Maybe she's some weird religion," Rose says. "I was reading the other day about this church where they make all the women—"

No child in this family has ever drowned, Brian thinks to himself.

"—wear these little kerchiefs. All the time. They're called triangles."

"She's *not* a weird religion," Maggie says. "She told me they're Methodist. That's not weird, is it, Ma?"

No mother has ever fled.

Mr. Kirkland says, "It depends on your perspective, doesn't it?

Just imagine if you were from Mars, and you were visiting Earth for the very first time, and there were these people who, even though they couldn't see him with their eyes, still believed that—"

Louise, beside Brian, asks, "What's so funny?"

eight

1981

Olivia's in the garden planting lettuce. Most years she would have done this by early May, but this spring has been unseasonably cold, and the few warm days have brought heavy rain—a death blow for tiny seedlings, which could easily wash away before taking root.

Before putting the seeds in the soil, she takes her hoe and breaks up the clumps that have formed since last fall. And then, very lightly with the tip of her blade, she scrapes away the small pebbles that seem to have magically manifested on the upper layer of the soil, back and forth, back and forth, until she's satisfied that the earth is loamy enough. Then she removes her gloves, which are too bulky to maneuver the tiny seeds from their paper packet into the ground.

It's the day after Memorial Day. Over breakfast yesterday morning, during her favorite radio show, the topic under discussion was the Tomb of the Unknown Soldier. Inscribed on the back of the monument, the host said, are the words "Here rests, in honored glory, an American soldier known but to God."

Out loud, Olivia speaks the words, which strike her as particularly sad.

With her fingertip she pokes into the soil a line of holes a quarter of an inch deep, then drops one or two seedlings into each. During her first spring in Vermont, not believing that seeds planted in such shallow soil could survive, she went an inch deep—and nothing grew. She's learned her lesson: stick with the rules until you've learned them well enough to break them. A good rule of thumb, actually, when it comes to most things in life.

She sprinkles a thin layer of soil over the seeds. The unknown soldier. What will her own grave say? The Mystery Woman of North Port, perhaps? When she dies, she imagines people going through her things. *What does she own?* she pictures them asking. *How much money does she have? Who should they notify?* And then, maybe: *Who was she?*

At the end of the row, she moves over a foot and, doubling back, plants a different variety of lettuce, a red butterhead she's been meaning to try. Elaine, a much better gardener than Olivia will ever be, raved about the lettuce. She also mentioned the eggplants that Olivia never believed would thrive in Vermont. They're a miniaturized version of the ones that grow in southern climes and are perfect for pickling. Olivia is excited about them, but her real thrill this year will be the heirloom tomatoes that resemble tiny purple pumpkins. She plans to plant them beneath the kitchen window, where she can view them while she's doing the dishes.

When she and Harry decided to move to New York City, Olivia's only hesitation had to do with the garden she would miss. Over the years she had planted masses of flowers, and each year she added more, until the patch of lawn in back of the house had grown so small that Harry had joked he'd soon be able to mow it with a pair of scissors. Now, brushing off her hands, she remembers the mock orange hedge she planted between the garden shed and the garage. She and Harry, on hot summer evenings before it grew dark, would get the boys to bed as early as possible. Then they would go out back and sit together at the picnic table, holding hands as they inhaled the scent the flowers released.

She stops herself from riding the memory any further. It isn't often that she allows her mind to wander backward, but sometimes it happens before she can stop it.

She checks her watch. There's less than an hour before her first student arrives, barely time to finish up the lettuce and consider where the peas will go. They should be in the ground by next weekend at the latest, which will mean more work with the shovel and hoe, not to mention the pea sticks she'll need to cut, having forgotten to save last year's. She reaches for the sprinkler head and positions it in the middle of the two rows, then walks over to the outdoor tap on the side of the house. Back inside finally, she strips off her shirt and jeans and, in the bathroom, turns on the bath.

A lot of Memorial Days have passed since she moved to Vermont. She counts back. Nine. She remembers the first one, when she got caught up in the North Port parade traffic. They closed off the main street while she was in the grocery store, and she had to sit on the curb, hot and miserable with her bags of melting groceries, beside flag-waving grannies in their yard chairs, cheering as the town's Brownies and Cubs marched past.

Never again, she thought at the time, vowing not to join a church or a club or any group of people with a common purpose. When the new calendar came out the following December, she circled, with a red marker, all the tricky dates, like Memorial Day and Labor Day and Christmas and the Fourth of July and Thanksgiving. On those days, when people gravitated toward one another to celebrate, she stayed home.

The first year was the hardest, she recalls as she climbs into the tub. That was when she felt she had a foot in each camp—at home in New Jersey, where she could never return, and in the schoolhouse in Vermont, among strangers.

She had taken back her maiden name. But *Olivia Somerville,* she said so many times, by mistake, before correcting it to Enright. Lord only knows what people thought.

Hiding her past was itself a bereavement, to be added to that original one. Everything she'd ever done and seen—the music she played, the books she read, the movies she loved, *her family*—all of it had to be put in a box labeled Do Not Open Ever Again.

At the same time, it was oddly freeing. When you reject your old life and everything and everyone in it, you have to pick a new one. *Who am I now?* she'd ask herself when she woke each morning. She pursued interests she'd never had, *because* she'd never had them. One winter she learned, from a book, how to make Amish quilts. Months were spent seated on the chair beside the woodstove working a needle through the somber-colored fabrics she would never have chosen years before. The chintzes and florals were what the old Olivia had liked. The new Olivia selected stark black and purple and emerald squares and triangles and rectangles, and she pieced them together to form a wall hanging she mounted on a pine frame put together with her own hands.

She taught herself basic and intermediate and then advanced French—written, of course, not spoken, because she attended no classes. She eventually sent away for French novels, which she consumed slowly, not knowing how the words were meant to sound but able, at the same time, to ascertain their meaning.

She read books on religion and on particle physics, understanding the former but clueless about the latter. Not giving up, she persisted, purchasing books on algebra, geometry, trigonometry, and, finally, calculus, until she tossed them all in the trash, concluding that she didn't possess the kind of mind required to comprehend how in the world the empty space around an electron could possibly be the equivalent of three American football fields surrounding a grape seed. Did this mean we were basically all just empty space?

It took several years for the new Olivia to replace the old, and although she never forgot who she'd been, nor the pain that had triggered the necessity for her to become the other, she found that it eventually became easier. It became beside the point. Over time she developed the knack for setting her old self aside—just outside her line of vision, so to speak. All it required was a brief mental gesture, something like an internal nod, and she was gone. Never completely, though. Just lurking somewhere in the shadows, where the new Olivia chose not to go.

Almost ten years, she marvels as she runs a bar of soap up and down her legs, and for the hundredth time she wonders whether she's still married—or divorced.

Harry may have been married for almost a decade by now, almost as long as he was married to Olivia. Men get married quickly after divorce or death. They love having wives. Marriage, for some reason, seems crucial to them, even though it's usually the women who have to talk them into it.

She reaches for the washcloth, wraps it around the soap, and swipes upward to clean as much of her back as possible. He was a good husband, Harry was, a good person. Despite her occasional moodiness, there was rarely a cross word between them.

They had met during a town ballet recital. Harry's younger sister, a high school student, was dancing the role of the Sugar Plum Fairy, and the regular class accompanist was ill. The teacher, a friend of Olivia's mother's, had at the last moment asked Olivia to play. During the intermission, as she was nervously scanning the score's second act, having had barely any time to learn the notes, a young man with a head of curly brown hair that grazed his shoulders appeared beside the piano and said, "That's some good piano you play."

"I had two days to learn it," Olivia said proudly and then thought, *He'll think I'm bragging.* And then, *So what? I don't even know him.* And then, *He's not bad looking. I wonder if he's with someone.*

He wasn't, she discovered later that night at the only coffee shop in town that was open. He was unlike most boys she knew. He asked her about herself and kept asking, and it was only as he walked her home that she discovered he was an architecture student at Cooper Union. Every day he rode the train into New York and back, because he couldn't afford to live in Manhattan, even in those days of rent control when practically everyone could afford it.

She reaches for the shampoo, rubs some of it in her hair, then ducks under the water to rinse it out. There's no way to find out whether she and Harry are still married without giving the whole game away. And that she won't do, having decided nine years ago that her presence would remain unknown.

A few years ago she'd gone to the library in search of information about divorcing a person who'd gone missing. She'd asked Elaine—that was the start of their friendship—and Elaine had quickly pulled a book from a shelf, as if she'd been anticipating the question all along and, leafing through it until she found the relevant passage, passed it wordlessly to Olivia. Then she went back to her desk while Olivia took the book to a quiet corner.

That was the reason Olivia had allowed them to become friends: the fact that Elaine hadn't asked why she needed to know such a thing. And now, years later, Elaine still has not asked.

Divorcing a disappeared spouse is easy, as Olivia discovered from the book. It's known as "divorce by publication" and involves little more than filling out some forms and publishing an intent-to-divorce notice in the newspaper closest to the area where the spouse had last been seen, along with the date and time of the court appearance, should she or he appear to contest it. Assuming no one turned up at the court on the assigned date, presto chango.

Reaching for a towel, she contemplates the afternoon ahead. She has three students. First is Robin, twelve, who isn't the least bit interested in music, but her mother, a violist with the Boston Symphony, will hear nothing about her daughter's lack of enthusiasm or talent. At some point Olivia will have to address the issue with her; it's not fair to poor Robin to have to keep failing to meet her mother's lofty expectations.

Following Robin is Seth, who at fifteen shows real promise. He's brilliant, actually, for his age, and she looks forward to their sessions together.

Her final student is Marcy, who will be having her first lesson. She's the daughter of the new minister at the town's Episcopal church, where in a month Olivia will be holding her year-end piano recital.

It was Elaine who suggested that she approach him about the church hall. "He's a widower," she'd said, as if that might matter to Olivia, who had never, to her knowledge, given the impression that she was on the prowl. If anyone was on the prowl it was Elaine, who was still trying to come to terms with the fact that her husband had left her the previous year for a much younger woman.

When Olivia turned up at the church office the next day, she was surprised to see seated in an armchair a man in blue jeans and a T-shirt. He was wearing Birkenstocks and eating peanuts from a packet. After introducing himself, not as Father So-and-So but as Jude, he held the packet out to Olivia, who shook her head. Then she asked him about the hall.

"Are you a churchgoer?" he asked, tilting his head back and shaking the rest of the nuts into his mouth.

She was stopped short by the question, which she had always considered rude at worst—and judgmental at best. She took a breath before responding. "Is belief in what you can't see a precondition for being allowed to give recitals in church halls? Because I'm not really into all that God-bothering." And then, to blunt the harshness of her words, she smiled and said, "Per se."

Jude threw back his head and laughed. "I haven't heard that expression since I was a kid in Liverpool."

"My mother was British. Anglican." She paused. "Episcopalian."

"Got it the first time. And none of it rubbed off, right?" But without waiting for her response, he explained how he himself had become a God-botherer.

His wife had died in a collision with a tree on the Quebec ski slopes. That was five years ago, when he was still selling life insurance. The year after it happened, he'd applied to seminary.

So, Olivia thought but did not say, *your wife dies under horrendous circumstances and you decide to throw in your lot with the deity you believe could have prevented it but chose not to?*

He seemed to guess what she was thinking. "Yes, well. Once something like that happens, it can go either way. With me, I thought there had to be a meaning in all that awfulness, and truthfully, I couldn't bear it if there wasn't." He paused. "I thought that if I looked hard enough—"

"And have you?" she asked, at the same time thinking, *What an attractive man.* "Have you found meaning in awfulness?"

He smiled at Olivia, still standing in the doorway. "I'm still working on it," he said briefly. "But you. What about you?"

"Never mind me," she said. "I never even believed in the tooth fairy." And they both laughed.

Back in the bedroom, she selects from her hanging rail a denim skirt and a blouse she hasn't worn in years. She bought it at Bloomingdale's when they decided to move to New York and she thought she'd need something a little more upscale than the faded T-shirts and jeans she usually wore around town.

When she's dressed, she examines herself in the mirror. She is, if she's honest with herself, dressing for Jude. Well, perhaps not dressing for him, but at least not willing to appear like the kind of middle-aged woman who's stopped caring about her looks.

She leans toward the mirror to apply pink lip gloss. It isn't exactly that she wants a connection with a man. Having been alone for nearly a decade, she's used to her own company. In a strange way, she's almost grown to love it—most of the time. But some days, she finds herself still saving up her observations and feelings for sharing at the end of the day, only to have it hit her: there's no one to share them with.

Robin is late, bearing apologies from her mother. When Olivia asks her to play the C Major scale, the child sits motionless on the bench, staring down at her lap.

"Move over a sec," Olivia says. "I'll play something for you." And when Robin slides over, Olivia launches into a vigorous performance of Scott Joplin's "Maple Leaf Rag."

When she's finished, she looks at Robin, who is grinning from ear to ear.

"Did you like that?"

Wordlessly, the child nods.

"You could do it, too, you know. You could play that. Eventually. If you want." She gets up from the bench and says, "But first, the scale. Let's get those little fingers going."

Seth arrives just as Robin is leaving. Removing his baseball cap and tossing it on a chair, he plunks himself down on the bench and places his hands on the keys, eager to demonstrate how far he's gotten with the Second Movement of the "Moonlight Sonata."

"Perhaps, a little less—" Olivia says, when he's finished, thinking she should offer up some sort of criticism but at the same time not really able to come up with anything.

"Energetic?" Seth says, using her word to describe a piece that's being played too fast.

She laughs. His mother is a lunch lady in a nearby school; his father works at the hardware store. Seth is their only child, and Olivia imagines that all their resources are directed toward him. She wonders if they realize the extent of his talent, how far he could go, provided that the money is there at the right time and that the right connections—nearly as important as talent and money—are made. She pulls down an exercise book and places it in front of the boy. Soon she'll have the talk with his parents.

When he's finished his scales, he says. "I heard something the other day. On the radio."

"Yes?"

"Mom said you might have it. It's called 'Doctor Gradus ad Parnassum.'"

A beat, before Olivia says, "Yes. Debussy. It's from *Children's Corner*. I'll play it for you if you like."

They switch places and Olivia begins. At the third measure Seth calls out, "That's it!"

When she reaches the slow part, marked *expressif*, she stops. She puts her hands in her lap. If she keeps on, she'll cry, and what will happen then? Seth will tell his mother that his piano teacher cries during his lessons, and word will get around that she is a little—

"Aren't you going to finish?" Seth prompts.

—*off*, she completes her thought. Well, everyone around here already thinks that.

"Yes," she says simply, and she plunges back in, attempting with all her being to unconjure the image that has risen up, a phantom presence, but still: Brian, with a puzzled expression on his face, as if he can't imagine how he managed to land here, in this strange house, beside a mother he is certain stopped loving him long before she left him.

After the accident, she couldn't imagine that she'd ever be able to breathe again. In those early days in the schoolhouse, the children were phantom presences, accompanying her during all of her daily activities. While she cooked her meal, Rory sat in his high chair, banging his tray with a spoon. As she swept out the schoolhouse, Andrew insisted, as he always had, on holding the dustpan for the crumbs. When she worked up the soil in the early spring, she could hear the notes of Brian's "Für Elise" floating out through the window.

Now, she can't even remember their birthdays. Brian, she knows, was born in the autumn, because she can recall that her water broke as she and Harry were raking leaves into a pile. But was that at the end of September—or early October? She's not sure. And the others? Well, Rory wasn't even two when she left, and that was in July, so he must have been born around Christmastime. As for Andrew, she hasn't a clue.

But they haven't completely vanished from her consciousness. There *is* that walk they accompany her on each day, the walk she's about to embark upon, now that Marcy's lesson is over and she and her father have gone.

She pulls on her boots and reaches in the cupboard for a sweater. Outside, she turns off the sprinkler she'd left on and sets off down the road, still thinking about her life, which, while not excessively busy, is hardly boring. Her students take up most of her afternoons. Then there's Elaine, whom she sees frequently for coffee or dinner now that Elaine is single. There's Cory, her neighbor from down the road, who arrives with his rototiller in spring and fall, and in the winter plows her driveway without being asked. He'll sit in Olivia's kitchen for hours if she lets him, drinking cup after cup of the strong black coffee she knows he likes, before her students arrive and she has to throw him out.

And there's Lorna, her hairdresser. Soon after Olivia moved into the schoolhouse, she'd taken a pair of scissors and hacked off her long black hair, thinking that in her new life it would be easier to take care of, and besides, there was no one around to appreciate it—and probably never would be again. But after she'd swept up the hair and spread it across the shrubs for the birds to use for their nests, she glanced in the mirror and immediately booked herself in with Lorna, who managed, in fifteen minutes, to make Olivia look like a woman whose new hairdo was intentional rather than a disastrous mistake.

She sees Lorna every month now and would go more often if it didn't seem odd. Lorna, whose magic scissors restore

Olivia to respectability and who doesn't bother to fill silences with idle chatter. Lorna, the only person in the world whose hands touch Olivia.

That counts for something.

She picks up the pace until, a few minutes later, she reaches the lake. It's begun to rain, lightly, the mist obscuring the water, and the gray sky bleeds into it, so that, looking across, she can barely see where the lake ends and the sky begins. She drops down onto the sand spit—that same sand spit she stood on when she decided to buy the place, just after the world changed. From there she can make out only the lodge's gables, emerging from the mist, and the large wooden dormer that juts off the top of the boathouse. She can't even see the dock.

Earlier today, Jude had stayed for his daughter's first lesson. After settling him into an armchair with a cup of tea, she sat Marcy at the piano and began, as she always did in a first lesson, with a simple little four-note song every child can master: C–D–E (beat) C–B–C. Four notes in all. The child caught on quickly, and after she played the tune a couple of times, Olivia had her repeat the notes while she herself clapped and sang the little ditty: *Sleepyhead. Go to bed.*

"See," Olivia said. "You can already play a song!" Then she moved on to the more boring part of the lesson: showing the child how to sit up straight and how to curve her fingers slightly before settling them on the keys. Through all of this she was conscious of being observed.

As they were getting ready to leave, he said, "I thought you might like to get a coffee sometime."

Inexplicably, alarm bells went off. Pretending not to hear the invitation, Olivia handed Marcy her music and instructed her to practice for ten minutes each day. Then she reached for the doorknob and said goodbye.

Now, on the sand spit, she imagines what it might be like to have someone like Jude—or any man—in her life. She pictures sitting across the breakfast table from him, chatting about the day to come. Or seeing a movie together and in a café afterward, discussing it. Then she envisions lying in bed beside him in the dark.

It begins to rain harder. She rises, tilts her head to the sky, and opens her mouth to let the drops settle on her tongue. Then she walks back down the path toward home, her feet taking up the old beat as she chants, very quietly, *I have three children. I have three children.*

That night Elaine calls. There's a modern production of *Romeo and Juliet* playing at Goddard College on Saturday night, and would she like to go?

Shakespeare has never held much interest for Olivia, but she says yes so quickly that Elaine says, "Is everything okay?"

"Fine," Olivia says. Then she adds, "Jude stayed while Marcy had her lesson today."

"And?"

"And, nothing." She stops. "He is kind of attractive, though, don't you think?"

Elaine waits, but when Olivia doesn't say anything further, she prods her. "Go on."

"He asked me for a coffee. Sort of."

"Well, that's good, isn't it? You like coffee."

"Very funny."

"You said he was attractive! You just said that. I heard you."

"Attractive, sure. Like a piece of jewelry or a flower or—a painting. One of those Pre-Raphaelites." Olivia pauses. "I said he was attractive; I didn't say I wanted him."

"So what's the big deal? Are you going?" Elaine pauses. "It's just coffee, Olivia! For Chrissakes!"

"Yes, well, there is that religious issue. Funny you should bring it up."

Elaine laughs. After debating where they might eat before the play, she returns to the topic. "I recently read that a significant number of Episcopal priests are agnostic."

"Okay—so why do they bother? The money couldn't be that good."

"The article didn't say. But have you ever been to one of their Advent services? Their robes are amazing. Purple or royal blue, with all this incredible embroidery. What plumage! I can see Jude now, with…"

"I thought purple was for Easter," Olivia interrupts.

"I'm pretty sure white is for Easter."

"So, what are you saying? That he's in it for the outfits?"

"Olivia!" Elaine repeats again. "It's just coffee!"

The point of marriage, she thinks, as she takes a novel Elaine has loaned her and curls up with it in her armchair, *is to save your spouse*. To save your spouse, and to be saved—from loneliness and from boredom, but also from fear and anxiety and despair and pain—and yes, if at all possible, even death.

But mostly from loneliness—the ordinary human loneliness of living inside one's head. When Harry asked her to marry him, Olivia was thrilled that such an amazing boy could be interested in sharing his life with her. And she never regretted it, not once, not even when they fought, as they sometimes did, over money, or where to live, or, after Brian, how many children to have. None of that mattered, because they had once been bold enough to stand before their friends and family and promise to save each other.

Once, before the children were born, Harry rented a small sailboat and they launched it off the jetty at the Jersey shore. Olivia was fearful—she was a terrible swimmer—but Harry had convinced her that he could handle it; he'd learned to sail at the camp he'd attended as a boy.

For a while the ocean was calm, and Olivia, forgetting her fears, leaned back and closed her eyes as the sun poured down on her and the boat rolled gently from side to side. But as the afternoon turned into early evening, and Harry attempted to tack and head for shore, a wind came up. And as he pulled on this line and that, trying to tame the boat as if it were a horse he needed to rein in, they nearly blew over.

Olivia was terrified. Although they were no more than one thousand feet from shore, it might have been ten miles as far as she was concerned. If the boat went over, Harry could make land quickly and easily. With her, there was no chance of it.

Finally, the wind ceased and the boat settled, and minutes later she and Harry were dragging it along the sand back to the marina. That night in bed, Olivia said, "You know, don't you, that if we'd tipped, I never would have made it back. I didn't stand a chance."

Harry reached out his hand in the half-light and touched her cheek. "Then we would have gone down together."

Harry. Sometimes, these many years later, she misses him so much she can hardly bear it. The other night she dreamed of their life together, from the beginning, when they met, and on through the birth of each child. But then the dream continued: the sons left home, Olivia and Harry grew old, and eventually Harry fell ill and died. It was then that Olivia discovered that their life together had in fact been a lie. It was merely a novel she'd been reading that she'd taken for true, a made-up story. There *were* no such people as Harry or Brian or Andrew or Rory; they were only characters in the book she now held in her hand. And realizing the truth of that, she closed its cover and replaced it on the shelf.

When she finally woke from that dream within a dream, Olivia found herself confused. What was real and what was not? Did they really exist—those people she thought she had so passionately loved?

And minutes later, when she finally came to herself, she grieved: *But who will save me now?*

She opens the novel and begins to read but halfway through the first chapter realizes she hasn't absorbed a single word. She's been thinking about Jude. Well, not just about Jude but, more broadly, about anyone who might in the future enter her life to take up psychological space. She likely has years ahead of her. It's bound to happen sometime.

But no. It won't work, and she knows it. It wouldn't be fair. No matter how ordinary she might appear—a piano teacher, a patron of the library, a maiden lady, yes, but not unattractive—she's not ordinary. She's deeply wounded, and that won't change; that dream she had proves it. To inflict herself on another person would be doing herself—and that future someone—a grave disservice.

She has her pupils and her music and her garden and helpful neighbors and a good friend. It's enough—and, all those years ago, it's more than she thought she'd have. This weekend she and Elaine will be going to see a play. They'll probably have dinner beforehand, maybe in that new Thai restaurant that's just opened outside Burlington.

But when she's getting ready for bed, she can't manage to banish the image of Jude—himself wounded—processing up the aisle in his purple robes and Birkenstocks, certain that even though this life has proved a disappointment, what lies ahead will more than make up for it. There's something about that certainty Olivia finds appealing.

But she will not, she tells herself again, have dinner, or lunch—or even a coffee—with him, or any other man. Ever. She's fine as she is. After all, the positive thing about love is that if you don't have it, there's no way you can lose it.

Still, deep inside she knows that if he'd repeated the invitation for coffee when she pretended not to hear it, she might have accepted.

nine

1985

The week before his father dies, Rory, sixteen years old, is walking home from Toni's through the cold evening, wondering whether that pasty stuff she just served him in between two slices of bread was really peanut butter. He'd eaten the sprouts, cucumber, and onion she'd put on his plate but couldn't manage the sandwich. She said it was peanut butter, but it smelled like burned sesame seeds.

"Call your brother," she'd said when he arrived. She'd summoned him earlier in the day. He knew something was up when he heard her voice, and feeling guilty, he agreed immediately. He hasn't been by in a couple of weeks, even though she only lives a few blocks away. But exams are looming, and then there's football practice—plus he's promised to meet his brother in the city sometime before Christmas. And of course there's the issue of his father.

When he got to Toni's, her twin daughters were seated in their high chairs, their faces smeared with jam. Toni looked tired.

Her face was pale and—unusual for her—makeup free. Each time the phone rang or a twin shouted, she startled, as if she'd spent the past hours quietly by herself and not in the company of two toddlers and, now, sitting across from a stepson who might not welcome her advice.

He knew she was worried about Harry but would never say it. It wasn't her way. *Probably guilt,* he thought, as she poured Coke into a glass and passed it to him. Guilt for abandoning him, in his early teenage years, she being really the only mother he'd known, and guilt, perhaps, for wanting her own children, her own family, as if the wanting of it was a statement that Harry and Rory—and Brian—were not, and never had been, enough for her.

"Brian's busy," Rory said, placing the top slice of bread back on his sandwich and putting the whole thing back on his plate. "He'll never come home."

Toni wiped one little face with a paper towel and bent over to pick up a piece of bread, jam-side down, from the floor. The other twin upended her cup on her tray; apple juice dripped over her mother's bare foot.

"He'll come," Toni said as she straightened and reached for another paper towel. "I can guarantee it."

She looked over at Rory. "Call him."

Well, maybe I will call him, Rory thinks now, rounding the corner to his house. It's late afternoon, the sun has set, and he can almost see the darkness rolling up the street. Every house except his own is decorated for Christmas. A plastic Santa sits in his sleigh atop the roof of the bungalow on the corner, clutching the reins of Prancer and Dancer, who list in the breeze. On front lawns, garish elves with stocking caps grin. Even the Atkinses next door, elderly and frail, have managed to thread a few strings of white lights through their cedar hedge.

As he turns in the driveway, Rory notes that the living room is in darkness. His father has either not woken from his nap or has lacked the energy to get off the couch and turn on the lights. He stops in front of the side porch and for a moment is tempted to turn around, to return to Toni's bright kitchen. She's probably getting ready to give the girls a bath before she prepares a meal for herself and her husband, Frank, due home from Manhattan on the commuter train. All the lights in her house would be on, and she'll have put on some music. Probably the Caribbean dance music she likes. It occurs to him, not for the first time, that he feels more at home at Toni's than he does here, in his own house.

He opens the door.

From the couch, his father's first words are "How's Toni?"

"She's okay." He throws his jacket over a peg and, in the living room, begins to turn on every lamp. "Are you okay?"

"I'm fine."

It's their ritual. Every day when Rory comes in from school and asks the question, the reply is always "*Fine.*" But in the past few weeks Rory can see that the cancer, which had until that point declared itself solely in the pain it caused, is impossible for him to deny. His father has become gaunt. His upper body has atrophied, causing his clavicle to protrude, and his skin, tinged with yellow, is so translucent that Rory is almost afraid to touch him, for fear that he'll crack open and bleed out.

"Shall I make us something to eat?"

Harry hauls himself to a sitting position and slowly places his slippered feet on the coffee table, which is littered with newspapers, magazines, medicine bottles, and a half-drunk bottle of ginger ale. "Nothing for me, thanks," he says. "I'll have something later."

Which they both know is a lie. Rory doesn't press the issue. He hasn't seen his father consume anything but ginger ale in almost a week. Eating is obviously in the past.

In the kitchen he takes a carton of eggs and some cheese from the fridge. Soon he has bread in the toaster and an omelet sizzling in a pan. When it's done, he flips the egg over the toast and douses the whole thing with ketchup, eating his meal seated at the kitchen table as he observes his own reflection in the uncurtained window.

He appears as he always has: clean black T-shirt, rectangular wire-rimmed glasses, hair sharply parted and slicked fiercely across his forehead in an attempt to combat its tendency to frizz. No one looking at him would suspect that his life is about to become torn apart—and he knows it. He looks like his usual self.

Everything else seems ordinary, as well—the blue-striped sugar bowl on the table, the glass vase filled with dusty silk nasturtiums on the windowsill, Harry's red plaid apron on a hook in the corner. The only thing out of place is Harry, on the couch instead of across the table from his son, quizzing him about his day, laughing about the pinochle game he'd won on the train to work, complaining good-naturedly about the Reuben sandwich he'd ordered at a deli where they'd left off the corned beef and, when questioned, claimed it was extra. Or enthusing about his latest project—an office tower in Lower Manhattan surrounded by a courtyard that would be paved with expensive gray stone to be hauled in, at great expense for the client, all the way from Scotland.

When his dad had arrived home with the news a few months ago, on a later train than usual, Rory's inane response (he cringes now as he recalls it) was, "Aren't there two of them? Can't they just take one of them out?"

His father had gone into the hospital later that week, where they'd removed his diseased pancreas and, as it turned out, a whole lot of other things he could apparently do without, at least temporarily. When he finally came home, Rory thought he looked great, better than he had for months. Even Brian, who had deigned to drive in from New York one Saturday afternoon, seemed unconcerned, and when Rory expressed his fear as his brother was leaving, Brian brushed it off: *He's a tough old soldier.*

But what will happen with his father's Scottish courtyard now? Will one of Harry's partners take over the project, or will it be canceled? Harry will never return to work—that, too, is over. He'll never play pinochle with his buddies on the train, he'll never again taste a Reuben sandwich, with corned beef or without. And for all his bluff, Harry knows that better than anyone.

Toni is right. He should call Brian. Rory picks up his plate and deposits it in the sink. Even if Brian won't come home and help, he has the right to know. He has the right to make that choice himself.

He squirts detergent in the sink and runs the water, thinking, *I can't do this anymore.* He scrubs out the frying pan, rinses it, and wipes it dry. In a moment he'll have to go into the other room, and he's dreading it. *I can't do this anymore.* He can't stand the silence. He can't bear the fact that his father will have turned off all the lights, as if in a dress rehearsal for what is shortly to occur. He can't take the smell of the room; it's damp and hot, and it smells like rotten eggs.

He can't, for one more minute, bear to watch his father die.

Nevertheless, when he's finished in the kitchen, he goes into the living room. His father hasn't turned off the lights, after all. He's sitting up on the couch, reading a back issue of *The New Yorker.*

When he sees Rory, he looks up and says, "Oh, I meant to mention. I called Brian this afternoon. He's coming out on Monday, and he says he'll stay through Christmas."

It's been a bad week, and the traffic through the tunnel—stop and start, stop and start—does nothing to improve Brian's mood.

At one point, when the heat from the car begins to make him woozy, he rolls down the window, only to be assaulted by the fetid air. How the armed, uniformed patrols on the platforms can bear working inside the tunnel for hours on end is anyone's guess. A very long time ago, Olivia said that the tunnel was where bad cops were sent to work, as punishment. At the time Brian believed she was joking.

Real estate is slow; it always is at this time of year. But true to Murphy's Law, as soon as he agreed to spend Christmas and New Year's in New Jersey, he received a call from a seller who lived in a large apartment in a Gramercy Park co-op. He wanted a quick sale, he said, unusual for the area but good for Brian. Or it would have been, had he been remaining in the city over the holidays. As it was, he had to pass the contract to Sondrine, a Riverside Drive matron in his office who was merely playing around with real estate, having lost interest in French lessons, ballet classes, and gymkhanas.

He exits the turnpike and pulls into a gas station at a service center, getting out of his car before he remembers that in New Jersey you can't pump your own gas. When he's paid the attendant, he pulls ahead and parks. It's only three o'clock. He told his father he'd be home—*home?*—before dinner. There's time for coffee.

A few minutes later he's sitting with a cheeseburger and fries at a table in the atrium, where he can watch the people who've come in for a leak exit the restrooms and take their place in the lineups for grease and caffeine, just as Brian has done, as he attempts to put off the inevitable.

Christmas with the family. Isn't there a bad movie called something like that? It holds no attraction for him. For him, home is a place filled with memories so sad and powerful that they occasionally cross the Hudson River to visit him as he's in bed asleep in his four-story walk-up.

An hour later he's in shock and trying not to show it. He and his father are in the living room, Brian seated in his father's recliner with a beer beside him, Harry lying on the couch under the pink afghan Toni once crocheted. He's nearly gone, Brian realizes. In only a few short months, how had this happened?

He wishes desperately for Rory's presence, but his brother is playing football after school and won't be in until dinnertime.

Reading Brian's mind, Harry says, "Tomorrow's his last day before Christmas break."

"Doesn't he have exams?"

"Finished yesterday."

"How's he doing?"

Harry's face breaks into a smile for the first time since Brian's arrival. "So far, his trajectory has been without wobble. I'm hoping this whole thing won't throw him off course."

"Is med school still in the cards?"

"That's never been in doubt." Harry pauses and takes a sip from his water glass, then leans his head back on the cushion. "It's why I called you."

Brian raises his eyebrows and waits for his father to go on.

"Your brother can't do this on his own." Harry spreads his arms wide, as if to include not only himself but the whole existential issue of life and death. "He needs time to study, time to kick around a football, hang out with friends. The whole package."

He looks over at his elder son. "He's a kid." He closes his eyes.

Brian says, "Life isn't fair, is it, Dad? If you taught me nothing else, you taught me that."

He watches Harry drift off for a few moments, staring hard at his father's face in an attempt to memorize it, while at the same time knowing that it's already too late. Harry's face is already only vaguely familiar, just a reminder, really, of the person Brian used to live with. He closes his own eyes.

When he opens them a few minutes later, his father is staring at him. Harry's eyes, unblinking, appear to be all pupil, and for a moment Brian thinks that he's gone.

Until he says, "Now, son. What shall we do about Christmas? It's on Wednesday, isn't it?"

After his father has settled down in the portable bed, Brian goes into his own room, first grabbing the bottle of whiskey from the dining room cabinet. He downs one shot while sitting on his bed, then undresses and, without turning off the bedside lamp, pours another and slides under the covers.

The room hasn't changed since he was a teenager. A few summers back he stripped his childhood books from the shelf and put them in a box to take back with him to the city. Toni suggested that he might want some of his old clothes as well—although what he would do with the ragged T-shirts and camouflage pants that remained in the closet, he couldn't imagine.

The boxes of books and clothes he had half-heartedly packed still stand in the corner of the room, a testament, he supposes, to the fact that although he hates the place, and resents it when he has to come back, a part of him still lives here. If he gets rid of all his old things, he might lose the part of himself that had once collected comic books with a view to getting rich off them one day. The part that once wanted, so badly it hurt, to make the soccer team. The part that loved to play the piano. The part that wanted to graduate from Princeton with a degree in psychology.

The part of him that is still waiting for his mother to reappear.

During the dinner that Harry hadn't eaten, and the coffee Brian had drunk with Rory when he finally came home from practice, his father never once asked Brian how his life was going. Nor did he ask whether Brian had a girlfriend, if he still liked living in Manhattan, or what he did in his spare time.

Which was par for the course. After Brian dropped out of Princeton and took the real estate course, Harry didn't—exactly—express disappointment. But he didn't offer any financial assistance to help his son reorient his life. It was as if Brian had disappeared from the family radar. On the rare occasions that Harry came into the city, mostly with Toni, once or twice with

Rory, he never came to Brian's apartment. He had never even seen it. Instead, they met at a restaurant or a club, or in the lobby of a theater. It was almost as if his father engineered things so that he and Brian would never spend any time alone together.

Although, Brian thinks now, finishing off the last of the bottle of whiskey, what has there ever been to say, between two people who have nothing in common but a strange and awful memory? He places the empty glass back on the night table. How ironic is it that he's spent the whole of his life yearning for the golden glow of family life? Something like *Leave It to Beaver,* which irritates the hell out of him but which he's compelled to watch, even in reruns—provided that there's no one around to see him do it.

But despite all this yearning for stability, he's never had a relationship with a woman that's lasted for more than a few months. The last girl, Deirdre, who had planned to move in with him during the past spring, chickened out the day before the move, with no explanation except that she wasn't ready to "get serious." He'd liked Deirdre. The other women—the women before Deirdre—all run together in his mind. He can barely remember a name, much less a face.

Except, of course, for his first girl. Louise. He'll never forget her. Their only problem was that they were too young when they met. He would have liked to become part of her family. He wonders what happened to her, imagining that, even now, in her late twenties, she must still be a free spirit, enthusiastic and full of life. He hopes that whoever has won her treats her well—as he would, if they were still together.

Rory opens the bedroom and sticks his head in. "I saw your light. I just wanted to say thanks."

"For what?"

"For coming home."

"Sure." He studies his brother. Rory had surprised him when he came home from practice. He expected to see the boy who had managed, all of a sudden, to grow taller than him, smarter than him. Friendlier than him. The brother who had cornered the market on all the family self-confidence. The brother who was undoubtedly heading for big things in life. Who had an unwobbly trajectory, as Harry had put it.

Instead Brian saw an insecure, anxious adolescent, almost trembling when he entered the room. A picture flashed through his mind of a young woman in a blue dress standing beside an open window and holding in her arms a tiny boy wearing a red jacket. Was that a picture—or a memory? Was that Rory? *Was that his mother?*

"It won't be long, you know," Brian says to his brother, and immediately wishes he hadn't.

"I know."

As if to make up for it, Brian says, "We'll get a tree tomorrow morning."

"Okay."

When his brother has gone, Brian turns out the light. He lies there for a while with his eyes open. The streetlight shines through the window, its pole festooned with a wreath of fake holly. The headlights of the cars driving by the house throw their reflections on the wall opposite the bed.

He sits back up. Something's missing. He feels at the bottom of the bed. It's still there, his old blue-and-white quilt. He spreads it up around his shoulders, tucking the soft material beneath his neck and, hood-like, around his head. Only then does he fall asleep.

In the morning Harry seems a little better. He appears in the kitchen where Brian and Rory are eating toast.

"Ready to get the tree, boys?"

Brian has his doubts. "Are you sure you're up for it? Rory and I can find something nearby, no problem."

"I won't have a Charlie Brown tree in this house," Harry jokes.

Rory helps to bundle him into his winter jacket, by now way too large, and together the brothers help him into the front seat of the car. Rory drives.

Harry has insisted that they buy the tree from the tree farm outside town, the way they always have. But when they arrive at the nursery, Harry says he'll stay in the car.

They leave the car running with the heat on. The place is packed with families, many of them there to cut their own trees.

"Why don't we do that?" Rory says.

"What—cut our own? You must be kidding. That takes ages. He might not last that long."

The joke falls flat.

Rory walks toward the ornament aisles, leaving Brian to pick through the trees that are sorted by size beneath the shed roof at the back of the glassed-in building. He grabs the first Scotch pine he sees on the top of the bundle labeled Six Feet and wrestles it to the checkout counter, where Rory joins him with a wooden ornament—a Santa on skis, perched inside a circle of shaved cedar.

"Didn't we have an ornament like this when we were little?"

"I don't remember." Brian pulls his credit card from his wallet.

Harry's asleep by the time they return to the car. The tree doesn't quite fit in the trunk, and Brian goes back to the store to purchase twine, which he uses to fasten the tip of the tree to the trunk latch. Finally, Rory backs the car out of the parking lot and turns on the radio. His favorite band, Queen, is singing "Thank God It's Christmas," and Rory, pulling onto the road, joins in.

Brian, who has never liked Christmas, hasn't had a tree since he left home, but the pungent aroma of evergreen that fills the car makes him ache with nostalgia. He remembers, in the distant past, stringing through the branches of the tree the little blue lights his mother had loved. Rooting out from the basement the painted and lacquered ornaments his father had made when he was young. Drinking cocoa with a marshmallow floating on top.

But were all of those his own, real memories? Or did he appropriate them from someone else, from some other, happier boy? He'll never know. Maybe they were just from his favorite Brady Bunch Christmas special.

Back home, Harry falls asleep in his usual spot on the living room couch. Rory flicks on the TV and turns the sound down low.

"Maybe we should do the tree tomorrow," he says. "Since morning's his good time."

He's watching football, and every few minutes he stifles, behind his palm, a shriek of joy or outrage. Harry snores softly. Outside the window, the day darkens.

Brian, standing by the window, feels deflated. It's barely three in the afternoon. How will he fill the remaining hours before bed?

"I don't care when we do it," he says to Rory gruffly. "Or *if* we do it." Then, telling himself he needs a drink, he goes to his father's liquor cabinet. Pouring himself a gin, straight, he lets himself out the front door and reaches into his pocket for his Marlboros.

How can this be happening? he asks himself in frustration as he lights a cigarette, takes a drag, then knocks back the gin in two gulps. Placing the glass on the frosty grass beside him, he walks over to the garage and retrieves a canvas chair from a pile of summer furniture. He unfolds it and sits with his cigarette. He's determined to manage some level of comfort for however long he's here.

He's spent the whole of his adult life manipulating events so that this sort of situation—he, an adult of twenty-three, trapped in his father's house in New Jersey on a winter afternoon with nothing but the TV for amusement—would never occur. He thinks about his own place in the city: the sleek black sofa covered with striped cushions, the wood floor he spent a week sanding and staining, the red curtains a past girlfriend (Deirdre?) found in Bloomingdale's, his bedroom window that faces across Macdougal, a stone's throw from Caffe Reggio, where he sometimes takes his female clients. If only he were there now.

But he wouldn't be there now. It's Thursday afternoon. He'd probably be showing some dark-suited banker and his fancy wife that co-op in Gramercy Park he had to pass up in order to drive out here.

On the way back from the nursery with the tree, his father, from the front seat, had surprised him by asking, "What are you up to in New York these days, son?"

"I sell real estate, Dad."

"I know that. I meant, what do you do besides that? It's a big city; there must be a lot going on."

For a moment Brian didn't reply. He remembered the excitement he felt when he moved to the city. He'd always thought of it as the center of the universe. Everything he could possibly want was there: good food, entertainment, beautiful women. And for a while, after he received his real estate certification, he went wild—the theater, art-house movies, restaurants, local watering holes. Out every night with a different woman. When had that changed?

He said, "I don't know, Dad. New York is pretty much like every other place, once you live there. I buy my groceries. I go out with friends sometimes. The usual stuff you do."

His father was quiet as Rory pulled the car into the driveway. The radio was still on, but now it was Elvis singing "Blue Christmas."

Harry finally said, "Your mother wanted to live in the city. Did I ever mention that? We were going to move that fall, just after—"

"I know." There was a silence as they both remembered.

Rory opened the car door and passed Brian the little bag with the wooden ornament. Then he went around to the passenger side, opened the door, and reached for his father's arm.

As he was being helped into the house, Harry turned to Brian and said, "I'm glad you have friends, son."

He's stubbing out his third cigarette when it begins to snow. Large, dry flakes drift lazily down, settling on the roof of the garage and the birdhouse, coating the shrubs and the front lawn and Brian's shoulders and head and lap. The flakes hitting his cheeks make little cold pinpricks.

He stands up. It's growing dark. Leaving the chair beside the garage for later, he picks up his glass and lets himself in the back door. Rory's in the kitchen, frying bacon.

"Can you grate some cheddar?" he says. "It's Cheese Dreams. Dad won't want any."

Brian holds up his glass. "I just need a refill."

When he comes back in the kitchen and opens the fridge for the cheese, Rory says, "You drink too much."

"Oh, I don't know, little brother," Brian says easily. "I don't think I drink nearly enough."

Harry hasn't had any liquids since that morning. "The man's an air plant," Brian says as he and Rory go down to the basement after dinner for the decorations. There's a small storage room off the main area, behind the old Ping-Pong table. It's filled with cardboard boxes stacked one on top of the other.

Brian hasn't been down here in years. "What's in these?" he asks.

Rory, dribbling a plastic ball across the Ping-Pong table with his palm, ducks under the low doorway, squints his eyes, and frowns. "Just stuff. My old stuff. Yours, probably. Maybe Andrew's—"

"Andrew's? Really? And Mom's?"

"I don't know. Probably not. I don't think Dad kept anything of hers, to speak of."

Brian pulls open the flaps from one carton. It's packed with baby blankets and children's picture books. He shoves it aside and opens two more, which are filled with games and old records. The Beatles. The Stones. The Velvet Underground.

Beneath this stack is a small, carved wooden box.

"They're over here," Rory says from the corner under the window. "Give me a hand, would you?"

"Just a minute." Brian opens the box. There are two compartments, the top filled with earrings and rings and a single strand of pearls. He holds up the pearls. They appear garish under the single light bulb suspended from the ceiling. He wonders if they're real.

"Here's that pine-cone thing I made in third grade," Rory says. "Come look!"

"Just a sec."

He drops the pearls back into their section, then tugs on the frayed ribbon to release the bottom compartment. Paperwork. Old bills. A few envelopes bearing Olivia's name.

One is a birthday card from her father, sent to her when she was five, another a valentine from Harry just after they met. Brian opens the third envelope, Rory squatting beside him as he unfolds a single sheet of paper.

Liv,

When I gave you the Constable last week I believe I made my feelings clear—that you should keep it in the bank as security against your future. None of us can predict where life will take us.

But you make your own decisions. I can understand your wanting to hang the painting in your bedroom where you will see it every day. It is very beautiful, I suppose, although I can't really say I appreciate art of that sort. He was a romantic, wasn't he, Constable?

I enclose here a check that should cover the insurance for at least twenty years.

I hope you are taking care of yourself and not running around too much. I also hope you will reconsider my advice on "natural" childbirth. You will shortly discover that there is nothing the least bit natural about giving birth. In other words, take whatever they offer!

Love, Mum

"What painting?" Rory asks when they've finished reading it.

Brian shakes the envelope, but there is, of course, no check. He puts the letter back in the box. There's not much else there, just a receipt for some sheet music and what must once have been a corsage, now brown and flaking.

"What painting?"

"It hung in her bedroom," Brian says. "Their bedroom. I'd forgotten."

"What was it a picture of?"

Brian thinks. "Grass. Trees. Sky. A house. A boy. Water. It was nice."

"Is that all?"

"I think she must have sold it. Constable was a very famous painter. She would have gotten a bundle."

He stands up, brushes the flakes from the corsage off his pants, and says, "Right. Let's go up and do the tree."

Later the brothers settle their father in his bed in the den. Then they light a fire in the fireplace.

"Against the dark," Rory says as they take their seats on the sofa, having removed the blankets that were piled at one end to keep their father warm.

"What's that?"

Rory says, "Something I heard once. In church."

"Do you go to church?"

"Not anymore. I used to go to Mass with Toni."

Another part of family life Brian was never part of.

He says, staring into the flames, "She's probably not dead, you know."

"Mom? So what! She is to Dad! She is to me!"

Brian pulls a cigarette from his pack and lights it. He leans back against the cushion and blows a thin stream of smoke toward the ceiling. "She'd only be forty-seven now. She was two years younger than Dad. He must wonder, even now—"

"Then why hasn't he tried to find her?"

Why had he waited all these years to have this conversation with his little brother? Had he held back because he felt that in doing so, he'd be keeping his mother for himself?

"He explained it to me once. Just before he and Toni got married. He said he thought it would be unkind to look for her."

"Unkind," Rory repeats. "What does that even mean, unkind?" He reaches for a cigarette. "It was Mom who was being unkind."

Brian holds out his lighter, then explains to his brother, "Dad says Mom knew one of us had drowned."

Brian wakes in the middle of the night, thinking he's heard a noise. He'd been dreaming that he was at a strip club and was sitting at a table drinking wine and watching a woman dressed as a nurse remove her white cap and toss it at the audience, followed by her blouse and skirt, until she was down to a bra and a pair of virginal white stockings held up by a black suspender belt. As she bent her head to unhook one stocking, she made eye contact with Brian, who realized with a shock who she was: Louise. Lovely, beautiful, generous Louise.

Despair threatens to engulf him, and he turns and pulls the covers up around his chin. As he begins to fall back to sleep, he hears another noise. Something between a groan and a shriek.

A second later Rory is in the room. "It's Dad."

During a crisis, Brian thinks, as he lights his twentieth cigarette of the night, you have a choice: to either fall apart or become an automaton.

He's alone in the hospital basement in a small room furnished with Formica tables and chairs and various snack machines. Rory is upstairs, supposedly sleeping on the foldout armchair beside his father's bed. Harry is out, doped to the gills, tubes and wires protruding from his body. The flickering screen behind his bed reflects the frail thread of his pulse. Twice during the night a buzzer had sounded; each time a weary-looking nurse had entered the room, glanced at the machine, jiggled a wire, and left.

Brian chooses to become an automaton. Or perhaps that isn't quite accurate. Maybe it's just that he lacks the strong emotions that seem to be expected during an event of such significance.

He feels in his pockets for change and feeds two quarters into the coffee machine. A whirring sound, followed by the discharge, off-kilter, of a Styrofoam cup. Before Brian can place the cup under the spout, murky brown liquid floods the drain beneath the stainless grid. He swears and digs back into his pocket. Only a few pennies and a nickel. Defeated, he sits back down. The clock over the doorway says 6:47. The lights in the hallway have been dimmed, but through the small window on the far side of the room he can see a lightening of the sky above the park that surrounds the south side of the hospital complex. Soon the place will be bustling with nurses and doctors and technicians and porters wheeling patients in and out of the hospital. And families, relieved or grieving—or both.

After Harry, in Intensive Care, had fallen asleep, the resident on call motioned Brian and Rory into the hallway.

"Is there anyone you need to call?"

Neither brother responded.

"What I mean is," the doctor said, meeting their eyes, "is there a wife or a mother on the scene? Or another close relative?"

"There's just us," Brian said.

Rory pulled the straw out of the can of Coke he had just finished and tossed it in the trash. Then he looked at Brian and said, "There's Toni. Isn't there, Bri?"

As he's reaching for another cigarette, he hears someone coming down the hall. After his smoke he'll go back upstairs and get Rory. They may as well go home. They can do nothing for their father; there is nothing to be done. Brian needs to eat, he needs to wash. He needs to brush his teeth. Mostly, he needs to sleep.

"Brian?"

Toni is standing in the doorway. She's wearing a beige trench coat and white sneakers. Dipping below the hem of her coat is what appears to be the bottom of a red flannel nightgown.

She says, "Your brother called."

He stands up then. Toni wraps her arms around him and lays her head against his shoulder. After a moment he pulls away.

"Is this it, then?" she says.

"It will be. Pretty soon, apparently."

"I'm so sorry."

It's on the tip of his tongue to say, *What have you got to be sorry about?* But he's hardly one to call her out on her leaving. He never accepted her as part of his family in the first place.

He motions her to a seat, then lights his cigarette, aware that she never approved of his smoking.

But she reaches her hand out for his pack and says, "May I?"

Time plays funny tricks on the dying. Sometimes it speeds up, like a train that's pulling away from the station just as you burst through the gate, ticket in hand, and it hits you that if you'd arrived a mere ten seconds earlier you'd be on it, bound for that place you always yearned for, the place you just knew would change your life from something ordinary to something so exquisite you can only guess at it. *(Dang! If only the phone hadn't rung on your way out the door. If only you hadn't forgotten your keys and had to run back in for them. If only you'd remembered that Montclair Road was closed for construction.)*

But sometimes time seems to grind to a halt, so that you—the dying person—can lose sight of how long you've been in this particular state, in this particular bed, in this particular room. Nor can you recall how long it's been since you've seen the face—or heard the voice—of another human being. Or, for that matter, heard any sound at all, except for the beeping above your bed that tells you that you still—barely—inhabit this world.

How is it that no one has figured out that you might like to be in your own bed for such a momentous event? There's surely nothing anyone can do for you here.

But really, in the scheme of things, it doesn't matter. If you keep your eyes closed, you can imagine you *are* home, in your own bedroom and in your own bed, where you slept with Olivia (*such a very brief time you had with her*) and later with Toni (*oh, why hadn't you loved her more?*).

But it's difficult to think about all of this now. As a matter of fact, you're having trouble thinking at all, at least in any systematic, sequential fashion, with one thought leading to another. Earlier, you heard the boys talking. Brian was saying, "I can't understand a thing he says." And Rory responded, "Yeah. It's like he's on a different plane."

The boys. *Your* boys. And now you feel a pang in your heart, and as you reach for it, you manage to catch hold of another thought: regret that you'd worried so much about Brian and so little about Rory, with his insatiable need to please everyone. You could have helped him.

That thought evaporates and you realize that your boys were right. You *are* on a different plane. Your thoughts are all jumbled up. But they're wrong if they think you can't feel them. Why really, your feelings are so much better than thoughts. They're almost pictures!

Right now, on your back under the covers, the image you see is that of your mother. She is wearing a purple hat and laughing. Her bingo hat, she'd always called it, but she wore it everywhere—to ladies' teas, to supper bridge club, to Mass. And, of course, to bingo. She appears to you clear as day. As a matter of fact, you can tell from the way her lipstick has been applied that she's had a few.

She was so full of sorrow those years before she died. She couldn't fathom going on without your father. But you knew her sadness had also to do with the fact that you had renounced your faith shortly after you met Olivia—and you'd stuck to your guns. You refused a church wedding, even though you knew how much it meant to her. She'd been so convinced, on her deathbed, that she'd never see you again.

But here she is anyway, and not a minute too soon, so close that you can make out the crucifix that has always hung from her neck, the tiny Jesus with his arms outstretched, the palms of his hands pinned to the cross. You twist your fingers together and, with a huge effort, manage to make a thought: You'd like to summon a priest.

But it's too late for that. You can finally feel yourself going, and besides, it doesn't matter. It's just silliness. All the same, though—and just in case—you trace, with the thumb of one hand onto the palm of the other, the four points of the cross.

The funeral is a small affair, attended by only a few of Harry's friends and coworkers and Toni and her family. That evening Rory asks Brian to stay and is relieved when his brother agrees. There are meetings with lawyers about the will, phone calls with Harry's partners about insurance policies, papers to sort through, and all of that will take at least another week. The house will be sold, but not until the following summer, which means that Rory can have a comfortable place to live while he finishes high school and goes on, hopefully, to Columbia, his first choice.

Toni stops by most days, ostensibly to help with the sorting and cleaning, but Rory suspects it's a pretense for checking up on him. During the hours she's there, Brian disappears—Rory has no idea where—but often when he returns, he slurs his words and staggers.

There are no further conversations between the brothers about Olivia, but often Rory finds himself thinking about her. He saw a few photos of her in an album once, a long time ago, but the album has since disappeared—probably his father's doing. His mother was slight, he recalls, from the one photo he does remember seeing, with long black hair. She was wearing a droopy pink dress studded with tiny mirrors—the kind of dress you see in pictures of young girls in the sixties and seventies.

My mother. What a strange concept! If she turned up on his doorstep, he wouldn't recognize her. She probably has curly gray hair by now, like all the other middle-aged ladies he knows, the mothers of his friends. Maybe she's even fat.

Although he knows his brother has to get back to his work—and to his life—Rory wishes he would stay, until Columbia. It's not that he's afraid to be alone; Toni and her family are just around the corner, and he does have his friends. But over the past couple of weeks, the brothers have spent more time together than ever before, and he feels a connection—and, therefore, an impending *loss* of connection.

The day Brian is to return to New York is Rory's first day back at school after the Christmas holidays and the funeral. Rory had expected his brother to be gone by the time he arrived home that afternoon—they'd already said their goodbyes in the morning. But when he opens the front door, he can hear music coming from the living room. Brian, seated at the piano, is playing a piece that sounds familiar. Rory stands at the doorway listening until his brother finishes.

"What was that?" he asks as Brian closes the dusty lid.

"Oh, it's just a piece Mom taught me. I haven't played it since she left." He pauses. "I haven't played anything since she left."

"You haven't played the piano at all? And still, you can remember it?"

Brian gets up and retrieves his packed suitcase, standing in the corner. "I can remember every single thing," he says, opening the front door. "That's the problem."

ten

1985

The night of the Christmas piano recital Olivia's head is spinning from having to be in several places all at once: in one of the Sunday-school classrooms, giving last-minute instructions to her students (*bow before and after your performance, don't run to your seats when you've finished*); in the girls' bathroom, tinkering with the paper towel machine six-year-old Katie caught her hand in; in the parish hall, checking that the piano lid has been lifted, adjusting the music stand, bringing the lamp closer for the children who haven't memorized their pieces.

At seven thirty she'll lead her students into the hall. Recitals always begin with the youngest and end with the oldest, so the little ones can depart early if they get cranky. Which tonight really isn't likely, since after the final performance (a Schubert impromptu, played by Eddie Mercer) they've been promised that Santa will arrive with a sack full of the candies Olivia had selected from the Grand Union.

She switches on the piano lamp and looks out over the audience, noting that Elaine is seated in the third row beside Jude. Olivia waves, and Elaine smiles back. On Elaine's other side is Peter, fidgeting with his program.

Peter. Just his being there, supporting her, makes Olivia happy. When they met a year ago, he was a relatively new widower. He was seated across from Olivia at Elaine's dinner table waiting for the meal to be served, and she watched, amused, as he turned to the woman on his left during the soup and engaged her in a spirited conversation and then, a few minutes later, when the main course was served, did the same with the woman on his right. Isn't that what British royalty did during dinner? When he caught sight of Olivia observing him, he winked.

She consults her watch. It's time. She returns to the Sunday-school room and seconds later appears in the hallway leading the line of young musicians, eight girls, most of them in princess dresses in varying shades of pink, and two boys, both in jackets and tiny bow ties, to the row of empty seats at the front. After a quick introduction to the audience, she claps her hands three times and nods at Katie, who gets up from her seat, runs to the piano, and without bowing plunges into "The Jolly Farmer." When she's finished she spins around in the stool, twice, and then, failing again to bow, runs back to where her parents are seated, beaming proudly.

The night before, Peter had proposed that he move in with her. They had just finished dinner and were seated on Olivia's couch drinking coffee when he reached for her hand and said, "Would you like a roommate?"

For a moment she was confused. It surely couldn't be one of Peter's twin daughters. Jeannette was happily married and soon to give birth. And Caroline, who had recently emerged from a bad relationship, disliked Olivia—no matter how often Peter denied it.

Seeing her confusion, he said, "It's me, silly! I think we're ready to move on to something more permanent, unless, of course, you think—" He shrugged, letting his voice trail off, offering her the space to say no.

She placed her mug on the coffee table. What he was proposing would be hardly different from the arrangement they'd gradually fallen into, with him spending most nights with her in the schoolhouse, even though he owned a large brick house on a fine street in Burlington. The main difference would be that some of his furniture would come over, along with the rest of his clothes, the ones he didn't already keep at the schoolhouse.

"I know you don't have much space," he said. "But if you want me—and I realize that's a big if—we'll figure something out down the road."

In bed later, he said she should think about it, that he didn't need an immediate answer. That he didn't even want an immediate answer. But hell yes, she wanted him. He was—by far—the best thing that had happened to her in years.

She never imagined she'd find love so late in life, she told herself at the end of the evening when she was putting on her coat, after the students, stuffed with chocolate, had finally left with their parents.

The first night they slept together, he'd traced his finger along her stretch marks, those silvery stripes between her breasts and pubic hair that had multiplied after the birth of each child. Up and down went the tip of his finger, up and down, letting her know that he knew she'd had at least one child but that he wouldn't ask, he'd wait to be told. She wouldn't tell him, though, she decided then. She would not. Not even now, after he proposed to move in. The last thing she wanted was to lose him.

She hadn't told anyone about her past, not even Elaine. A few times over the years she'd been tempted. It was difficult, hiding a significant past event from someone you saw every week for lunch or coffee or a movie. Once, she and Elaine were out for a walk, and as they passed the spot where they could see the resort, Olivia grew pale. Elaine remarked on it, saying, "I don't know what just happened, but you're white as a sheet. You know, Liv, you don't have to tell me, but if you ever do decide to trust me with whatever happened to you—"

Olivia almost blurted it out right then. She almost pointed across the lake and said, *That place, that exact spot there, is where one of my children died.*

She wanted to, wanted to relieve herself of the burden of that long-ago action. But who knew how Elaine would take it?

She might see it as an act of pure selfishness—and who could blame her? So Olivia just said "Thank you" and continued on up the road. A moment later Elaine caught up with her and began describing a dress she'd seen in a store window that day, an emerald-green sheath with shoulder pads and a plunging neckline she thought she'd buy—it was the perfect thing…

She joins Elaine and Jude and Peter in the hallway.

"Another triumph," Elaine says, as if the recital had been held at Lincoln Center rather than in the parish hall of North Port's St. John's Episcopal. "I thought little Katie did well."

"I have great hopes for her." Olivia pulls her coat collar around her neck as they leave the building. Why do recitals always seem to occur on the hottest day of summer and the coldest day of winter? "Not many six-year-olds can play 'The Jolly Farmer.'"

Peter, opening the car door, says, "That was the first piece I learned. Also, thank God, the last."

Jude says, "What's happened to Seth? Your old student, Liv? I remember him—he took lessons at the same time Marcy did. He was a fantastic musician, I thought."

"He *is* fantastic. He's at Juilliard. He's only nineteen, and he's doing a summer tour in Tokyo and playing only Schubert. He recently came upon a trove of Schubert pieces that no one knew existed."

"You went to Juilliard, too, didn't you?" Elaine says.

Olivia's heart stops. How did Elaine know that? And what else does she know? She can feel her face grow hot. "I did."

"Seth told me. He used to come to the library to order sheet music. I could get it for him free."

"Ah. Yes." Funny. Elaine had never mentioned that she knew.

Peter, from the front seat, turns around and gives Olivia a quizzical look that she reads as *Juilliard? What other tricks do you have up your sleeve?*

The morning after the recital, she and Peter discuss Christmas. Last year Olivia had had Christmas dinner with Elaine and Jude, and Peter had gone by himself to Jeannette's. The relationship was too new, they'd agreed, to involve other family members. This year Peter wants them both to go to Jeannette's.

"It was her idea," he says as he refills Olivia's mug.

He's about to leave for San Francisco, where he'll spend a week visiting his mother, who's in a nursing home. He drains his own mug and stands up.

"Well, okay," Olivia says, following him into the hallway. "If you really think it won't be too much for her, this late in her pregnancy. I can bring something."

"Tell her that. Give her a call." He grabs his briefcase from the stand in the hall. "It'll be good for her to have another woman around. Next Christmas, though—"

She knows what he's thinking. He's excited about the birth

of his first grandchild. She feels a pang as she realizes that if she herself had grandchildren, she wouldn't know it.

He continues the conversation as he opens the front door. "When I'm back," he says, "we'll tell the girls about our decision. They'll be thrilled."

Well, maybe Jeannette will, Olivia thinks, as she closes the door behind him. She's not so sure about Caroline.

Watching through the window as his car backs out of the driveway, she vows to make the most of his absence. It will be the last time that she's utterly on her own. In ten days he'll be back, the week after that will be Christmas at Jeannette and Jeb's cottage outside of Burlington, and in the new year—she smiles and shivers in anticipation. It's been a long time since she's allowed herself to look forward to something.

After finishing the breakfast dishes, she puts on her coat to go Christmas shopping. Perhaps she'll buy Peter a sweater, or maybe that new novel he mentioned a couple of days ago. Or both. She'll also pick up a present for Jeannette. And of course something for Peter's first grandchild.

She has some free time now, until the middle of January when her lessons begin again. She'll spend some of it turning out closets and shelves, maybe toss out the clothes she no longer wears. Space will be tight when Peter moves in, although this morning, when they woke, he mentioned that they might consider expanding the schoolhouse out the back and renovating the kitchen.

She must call Elaine. Elaine will be excited at her news.

A couple of months after Olivia and Peter began seeing each other, Peter had brought his daughters to meet her.

"You're going to love them," he said before they arrived. "They're intelligent, beautiful, generous—" He caught her eye, as if waiting for her to chime in with a superlative he may have missed.

"I get the picture," she said, laughing. But later, when she remembered the conversation, she wondered how he could have gotten Caroline so wrong. How he'd managed to miss how jealous, how proprietorial she was of her father.

They arrived an hour late. He'd gone into Burlington to pick up the girls, and Caroline, he said, had had to do a couple of errands before she could join them.

"What a beautiful spot," Jeannette said when she stepped out of the car, taking in the view of the trees that lined the property, the rugosa bushes in full bloom, and the lone magnolia Olivia had planted the year after she bought the place.

Indoors, the table was set. Olivia had picked a bouquet of wildflowers from along the roadside and placed them in a glass jar that she set in the middle of the table. The lamb and vegetables were on warming plates in the oven.

Caroline took a look around and said, "It's such a nice night. Why don't we eat outdoors?"

Peter glanced over at Olivia, who was trying not to show her annoyance. The dinner had been ready for an hour.

"What a good idea!" she said, clapping her hands together. "But I don't have an outdoor table. Why don't we just unset this one and carry it outdoors."

Peter seemed relieved, and as he and Jeannette sprang into action and Olivia assembled four trays, Caroline walked over to the end of the room and stood in front of the bookshelves, scanning the titles and pulling out the odd book to examine before replacing it.

"Are you from Baltimore?" she asked Olivia, who was stacking dinner plates. "You sure read a lot of Anne Tyler."

"New Jersey," Olivia said. "Originally." Who was this girl, to come and disrupt all of her careful plans? The lamb would probably be dried out, the vegetables cold by the time they got around to eating. All of that would reflect badly on Olivia—and she'd so wanted things to be perfect.

"I love Anne Tyler," Olivia said. "But strangely, I don't actually select my reading material according to where the book is set."

When Peter and Jeannette came back inside, Olivia handed them each a tray. A moment later, they were all seated outdoors chatting. It was a lovely night. Olivia felt silly for having had reservations—and hoped it hadn't shown.

The girls spent much of the meal focused on each other. If there was really such a thing as a dominant twin, Caroline was obviously it. She was the one who asked most of the questions, the one who finished her sister's sentences. Toward the end of the meal she asked to use the bathroom and disappeared back inside.

While she was gone, Peter and Jeannette discussed the

coming grandchild, speculating about its gender—shortly to be determined—and about its possible physical appearance and temperament. Would they hire a nanny, Peter asked, or send the child to day care? Olivia left them to it and began stacking plates. When she went back inside for coffee, Caroline was nowhere to be seen. A moment later she appeared from Olivia's bedroom, saying she hadn't been able to find the bathroom.

Olivia pointed. It was in an obvious spot, next to the bedroom, and its door had been open, revealing the bilious orange tile Olivia had never bothered to replace.

After apple tart and further baby discussion, Caroline began to aim a series of questions at Olivia. When did she come to Vermont? Why? Didn't she like New Jersey? Did she still have family back there? When did she start teaching piano? And why, if she had studied music, hadn't she become a performer?

"Those who can't do, teach," Olivia said lightly and then cringed as she remembered her mother saying exactly that when told her daughter would be teaching instead of performing.

"Woody Allen," Caroline said.

"I believe it was actually George Bernard Shaw." *Score one for me.*

"Hey, girls," Peter said. "Enough questions, don't you think?" even though Jeannette had been silent during the interrogation.

At the end of the evening, Jeannette pointed to the little graveyard behind the church. "Is that yours? Your very own cemetery?"

"It belongs to the church actually. Well, at least technically, since the church is abandoned. Someone told me it was deconsecrated, so I guess you can't even call it a church."

The girls and Peter went over to examine the markers, and when they returned Jeannette said, "How sad. How beautiful and how sad. Especially that mother, with all those dead children. I can't imagine how she could have borne it."

"It's surprising how much one can bear," Olivia said, then bit her tongue.

Caroline gave her a sharp look.

When they were gone, Olivia went inside and began cleaning up. It could have gone better, she thought, but thank God it was over. Caroline was a force to reckon with. Olivia would have to be very careful when her name came up in conversation with Peter.

Then she recalled that the girl had been in her bedroom. She went into the room. Everything seemed as usual, until she noticed that her handbag, which always hung on its own hook on the closet door, was slightly askew. She brought the bag to her bed, where she sat and examined its contents. All present and accounted for, she thought, until she opened her wallet and noticed that her driver's license was in the pocket beneath her credit card, instead of above it. She pulled it out. Olivia Jane Somerville, it read. It was the only piece of ID she hadn't bothered to change back to her maiden name, assuming that it would be too complicated without a record of divorce.

She returned the handbag to its hook. Then she went over to her night table and sat back down on the edge of the bed, considering. Inside the drawer were the three items she'd grabbed from her children's bedrooms when she went back home for the painting. At the time she wasn't sure why she did it; she only knew that she needed to. In her new life, if she should have one, those items would be the only record of proof that her boys had existed. The only proof that once she had been a mother.

She has never opened the drawer—it's been enough just to know that they were there—but now she slides it open. Had Caroline looked inside? And if so, had she wondered what part its contents played in Olivia's past?

She pulled them out—the hat, the bear, and the purple blanket fragment. She brought this last item to her face. Was it her imagination, or could she still smell Andrew?

Without replacing them, she undressed for bed. Then she turned out the light and hugged them to herself, tight.

Cleaning out dresser drawers and kitchen cabinets is no way to spend the day when there's Christmas shopping to be done. After Peter has departed, she calls Elaine, who says she's getting off work early.

"Come for an eggnog," she offers. "Sometime after two?"

Olivia decides to make headway on her Christmas list before joining her friend. She drives into town and parks behind the new pop-up Christmas shop. The sidewalks are crowded, forcing her to elbow her way around mothers pushing strollers, through groups of skateboarding teenage boys. Multicolored lights wink off and on between the branches of the blue spruces that line each side of the canal. The front lawn of St. John's contains a wooden crèche with Mary and Joseph, life-size, bending over the cradle. On top of the crèche is an angel holding up a gold star.

She's briefly reminded of that first Christmas she spent in North Port, when Bing Crosby was piped through the town, and it was all she could do to stop herself from screaming from memories of past Christmases—and loneliness. Well, that's over, now.

Across from the church is the department store. Inside, she makes her way through to the children's section. In mind is a quilt for Jeannette's new baby. The selection is huge, and she spends a happy half hour examining each quilt before finally deciding on a blue-and-yellow one appliquéd with giraffes.

The men's section is practically empty. In minutes Olivia has selected and paid for a gray cashmere sweater and is back outside again, heading for the bookstore. What was the name of that book Peter mentioned? It was by someone Cornwell, and he'd mentioned the word *sharp* in the title. *Bingo,* she thinks as she scans the mystery shelf. It's Bernard, Bernard Cornwell, and most of his titles have the word *Sharpe* in them. She checks the date in each book and buys the latest.

She consults her watch. It's nearly time to meet Elaine. After coffee, she'll pop into the crafts store, where she'll probably find some candles for Jeannette and for her own house, too, and, hopefully, some boughs of spruce. And a tree, she must have a tree! It will be her first here in Vermont. They're selling them in the parking lot of the Grand Union. She imagines Peter coming in the door from California to a house lit up with candles and, in one corner, a beautifully decorated Christmas tree. She'll stop there on the way home from Elaine's.

Christmas! she thinks, suddenly suffused with the spirit of the season. *Wrapped presents! Snow globes! Carols! Colored lights!*

And now it's starting to snow, not a lot, just a few flakes here and there that seem to drift horizontally through the air rather than fall. The temperature has dropped, and Olivia tucks her scarf under her collar. By the time she reaches Elaine's house, it's really coming down.

She sits by herself in the sunroom while Elaine prepares a tray. Through the window she can see a bank of oaks and maples, their trunks spun with ivy. Beyond them is a tangle of lilac, untended and out of control, that leads to a wooded area Elaine has often spoken of doing something with but—so far—hasn't. One summer a bear and her two cubs took up residence there.

When Elaine appears with a tray, Olivia tells her her news. She talks about Jeannette and how excited she is to become, in essence, a grandmother. When it's time to leave, she mentions Caroline and how the girl has never warmed to her.

"She snooped around in my bedroom one time last spring. She went through my wallet, and my night table."

"How brave of her," Elaine says. "Everyone around here would jump at the chance to go through your wallet and night table."

Is she joking?

Elaine hands her a little plate of cookies, shaped like stars. "Taste these. I thought, maybe, too much anise. What do you think?"

The next nine days pass quickly. Olivia manages to empty a couple of drawers for Peter, hauling the clothes she's discarded to Goodwill. She buys extra hangers and places her out-of-season clothes in a box under the bed. She makes a fruitcake to bring to Jeannette's and ices it with marzipan she made by grinding her own almonds, even though there's a whole shelf of it to be had at the Grand Union.

She purchases a Le Creuset casserole dish for Jeannette and wraps it in silver foil. The next day, vowing to keep putting her best foot forward no matter how much she is disliked, she returns to the same store and buys another for Caroline, but in black, for when she returns from Florida.

Then she turns her attention to the house, putting candles into glass ramekins and placing one in each window. She buys a small crèche, the manger made of twisted willow, which she fills with tiny porcelain figurines of the Holy Family. The tree she picked up at the supermarket stands on a table beside the bookcase, decorated with silver balls and blue lights. She bakes gingerbread men, outlining the fronts of each with green and red frosting and suspending them from the tree branches. She cuts out a cardboard star and applies gold paint to each side, then, when it's sufficiently dry, attaches it to the top of the tree with paper clips and string.

Peter calls each night, sometimes twice. His mother is holding her own, he says. He can't wait to get back home.

He's already calling the place home! She gazes around the house with satisfaction at the lights and decorations and candles.

The night before he's due back, he doesn't call. Olivia doesn't think much about it. He'll be saying his final goodbyes to his mother, wishing her Merry Christmas, before going back to his hotel to pack for his morning flight. He should arrive back by early afternoon. She can barely wait.

But by three the next afternoon, she still hasn't heard from him. Could his plane be late? Perhaps the weather has closed in, somewhere between California and Vermont. Surely, though, he would have managed to contact her if it had.

By seven, she's frantic and can't manage even one bite of the dinner she's prepared for his welcome home: sole almondine, green beans, wild rice, and a lemon pie. At nine, she clears away the meal, goes into her bedroom, and lies down. A little later, the phone rings.

"Hello?"

Without even a greeting, he says, "Caroline told me something today."

Olivia takes a slow breath and waits, knowing that nothing he says will she want to hear.

"Are you still there?"

"I'm here." Inside her head is a beating noise. *Thump, thump. Thump, thump.* She closes her eyes.

He pauses for a moment, then says, "She told me she found a report on women missing in the 1970s." He waits. When she doesn't respond, he goes on. "The report states that an Olivia

Somerville from Montclair, New Jersey, was reported missing on August 11, 1971."

Olivia doesn't say anything.

"'Race: white,'" he goes on.

She remains silent.

He continues, his voice flat and cold, as if he's reading a weather report. "'Gender: female. Hair: black, long, straight. Eye color: blue.'" He stops.

"Yes," she finally says.

"Under the heading Details of Disappearance, it reads, 'Mrs. Somerville was last seen on the day of her son's death at the bus station in North Port, Vermont, where she was assumed to have boarded a bus to New York City.'"

As he says the words "her son's death," she holds the phone away from her ear. If she could allow herself to hear what he's saying, she might say some things herself. She could advise him to tell his daughter that if she cared about him, she should mind her own business. Or she could tell him that sometimes very well-intentioned people, when damaged or in shock, do things they may regret, things they may be unable to ever undo. Or she could just plead with him to trust her, to disregard everything Caroline has told him, everything he's just read out to her on the phone. They've loved each other for almost a year. What they have is working...

But she can't do any of this. Instead, she very quietly—so quietly she's not sure he can even hear her—says, "Goodbye, Peter." And then she carefully replaces the phone.

For a long while she remains seated in her chair, stunned. She could almost convince herself that he will call her back, tell her the whole thing was a misunderstanding, but somewhere inside she knows he won't.

The light makes its way around the curtains. A whole night has gone by. From outside comes the sound of chirping. And there are other noises, too: a car engine rhythmically turning over, then dying. Two women chatting as they walk by. She gets out of bed, goes into the kitchen, fills a glass with water, and drinks.

I've done it again, she thinks as she dumps into the sink the plates from the night before. The happiness she's felt this past year has been false. But her mistake wasn't giving away too much of herself, as her mother had once said when Olivia was pining after a boy who was quite obviously not pining back. Her mistake was giving herself away at all.

It wouldn't have worked, she tells herself as she scrapes the fish skin from a serving platter and plunges it into the steaming water, then reaches for the salad bowl and tips the wilted leaves into the trash. It wouldn't have worked at all.

eleven

1987

He should have called first, instead of just turning up. But what if she'd said no, which she had every right to do? The last time Brian saw Toni was two years ago, at his father's funeral, and although she was very helpful with the organization of the service and the reception, he never thanked her. And he hasn't been in touch since.

But there are some things he needs to know, things Rory doesn't know and has no interest in finding out about. Things only Toni might be able to tell him.

Funny little neighborhood, he thinks, striding past rows of small Cape Cod houses, identical except for their color. So unlike the sprawling house he grew up in, only a couple of blocks away. He noticed, when he passed their old place a few minutes ago, that the new owners had expanded the kitchen outward and built a conservatory off the back. He wonders why his father, an architect, never thought to do that. But of course there's that old saying about the shoemaker's children going barefoot.

Toni's house, at the end of the block, is painted Williamsburg blue. Like the other houses on the street, it has a front door that's positioned smack in the middle of its plain exterior, with two windows at either end. All the place needs is smoke curling from its chimney and a family of stick figures standing in front of the door.

She's lived here for years, and Brian has never even seen it, much less been inside. Not that he hasn't been asked. But he'd just dropped out of Princeton when she left Harry, and soon after that—very soon after that—she met Frank. By that time, Brian had decided he didn't want to come home. He didn't want to come anywhere near home. And so he'd moved into the city, where he rented a room on Perry Street—a shabby room where bugs crawled up the walls, a small, hot cell with a window that faced a courtyard where teenagers slouched all day and broke bottles all night.

He steps up onto the porch and rings the bell. A minute goes by. He lifts the brass knocker and releases it. When the door finally opens, it takes a moment for him to recognize her. She's wearing a funny floral wraparound thing that doesn't resemble any woman's daytime garment he's ever seen, and her feet are bare. Also, her face is red, so red it appears to have been dipped in a lobster pot.

She's been crying.

"Toni?"

"Brian? Is that—?" For a moment she just stands there, staring at him.

"It's me," he says.

She steps forward to hug him. "Come in."

He follows her to the kitchen, catching sight of a neat, spare interior. Plain furniture made of light wood, all straight lines and smooth surfaces. Navy drapes at every window. A flowering houseplant set in the middle of a narrow trestle table.

"I was just—" He shrugs.

"—in the neighborhood?" she says, and they both laugh. "Have a seat. I was just about to have some coffee. Would you like that, or tea? I have tea."

"Coffee would be good."

She pulls a Kleenex from the sleeve of the odd-looking garment and blows her nose. "You caught me at a bad moment. It's the twins' first day at preschool."

Twins? Had Rory ever mentioned that?

"I'm sorry," he says. "To come by without calling first."

"No matter. You're the perfect distraction. And since I didn't expect you, I can't feel guilty that my—outfit—is less than presentable." She laughs again and says, "It's called a muumuu—the latest thing in ladies' wear," and taking a can of coffee from the fridge, she busies herself with the coffee maker. It's not until she turns her back to fetch the mugs from a shelf that he feels courageous enough to say, "I've come about my mother."

"It's their first day of school," she says again, passing the sugar bowl to Brian. "That's why my face is so red."

They're in the family room, seated on the low-slung couch

beneath the window, through which Brian can see two bikes leaning against the garage, both pink, with training wheels attached. There's a sandbox filled with toys, and a swing set with a slide. A lone bare doll lies on the grass under a tree.

Brian fishes about for something to say to break the ice, finally settling on, "Did they cry?"

"*I* cried. They went into the classroom without looking back. I stood beside the door for a few minutes, then peeked in through the little window. Sarah was sitting on the floor under a huge stuffed giraffe, looking at a picture book. Anna was staring into a goldfish bowl."

She reaches for another Kleenex from the box on the coffee table and wipes her eyes. Then she says, "How long has it been, Brian?"

"Two years, I think. Nearly three. When Dad died."

They fall silent, Brian thinking about that day, the day of Harry's funeral. It was just before Christmas, and there was a blizzard. After the reception, Toni had tidied up the church hall, clearing away all of the dishes, washing the various parts of the coffee maker, and sliding the chairs back against the wall. Then she'd put on her coat and walked back home through the snowstorm. Remembering all of this now, Brian's face reddens. He should have thanked her. He should have driven her home. He hopes she doesn't remember, hopes she doesn't hold it against him.

"So, your mother," she says. "You do know, don't you, that I never met her?"

"Yes, of course. But I thought you might have, well, absorbed something about her. Through Dad, maybe?"

Toni places her mug on the coffee table. "Your father didn't talk a lot about her. As you know. But yes, you're right, I did absorb quite a bit, over the years. The few years we were married, that is. I knew from the beginning, of course, that she'd disappeared."

"Because of Andrew." He holds his mug very still, not wanting to break her train of thought.

"Yes, because of Andrew. And then there was that painting. I think it was you who first realized it was gone."

Brian nods. "I'd forgotten that."

Toni runs her thumb along the rim of her mug. "She was thirty-three years old when she left. So young."

I'm twenty-five, he thinks. *At my age, she already had a husband. She had a child—maybe two by then—and a house and a whole settled life. And then a death.*

Seeming to read his mind, she asks, "Do you have anyone?"

He looks at her blankly.

"A girlfriend? A wife? But I guess Rory would have told me."

He gives his head a little shake. "No. I'm not married. But there *is* someone I met recently. Her name is Ava. But it's too soon, yet, to—" He shrugs.

Toni nods. She drinks from her mug, then sets it down on the table. "So, Olivia. Hmm. Let me think. Did you know that when your father met her, she was a flower child?"

"You mean beads and incense. The whole bit?" He smiles, unable to reconcile the memory of his mother with such an unlikely creature.

"She went to Woodstock. She had friends who were going,

and your father encouraged her to go along. She went for the music, your dad said. It was originally billed as a weekend of music. No one knew, of course, what would happen, that it would become this incredible legend—"

"The summer of '69. I was nine. Andrew was what—three? Or four?" He smiles, thinking of it. "Funny—I don't really remember."

"Your mother hated it! She told your father it was worse than Girl Scout camp, that at Girl Scout camp they at least had showers."

She goes back into the kitchen, returns with the coffeepot, and tops off their mugs. Back seated on the couch, she says, "When I first came—not long after your mother left—everything in the house was exactly as she'd left it. Your father was living—well, not exactly in a state of suspended animation, but something close to it. Even though he accepted—he knew—that your mother was gone for good, he said he felt that at any moment she'd be coming through the door.

"I was supposed to clean, shop, get the meals, et cetera, as well as take care of you and Rory. Everything, or nearly everything, that your mother did. I remember doing the laundry the first week I was with you. Your mother had left some of her dirty clothes in her hamper before you all went away that weekend." She pauses, then says, "That last weekend."

Brian closes his eyes, trying—but failing—to recall that morning before they left.

"When I pulled the hamper out of her closet, your father saw what I was about to do. He insisted that I not touch it. He put it back and closed the closet door.

"Your mother's dirty clothes remained in that hamper until the week after your father and I were married. Nine years. When we got back from our honeymoon, the first thing I did was haul that dirty laundry out of the closet. I stuffed it into garbage bags, along with the rest of the things she didn't take with her. Your father came into the room at one point, and when he saw what I was doing he turned white and went back out. I hauled the bags out to the curb myself. Then I went back inside and filled your mother's closet with my things."

She looks at her watch. "Goodness, it's nearly time to pick up the girls." She looks at Brian. "Stay, Brian. Stay and have lunch with us. We can keep talking."

While she's gone, he's tempted to explore the house. Even though he lives in a small, one-bedroom apartment, houses are his thing, and it's been ages since he's been in one. He looks around, taking in the polished buffet and the jar of anemones on top, the TV in the corner, the basket of newspapers and magazines. A dollhouse underneath the window. It's a real home, a family home. He kicks off his shoes and, pulling the crocheted afghan from the arm of the couch, spreads it over himself. What he'd really like to do most in the world is stay here on this couch in this puddle of sunshine. He closes his eyes.

When Toni arrives back a little later, his eyes fly open. She's carrying one twin in her arms, and the other is trailing behind. Struggling to get his bearings, he sits up.

"This is Brian," she says as both girls stare at him. "He's your brother—sort of. Say hi."

"Why is he sleeping in our house?" one twin asks.

He feels embarrassed, as if he's done something wrong. "Hi, girls," he says lamely.

"Hi," they respond, in small, shy voices. They are identical, although they're dressed differently, one in a blue jumper and a blouse, the other in a pink dress. They are obviously suspicious of this stranger their mother calls a brother, who for some unknown reason has ended up on the sofa in their living room.

He joins them in the kitchen while Toni prepares their sandwiches, the girls chattering away about their first day at school. One twin says she looked through a microscope and saw the legs of a spider. Her sister begins to cry. She didn't get to see the spider.

"It was too late," Twin One points out. "It was time for Circle. You were playing with the Harriet doll, remember?"

"Never mind," Toni says, pulling two bananas from the fruit bowl. "You can see the spider legs tomorrow."

Twin Two stops crying and begins kicking the seat of her chair. She stares over at Brian and says, "Are you really our brother?"

Her sister takes a bite of banana and, looking him up and down, observes, "He's too big to be a brother."

"He's not big, he's just old," Twin Two says.

Brian smiles helplessly at Toni, who says, "Come on, girls. Nap time."

Despite cries and pleas and a mild temper tantrum from Twin Two, Toni takes them upstairs. He can hear them overhead, one girl jumping on a bed, the other pleading for something her mother is obviously not going to give her.

Until recently, Brian assumed he would eventually have children. If he had kids, he always vowed, he'd make sure they had a mother in the house, and if he ever had to leave them, even for a short time, he'd always tell them where he was going. And he'd be back when he said he would.

Lately, though, he's been wondering if it would be wise for him to inflict himself on small, innocent people, who, like Toni's girls, could obviously sense that there's something wrong with him. And why wouldn't there be? His life, so far, has been a disappointment, and most of that has been his fault. The reason he couldn't finish school was not that the work was too hard but that he couldn't focus on it properly. There was something wrong with his brain.

Which was why, after Princeton, he was determined to prove to himself—and to the world—that he was capable of doing something right, something ordinary that nearly everyone managed to do. So far, he's failed. He's almost twenty-six, and he hasn't got a house, or a wife, or kids. And he drinks too much, he knows that. At the moment there doesn't seem to be any point in not drinking.

Toni comes back down and makes sandwiches for both of them. As they eat, he summons up his courage.

"Why did you and Dad break up?"

She ponders the question for a moment. "Your dad was my first real love. Without your mom having gotten there first, I think it would have worked. But, truthfully, I found it difficult to lie in bed beside someone who was always yearning for someone else." She smiles. "It's difficult to compete with a ghost. A better way to put it might be that your mother's absence was almost as strong as her presence. Or at least, it was to me."

"But I was telling you what she was like." She bites into her sandwich and a moment later says, "When I went through the few clothes she left when we were first married, it occurred to me how much she liked bright colors. Her dresses and blouses were red or yellow or orange or bright pink. Even her underwear. Her top dresser drawer was filled with beads and ribbons. And she had a feather boa! It made me wonder: What kind of woman wears a boa? And I concluded, a confident woman! I remember thinking how strange it was that for years I'd imagined that she was a dark, gloomy, depressed sort of person—but her clothes proved me wrong.

"And there were other hints to her personality. Her choice of books, for one. She kept her childhood books; they were on a shelf opposite the bed. Her favorite stories were about girls who were passionate about music, or ballet, or social work, or flying airplanes. You know the kind of thing: 'Against all odds, Veronica gets accepted into the American Ballet Theatre,' or 'Amelia Earhart finally learns to fly a plane.'"

"She wanted to be a pianist," Brian says. "But she wasn't good enough. At least, that's what my father said."

"Yes. Your dad said it was her one big sorrow."

"Until Andrew."

"Yes."

A few minutes pass. Brian wonders if he should go. Maybe she'd planned to do something when the girls were napping that she couldn't do when they were awake.

But she shows no signs of wanting him to leave. She says, "I even thought I found evidence of her personality in the recipes she collected."

Brian lights up. "I remember that mandarin orange salad she made with marshmallows and whipped cream." He laughs. "I've looked everywhere for that recipe!"

Toni says, "Would you believe that in her recipe box, under *P*, she filed the recipe for Play-Doh?"

"I helped her make that. You had to use a lot of salt and flour. Then we colored it pink and she added vanilla—for the smell, she said. I remember Rory eating it."

"She wasn't dark," Toni says. "That's my point—she couldn't have been a dark person, even though you might have thought she was. In light of things."

"I've never known what to think."

"How *is* Rory?" she asks after a moment.

"He's fine, I guess. In another couple of years it'll be med school. As planned."

"He's always wanted to deliver babies. He'll make a good doctor. He has the touch, and the sensitivity." She toys with her crust, then sets her sandwich down. "I wonder if he still has those night terrors."

"What night terrors? I wasn't aware of anything like that."

"Oh yes," Toni says. "I'm surprised you never noticed—although I guess you were always asleep by that time. When he was very little he had night terrors, which are something quite different from nightmares. He'd turn up in the living room hours after he'd been tucked in, shaking and screaming. Making no sense. Your father would lead him back to bed, at which point he'd quiet down. He never remembered anything about it in the morning. Then, much later, when he was in high school, he had regular nightmares. Sometimes we'd wake up and hear him shouting. But if we mentioned it the next day, he'd get embarrassed, so we learned not to." Toni eyes Brian's empty mug. "I could make more coffee, if you like. And I have cookies."

"No thanks. I'm good. I should think about getting back to the city." But he remains seated. "Do you think," he says, "that any of that—Rory's nightmares, that is—had to do with our mother leaving?"

"Your father thought so. No one really knows what two-year-olds think, do they? Basically, since they don't remember."

"'The amnesia of childhood.' I've heard it described. How convenient."

"Yes."

Brian finally gets to his feet and Toni says, "Rory was here in July, by the way. He stayed the weekend. He and Frank went fishing on Long Beach Island."

"Ah," Brian says. "Well, you've obviously seen him more recently than I have. I think Christmas was the last time he and I got together. We went for drinks in SoHo." He looks at the wall clock.

From the couch Toni says, so quietly Brian can barely make it out, "So, have you decided to look for your mother? Is that what this has been all about?"

"No," Brian says, not meeting her eyes. "I mean, yes, that's what this has been about, but no, I haven't decided. Yet."

"Do you want my opinion?"

He avoids the question. "I'm not sure I want to find her. And that's the truth. If she wanted to be found, I imagine she would have made the move to find us. Although, maybe she's afraid. And maybe she has regrets about leaving—"

Go on, go on, he can almost hear Toni thinking. *Keep talking!*

The sun, streaming through the window above the dollhouse, disappears behind a cloud, and when Brian glances down at Toni, her face is cast in shadow, her features blurred. He wonders what she's thinking.

He plows on. "I always thought she must not have loved me. Or else…" He shrugs.

There's a long silence. Brian puts his hand on the doorknob, but before he can open the door, Toni says, "You can't just assume such a thing."

"Can't I? Why not?"

"Speaking as a mother, I think I can understand what she did. If I imagined myself in her position, the temptation might be very strong to just not know. And then just leave."

"Really? You could see yourself leaving your family forever?"

Toni sighs. "I don't know, Brian. I'm not sure. I just can't tell you for sure that I wouldn't."

He opens the door, but before he steps out, she says, "Brian."

He turns.

"I'm sorry."

He waits.

"I'm sorry. I'm sorry for your childhood. Rory may have had some deep-rooted problems, but I was the only mother he knew. With you there was a lack, and I didn't know how to fill it. I saw the problem, but I couldn't solve it. I'm sorry."

"That's okay," he says, smiling. "How could you solve it? There was only one person in the world who could do that."

PART THREE

twelve

1995

One morning Olivia wakes early, thinking that there's something about the day that's significant, only she can't remember what. It's gnawing away at the back of her mind. She sits up. It's still dark, but through the window she can hear the introductory peep of the dawn chorus.

What is it? She lies back down. Her brain is foggy, and it's way too early to get up. She'll try to go back to sleep. Whatever the day is meant to bring, it won't begin at this ungodly hour. She brings her hands to her face and cups her eyes with her palms, the way she did as a child when she wanted to soothe herself. It doesn't work. Then she strokes her cheeks and her shoulders and smooths her fingertips over her breasts.

And there it is, on the inner side of her right breast. A small, hard lump. She runs her finger around its perimeter, slowly wiggling it, back and forth. It moves with her finger.

Didn't she read something about that recently? That if it moves, it's cancer, and if it stays put, it's not?

Or was it the reverse?

She gets out of bed and goes over to the full-length mirror. Both breasts appear fine. They are, as far as she can tell, symmetrical. There's no redness, no swelling, nor is there any puckering in her breast. Didn't that article mention something about puckering?

It's probably nothing. She surveys the rest of her body. She's slimmer than most women her age, much slimmer than Elaine, who's constantly trying to diet away her menopausal weight. Olivia has never gained an ounce. Her waist tapers in, then flares slightly at the hips. She turns and looks over her shoulder. Her buttocks are smooth and undimpled. As far as she can see, she has no cellulite, whatever that is. Her thighs and calves are, happily, devoid of the bulging veins that afflict so many women of her age. And her hair is as dark as it ever was, except for a half-inch band of gray in the front that Lorna trims when it falls over her eyes.

As near as she can tell, she looks fine. And she feels energetic, still teaching, still able to go for those walks to the resort and back every day. All seems well.

Except for that lump.

She goes back to her bedroom to get dressed when the significance of the day hits her. Today she is fifty-seven years old.

Over the next week she finds herself constantly checking. Is it still there? In the middle of a piano lesson, she excuses herself to go into the bedroom to feel underneath her bra. At the supermarket she finds her hand sliding between the top buttons of her blouse, pulling it out when she sees a young man eyeing her strangely.

That evening she can barely find the lump and concludes that the whole thing must have been her imagination. But the next morning it's back.

Over the next several weeks she and the lump coexist. It's her secret from the world. She doesn't even mention it to Elaine when they drive into Burlington to see *Braveheart*. She still checks it often, though, and when she does, it feels exactly the same. But of course, if it were growing slowly, she probably wouldn't notice it.

Why is she hesitating to call the doctor? Everyone knows that early diagnosis is the key to survival. But there's something about having a breast lump that she finds—well—interesting. That's the word for it. The lump has made her life interesting.

Sometimes in the afternoon she'll lie down, close her eyes, and move her fingers over its boundaries, marveling at its potential significance. This slight, less-than-one-inch sphere—a tiny planet—might contain within itself the story of the end of her life.

She recalls some lines from a hymn she used to sing at the private girls' school she was sent to:

What though, in solemn silence, all
Move round the dark terrestrial ball?

What if it's cancer and she lets it go? It would grow bigger, of course, and spread into the glands in her armpit. And from there it would travel to her stomach and her lungs and maybe to her brain. Eventually it would win.

And what's so bad about that? She ponders this question for days, before reaching the conclusion: Because then I'll never know.

She phones her doctor's office. The nurse states that there isn't a spot available for a few weeks, but when Olivia says those two words, out loud and for the first time—*breast lump*—a space is suddenly cleared for the next morning.

Several times that day Olivia almost calls to cancel. The alacrity with which the nurse gave her the appointment has alarmed her. But not only that, she realizes that whatever happens—whether the lump proves to be cancer or something quite innocuous—she's about to be swallowed up by a machine that switches into gear at the words *breast lump*, and, following its own immutable laws, leaves its patients childlike and helpless and frightened, until they're regurgitated from it, either healthy or dead.

"Well," the doctor says, after poking and kneading and rolling his hands over both of her breasts, "I'm not that impressed. I think it's a cyst. I'm 99 percent sure it's a cyst, but of course—" He pauses and, reaching for his pen, scrawls something on a pad of paper. For a moment Olivia thinks he's forgotten her.

"—of course?" she prods.

He caps his pen and tosses it on the desk. "We'll have to see. We'll just have to see. We'll need a biopsy, of course. Just in case. I'll give you a referral for that. There are a couple of surgeons in Burlington. But as I said—"

At home, she examines the paper, which lists the name of the surgeon, the address of the clinic, the phone number, and the date of her appointment, in ten days' time.

Step one, and into the machine.

Over the next few days she barely gives it a thought. It's out of her hands now. She even stops feeling for the lump. Her job is simply to follow the instructions on that piece of paper, and the piece of paper after that.

The night before her procedure she finally tells Elaine.

"My dear," she says, after Olivia has finished speaking.

"I'll be fine," she says quickly, because she doesn't want her friend to worry, even though she herself doesn't believe it.

"I'll bring potato soup," Elaine says, alarming Olivia even further. Whenever someone in Jude's parish is dying, Elaine is there with her potato soup.

The appointment is an early one. She's there by seven, and a few moments later, undressed and gowned, she's whisked on a gurney into a small, brightly lit room. Headphones with classical music are offered, and during the first section of the "Raindrop" Prelude, antiseptic pads cleanse the area surrounding the right nipple. A local anesthetic is injected into the site.

Before the Chopin resolves from C-sharp Minor to D-flat Major, Olivia's headphones are removed and a nurse is helping her off the table. Did it happen?

Apparently it did.

"It can take up to ten days," the nurse responds, to Olivia's question about the results. "Now go home and don't worry. Don't even think about it."

Olivia, incredulous, raises an eyebrow. *Don't even think about it.* Does the stupid cow tell every dying person the same thing?

For days she lies in bed or on the couch, getting up only to fix herself tea or a quick meal. She's tired and worried. She finds that it's only by lying absolutely still, on her side with the sheet pulled up around her head, hood-like, that she can quell the panic that keeps rising in her chest, making her heart beat so fast she wonders whether she'll survive it to fight the cancer, if that's what she has.

Elaine arrives one day with her soup and Margaret Atwood's *The Robber Bride*. "It's about betrayal," she says. "But it's also funny. I figure it might be something you'd like, right about now."

Because it's starting to rain, the women eat their meal in

the living room beside the window. Outside, sodden chickadees huddle around the edge of the bird feeder. After they peck up the seeds, they hurry back to their refuge in the trees. Occasionally Elaine mentions a parishioner of Jude's, or repeats an anecdote about a library patron, but for the most part the women are silent. It's the lump, Olivia realizes, that's the focus of attention, although Olivia doesn't bring it up and Elaine doesn't mention it. The lump is the elephant in the room. The ghost at the party.

When Elaine rises to go, she asks, "Have you told anyone else?"

What she means, obviously, is who should she tell if something happens to Olivia? It's the perfect opening for her to speak about her life—her whole life, not just the Vermont bit. But what would be the point? It might, briefly, be a relief to share the pain that occasionally bubbles to the surface, but she's lived with it long enough to know that sharing would bring only temporary comfort. It wouldn't change a thing.

She gets up from the table and reaches for the soup bowls. "No," she finally says. "There's no one *to* tell."

She stands and leans against the doorframe, watching as her friend drives away.

A few days later, the nurse from the doctor's office calls. Her biopsy results are back. She makes an appointment for Olivia to come in the next day.

"Am I okay?" she asks, but the nurse says, "The doctor will explain everything when you come in."

Explain everything. *Ha,* she thinks, when she hangs up the phone. It's cancer, of course. *Cancer.* If it were nothing, there would be nothing to explain.

She lies awake for hours, and when she finally does sleep, it's in short bursts. In the morning her head is pounding. It frightens her, the feeling that her future is out of her control. If she even has a future. She thinks again of that ugly word. *Cancer.* Something growing inside her in the dark. Its raison d'être, her destruction.

She consults her watch. There's half an hour before she has to leave. She springs out of bed, a condemned woman eager to get her execution over and done with.

"The biopsy results are equivocal," the doctor says. He's seated behind his desk today, looking important, more important than he had two weeks before when he helped her up from the examining table and reassured her in a kindly voice that the lump was probably nothing. Which is now obviously not the case.

She eyes him, but he's gazing down at a piece of paper. Does he never look his patients in the eye?

"That means we're not sure. Sometimes that happens." He sighs. "We need to take it out."

Olivia slowly nods.

"It's called a lumpectomy—you've heard of it. It's just minor surgery. Very minor. A very small amount of anesthetic. We call it a 'light sleep.' You can leave right after."

Again she is presented with a piece of paper. A number to call, an appointment to make.

He doesn't do surgeries, he explains, not even minor ones like this. There are surgeons for this type of thing. Nor does he do biopsies, obviously. Olivia wonders about the qualifications he does possess. It appears that what he does best is feel ladies' tits and write on pieces of paper. A gas station attendant could do as much.

She goes home again and waits. Two whole weeks, this time, before she knows whether she will live or die.

The first week passes slowly. Olivia gives lessons most afternoons. She gets her hair cut one morning and spends another day at an art gallery in Burlington to distract herself. Elaine calls often. She'll be retiring in a couple of months and is caught up in retirement party plans. She's already picked a venue, and during every phone call she poses a different question. Should there be a vegetarian option? What about gluten-free? Would people be offended if they were asked to pay for their own drinks, or should there be an open bar?

It's a kindness, Olivia realizes, Elaine trying to distract her with party planning. But it doesn't work. What does Olivia care whether, on a night in three months' time, she eats strawberry Pavlova or lemon-curd layer cake? She actually prefers to contemplate her own mortality; she'd rather not be distracted from it. If she is dying, she'll need a good long time to get used to the idea.

The day of the procedure Elaine drives her to her appointment and waits in the waiting room to take her back home. The surgery for lump removal is similar to the one for the biopsy, only this time there are no unfinished Chopin preludes. Instead, a needle is inserted into Olivia's arm, and the next thing she knows, she's awake and the whole thing is over.

Back at home, Elaine hovers, making tea and slicing the quiche she brought with her. After the meal she fetches pillows and blankets so Olivia can lie on the couch and watch the bird feeder.

It's a relief when she goes. Olivia pulls the blanket around her shoulder and closes her eyes, but despite the after-effects of the anesthetic, sleep doesn't come. There will be time enough for that, she tells herself, at the same time knowing now that no one alive can assume such a thing.

When she first came to Vermont—had it really been almost twenty-five years ago?—she never thought she'd live this long. Sadness alone, she expected, would kill her. The only way to go on was to expunge the past from her mind. When she found herself thinking about what she had done, she directed her attention elsewhere—to her garden, her music, her books, her walks. But from time to time, the memories would creep back in, especially in her dreams and during the early morning hours. It was then that she would find herself thinking: *Could I? Could I go back?*

"The past is a foreign country: they do things differently there." Olivia's mother was fond of quoting that to her daughter. And Eleanor's experience was proof. She had never wanted to move from England to America, where Olivia's father had been offered a teaching job. Once settled into her new life with thirteen-year-old Olivia, she spent the next couple of years before Olivia's father's death trying to persuade him to return home. It wasn't until she flew back to London for her own father's funeral that she realized how much England had changed—and, along with it, her family and friends, whom she suddenly saw as small-minded and class-conscious.

Each time Olivia faced a decision, there it was again: "Don't burn your bridges, because you can't go back. You won't be the same person—and neither will the people you left." When Olivia decided to teach instead of perform, Eleanor had said it. When she decided to marry Harry, she had said it again.

In those early years in Vermont, Olivia tried to put her mother's words aside when she contemplated returning to her family. She'd written one letter to Harry soon after she'd left, telling him she wouldn't be back. What if she were to write another letter? What if she were to call? Turn up on their doorstep? What should she say? *Here I am, I'm sorry, please love me and let me love you?* That wouldn't be enough; it wouldn't be nearly enough. She would have to offer an explanation. But how could she do that when even she didn't fully understand the split-second decision that had led her to flee?

Lying on the couch as the afternoon darkens into evening, Olivia again finds herself thinking about her family. What it comes down to is forgiveness. Would they be able to forgive her? On the whole, she thinks not. And so, it's best to stop thinking about them. But facing, now, an uncertain future, she finds she can't stop. Since the discovery of the lump, she's been dreaming of her home in New Jersey, with its brick walls and dormered roof, and her bedroom, with that picture on the wall—the one she needed after all to finance her life. She's been dreaming of Harry, who never deserved what he got. Try as she might, she can't envision him as he must be now, a kind man with graying hair and wrinkled skin, an almost elderly man who, like herself, has lived most of his life.

And she's been dreaming of her three sons. Two of them would be men by now, adult men around the same age she was when she left, going about their lives with their partners and friends and—maybe even—children. They probably haven't spared their mother—and how can she claim that title?—a moment's thought in decades. They surely no longer have need of her.

The past is a foreign country.

One afternoon two women arrive at the door, both dressed in long skirts and long-sleeved blouses.

"Can we come in?" the older woman asks. "We have something to share." And because Olivia hasn't seen another human in almost a week, she leads them into the living room, where they introduce themselves and make themselves comfortable on the sofa, then remove from their large purses two Bibles and an assortment of small magazines.

Olivia waits politely until the younger woman informs her, as matter-of-factly as if she were relaying the Grand Union's new opening times, that the world will be ending in ten days.

Olivia leans back in her chair, regretting that she invited them in. "I had no idea."

The older woman—Lydia—speaks of the rapture, which will be occurring a week from Thursday. At 10:23 in the morning.

"The rapture," Olivia repeats. She's not sure what it is, but it sounds nice.

"When Jesus returns to Earth," Lydia explains, "and all believers, dead and alive, will rise in the air to meet him."

Both women are heavyset. Olivia imagines them lifting up their doughy arms and slowly and painfully rising until they're airborne. They are obviously mother and daughter—she can see that now.

"But we can help," the daughter says. "If you want to be one of the chosen few." She passes a magazine to Olivia. On the front is an illustration of a flame-engulfed cross. Olivia turns the page. The title of the first article reads, "My Journey: The Morning Our Daughter Stopped Breathing."

Which would be the least rude course of action? Olivia

wonders. To play along—or admit that she doesn't believe a word of it?

Lydia asks gently, "Have you been saved, my dear?"

"From what?" Olivia responds almost indignantly, at the same time appreciating the *my dear*. No one has called her *that* in a long time.

The women are prepared with their answers, and as she listens, they speak of repentance and faith. And if Olivia can repeat ten words, just ten, she, too, will rise in the air next Thursday morning, along with these two ladies. *Your sisters,* Lydia says.

"So what are the ten words?" Olivia asks. If she said them now, maybe they'd go without being prompted.

Lydia says slowly, "I accept you, Lord Jesus, as my—"

Olivia looks out the window. Through it she can just make out a corner of the tiny graveyard, the resting place of the seven children who never had a chance to utter those ten words. What would happen to them next Thursday at 10:23?

But she doesn't say that. Instead she says, "I could say it, but I wouldn't mean it."

She stands. Seeing this, the women reach for their bags and gather up their literature. As they do this, it occurs to Olivia that they have elected to spend a precious hour of their few remaining days on this planet to rescue a complete stranger.

What generosity! The least she can do is offer tea. When she comes back in the room with a tray, the atmosphere is lighter. They've done their job; they've acquitted themselves admirably.

No one can blame them if today, outside a small Vermont town, the soul of a sinner was not saved from eternal damnation.

What brought them to this point in their lives? Olivia wants to know, and asks, as she's pouring tea.

Lydia begins, "I was just seventeen. I was spending the weekend with a girlfriend, and on Sunday her family took me to their church. It wasn't buttoned up like the Presbyterian service I was used to. It was joyful! People got up to speak about their experience with the Lord, and I understood, finally I understood. Everything about birth and death and life and God and Jesus, everything I hadn't understood before. It all fit together.

"Near the end the pastor asked everyone who wanted to be saved to come up. I joined a huge crowd surging forwards, and at the front I repeated the ten words. After, people were dancing in the aisles and speaking in tongues and I was, too, even though moments before I never would have believed it. From then on, my old life was over and my new life had begun."

"What about your family?" Olivia says. "The Presbyterians. What did they think about your…conversion?"

"They hated it. They called me a Holy Roller. Which I took as a compliment. The next year I left and hitched to California, where I joined a church family. I met a man—"

"My father—" her daughter says.

"—and had nine children."

"And now you're back," Olivia concludes. Suddenly she's tired. She's ready for them to go.

"They disowned me," Lydia says. "Years later I wrote to inform them that they had four grandchildren, and my father wrote back and said that the family wanted nothing to do with me. I'd made my bed. Et cetera."

Olivia repeats, "And now you're back."

"My husband's sister is sick. We're helping to take care of her."

"So you haven't seen them? Your family?" Why is she pressing the issue? The faster they leave, the happier she'll be. Still, she needs to know.

"She tried," the daughter says. "She called my aunt as soon as we were back."

"Nothing had changed," Lydia says, reaching for her bag. "They're still mad. Thirty-two years ago I betrayed them by leaving."

"They don't want to see her," the daughter says as the women rise to go. "Can you imagine that?"

"I can imagine it," Olivia says.

The next morning the doctor's office calls, not to summon Olivia for another appointment but to say she's free and clear. She would, after all, live.

thirteen

1995

Although Rory had always wanted to be a doctor, Brian had a hard time believing it would actually happen. They were brothers: born of the same people, they attended the same schools and shared the same love of soccer, the Beatles, and pineapple upside-down cake. They were of the same stock. But, on the other hand, they couldn't be more different in their determination, their self-confidence, their ability to set goals and follow through on them. Rory has always believed he can do anything, and it seems to Brian that his thinking this has always made it so. If only Brian had one tenth of the confidence his little brother possessed, he'd have a totally different life.

He wakes early, pulls on his jeans, and goes into the kitchen. This afternoon Rory will climb the steps to the podium and be handed a framed page that announces to the world that he is qualified to practice medicine. After receiving his certificate, he will swear an oath that, for the rest of his life, he will do no harm.

Do no harm. Is that really how it goes? It seems to Brian that the phrase can be interpreted to mean whatever you want it to mean, depending on who you are and how you define the word "harm."

He hasn't had a drink in four days—no, make that five. Almost a week! The date is May 10, exactly a year since Ava left. He—along with his fellow compatriots—will remember it as the day John Wayne Gacy was executed. But for Brian, there was more to the day than the death of Gacy. When Ava came through the door he was glued to the TV. When she said "I'm pregnant," he waved his hand to shush her, as Gacy's last meal was described in detail: a bucket of Kentucky Fried, a dozen fried shrimp, fries, strawberries, and a Diet Coke. His final words, the anchor reported, were "Kiss my ass."

"Kiss my ass," Brian repeated, laughing, as Ava stood across the room staring at him. "Can you believe it? The guy is about to die. What balls he has." He reached for one of the bottles of Heineken on the TV table and took a swallow. "Had."

"You don't even bother to hide the fact that you're drinking again," she said flatly. Then repeating the words "I'm pregnant," she threw her jacket over a chair and left the room.

When the coffee's made, he cranks open the kitchen window and lights a cigarette. A couple of drags later, he's feeling almost human. Rory won't be up for a while, so he has an hour, at least, to savor his coffee and the silence, such as it is, standing in his brother's apartment two stories above the busier end of West Twenty-Third.

He stares down at the street, watching as a teenage boy throws his arms around the older woman who's just exited the bakery with a paper bag. They hug and continue up the street. A soda truck is trying to maneuver itself into a space between two Volvos. Brian reaches for another cigarette and mouths the words "Good luck, mate" as he strikes a match.

There's a soft thud from the other room. A moment later, Chimo pads into the kitchen and whines briefly at Brian, then trots over to the front door, where Brian can hear his tail thudding up and down. He grinds his cigarette into a tuna-fish can and goes back into the bedroom, pulls the T-shirt he'd worn the night before over his head, then grabs the leash from the doorknob. A moment later Chimo is pulling him along the pavement.

Although it's still early, the street is coming to life. The shopkeepers are sorting things into bins, putting sales signs in the windows or taking them down. The young Irishman who runs the magazine shop at the end of the block is puffing down the sidewalk—he's late to work—and the grocery store across the road, who waves at Brian, is training water from a hose into the flower buckets that appear, magically, overnight, every night. Brian wonders why the flowers are never stolen. It must have something to do with the gangs. The feeling among law enforcement is that it's gangs that cause the city's problems, but any New Yorker will tell you it's gangs that keep the place safe.

When he's back inside a half hour later, he finds Rory in the kitchen in his boxer shorts, slicing a green pepper. Across the bridge of his nose is a dilator strip.

"A cold?" Brian asks.

"Allergies. Something started pollinating in the middle of the night; I could feel it. I can't imagine what. The only thing growing between here and First Avenue is that pile of milk crates the city keeps refusing to pick up. Want a western?"

"Sure." Brian unhooks Chimo, and the dog takes his place in the puddle of sun that makes its way through the fire escape for about ten minutes each morning. "So. Big day."

"Umm." His brother reaches for an onion. "Honestly, I never thought I'd make it."

"Oh, come on. This is what you were meant for. Even Dad knew it. I was just remembering that stethoscope he bought you. A real one, not plastic—remember?" He reaches behind Rory and pulls two plates off a shelf.

"And when I stuck it in my ears, I couldn't hear a thing!"

"You were ten."

Rory puts down his knife and dumps the onions into a frying pan. "I keep having this dream that the whole thing is a mistake. And someone finds out." He cracks an egg into the pan. "With med school, there are so many points along the way where you can fail. I've always been aware of that. In my dreams, I step onto that stage, and the person who is supposed to be giving me my diploma starts laughing, and then the whole room erupts..."

Brian turns to see if his brother is joking, but it's obvious he isn't.

"Think of the money, Doc. Think of the prestige."

"If I was thinking of money or prestige, I wouldn't choose obstetrics, believe me. I'd choose brain surgery, or plastic surgery. *Any* kind of surgery." He pauses, then says, "You know what?"

"What?"

"I was thinking. I wish Dad were here. Today."

"And Mom."

Brian can remember a lot about his mother, but barely anything about the way she looked. Years ago he was able to call her to mind, and she'd appear exactly as she always had. Over time, though, she's become a barely remembered image—a fragment, really, of someone he once knew. A faceless woman in a floaty dress.

And, of course, Rory doesn't remember a thing.

"Anyway," Rory is saying, "Toni will be there. Which reminds me. She'll be dropping the twins off at the babysitter's late—probably not until four—and she said to tell you she'll meet you in the hall just before five. Can you save her a seat? She said she'll find you."

After breakfast Brian washes the dishes while Rory goes into the bedroom to gather up his things. He's spending the rest of the day—until the ceremony—uptown with his fiancée, Lily, and her family, before they drive out to Jersey for the commencement. On his way out the door, he pokes his head back in the kitchen.

"Come to the party after."

He's been talking about it for days. It's at Lily's apartment, for some of their fellow graduates. Lily will be graduating, too, along with Rory.

"I don't know—" Brian imagines a group of newly minted doctors, all standing around Lily's apartment, proud as can be, congratulating themselves that after years of hard work, they had finally become—by virtue of that framed certificate they would be handed during the ceremony—the cream that floats to the top. The mighty. The elite. The untouchable ones...

Shut up, Brian tells himself.

"Come," Rory pleads. "You know everyone there anyway. Come celebrate with me."

After his brother's gone, Brian swings into action. Later this morning he'll be showing an apartment on Gramercy Park, his own exclusive and the most expensive one he's ever had. His client is a young woman, the daughter of a popular TV anchor who has to be footing the bill, or most of it. The girl and her father came to his office the day before, and Brian recognized him immediately. As soon as they were seated, the girl pulled from her bag a list of ten of the most expensive apartments on the park. The largest, most spacious one was Brian's exclusive. After scheduling appointments to see several of the others, they agreed to start with his. Maybe he would luck out; maybe she would see it and fall in love with it. That kind of thing, although rare, does happen. It's what keeps real estate agents going.

In the bathroom he strips off his clothes and stands under the shower, letting the water wash away the grime the city tosses into the air every minute of every day. As he works the soap into a lather, he considers what he will do with the money he makes on that exclusive, should he sell it.

He'll get his own apartment, for sure. Rory will be moving in with Lily in August, and in December they'll be married, in a small church wedding in Connecticut. A Christmas wedding, with Brian as best man. *Rory's only man,* he thinks. It isn't very often he thinks of Andrew, and he wonders, as he pulls on a pair of neatly pressed khaki pants and takes a white dress shirt from its hanger, how the brotherly equation might have been different had Andrew still been alive. Would the three of them be sharing an apartment, with Rory in med school, Andrew maybe doing a postdoc somewhere, and him, the family drunk, consigned to the living room couch after a failed relationship had driven him back into the arms of his family?

Chimo pads over and with his cold nose reminds Brian to replenish his water and fill his bowl with wet food—the smelly, natural kind that Rory prefers, even though it costs three times as much as the supermarket brand. Then Brian fetches his clipboard and folder from the counter and tries, without success, to locate his jacket. Because there's no closet in his room, his clothes are jammed into the hallway coat closet, a two-foot sliver of a space that gobbles up or conceals items of clothing on a regular basis.

Even with Rory gone, the place would still be small. Brian would like something bigger, something in another location, something maybe uptown. Something other. He'll be needing a bigger space eventually, for he won't always be alone. There's a girl out there somewhere, a girl in his future who will love him—provided he can keep off the booze.

It all comes down to booze. Most of the problems in his life lead there: to booze consumed out in the open, and to booze unconsumed but there nonetheless. Booze hidden under his bed, waiting for bedtime. Booze hidden behind supersize cereal boxes, purchased for the purpose of concealment, since neither of the brothers eats cold cereal. Booze of whatever kind, constantly obsessed about, constantly drunk.

Numerous times, oh, maybe twenty or thirty, he's thought he had it licked. But it's never been quite the right time, or if it was, it didn't last. Something has always interfered with his good intentions.

Of course Rory knows about his problem, since Brian has spent much of the past year plastered, but it's never come up in conversation—at least not since the pregnant Ava left and Brian ended up on the floor, passed out after drinking three bottles of red wine. He never remembered calling his younger brother, although he must have, since the next thing he remembered was Lily and Rory hauling him off the floor of his apartment and into the back of Lily's Toyota. Shortly after that, he found himself on his brother's bathroom floor, retching into the toilet before passing out again.

The next morning he woke in the guest bed of the tiny room off the kitchen, a storage room, really.

When Rory came in with coffee, he said, mildly, "You can stay as long as you want. And if I were you, I'd cut back on the sauce."

And now he's only five days sober. Still, five days is better than no days.

He was sure he'd beaten it when he first met Ava. He was at an AA meeting, his first. He'd been sober almost a month by then, but one day all he could think of was beer—a long, cold one. He wanted it so badly he knew he was in trouble. So he looked up a number in the phone book and made a call, and that night he found himself in the basement of St. Michael's Episcopal, a stone's throw from his apartment.

They met at the end of the meeting. She'd been sitting across from him, and as he was helping himself to a third cup of coffee, she came up to introduce herself. When he told her he hadn't had a drink in a month, he could see she was impressed. Most people, she informed him, were out-of-control drunk the night before their first meeting. Which made Brian wonder whether he was an alcoholic at all.

She seemed to know what he was thinking. "If you've ever thought you're an alcoholic, you are. Go with that."

At the end of another meeting a few days later, they gravitated again toward each other. She wasn't particularly beautiful, he decided, but he was struck by her honesty. She got him talking in a way no one had, not for years, and she had a startling knack for seeing right through to his core. When he admitted to having a hard time believing that sobriety equaled happiness, and that drunkenness didn't, she acted as if that was the most logical way to feel. She didn't even try to talk him out of it.

A month later he asked her out. She refused. Not even for a coffee.

"A year," she said. They were standing outside the church in the chilly winter air as he smoked his cigarette. She stamped her feet and rubbed her hands together. "That's the rule. No involvement with another AA member until you've had your first year of sobriety."

"It's been almost a year," Brian had replied. "Only forty-eight and a half weeks left to go. Couldn't we just skip right on through them?"

But they didn't. The next winter, when he'd been sober for eleven months and three weeks, Ava turned up at his door with a tomato pie and tickets to see *Jurassic Park*, playing that night in Hudson Square.

He thinks, as he reaches around the back of the closet to the hook where his three ties hang, how useless it is to keep dwelling on the past. The past has proven to be the one place he hasn't been able to extricate himself from, not since Ava told him—no, strike that—not since he'd actually listened and heard Ava tell him that she was pregnant and the next day would be moving out. Even now he cringes as he remembers the last few words she spat out before slamming the door: "And I'll pay for my own damn abortion!"

He almost believed she was joking. He almost believed—and nearly said—a million things (*I'm sorry, I'll quit drinking forever, I love you, Let's have the baby, I want the baby, I would love a baby, Let's get married*), but he had no chance to say any of them, because before he knew it, she was out the door with her small, hastily packed suitcase and gone from his life forever.

Ah, Jersey, he thinks, cranking up the car window after he's left the Holland Tunnel and entered that section of the state that smells like something crawled up you and died. The Jersey Meadowlands, it's called, as if on a summer day it's filled with butterflies and bees. Instead what you get is an unbearable stench that stretches about five miles. Some say it's the smell of rotten eggs; others swear it's burning rubber. Regardless, it's what gives the state its reputation. People who've never left the Jersey Turnpike, who've driven from Manhattan straight down to D.C., believe the whole state stinks, and when someone mentions that it's called the Garden State, they think it's a joke.

The first time he smelled it was when he and his brothers were taken by their parents to the Bronx Zoo.

"Quick, roll up the windows," their father had said, laughing from the front seat, although even with the windows closed, the stink permeated the car's interior. The day was forever etched in Brian's mind, not only because of the smell but also because of what happened in the monkey house, where Andrew screamed in terror and wouldn't stop as monkeys swung from fake tree limb to fake tree limb and hissed spit through the bars, prompting Olivia to say, "Okay, Harry. Let's call it a day."

He hasn't been back to Jersey in years, and it hasn't anything to do with the stink. It's just that he has no reason to return. His parents are gone, his only brother lives in the city, and most of his friends—his former friends, that is—have moved on or are married with children and ensconced in those soulless developments that dot the Jersey landscape.

Moments later he turns on to the Garden State Parkway, and a half hour after that, as he passes a bar, he begins wrestling with himself. He'd love a beer. But is he really going to break down after five days of sobriety?

He can't decide. He drives around the block once, then twice. Consulting his watch, he sees it's only four thirty. The ceremony doesn't start until five. Just a quick one, he tells himself, and the third time around, he pulls the car to the curb. Without taking the time to lock the door, he sprints across the sidewalk and through the doors and into the dark interior, which is full of smoke and the smell of stale ale.

A few older men are hunched over the bar, silently drinking. The barman approaches Brian, who holds out a five-dollar bill and asks for a Heineken. When it's passed to him—ah, and in such a cold glass—he takes a long sip, then turns around to look out the window. From his vantage point he can just make out the back end of the car. Someone could open the unlocked door and let themselves in, and in a flash they could drive off, easy peasy.

The last thing Brian would see would be the rear bumper and the license plate before it disappeared out of sight.

He downs his beer, fast, then orders another and, looking again at his watch, drinks the second one as he's walking toward the door. He drains his glass and places it on the window ledge, and it isn't until he's opened the car door and is seated behind the wheel that he thinks, *I've blown it again.*

———

It's nearly five when he arrives at the PNC Arts Center. The lobby has already cleared out, except for a few people detailed to hand out programs at the auditorium's entrances.

"Brian?" someone calls, and he turns around.

It's Toni. If she hadn't called his name, he wouldn't have recognized her. She's lost weight, quite a lot of it, and grown her straight brown hair long, almost to her waist. She looks like a girl—a college student or a young professional—in her red, hooded trench coat. But of course she isn't; she's more than a decade older than Brian. Probably around forty-five.

They go in together. There are only a few seats left in the auditorium. Toni grabs his arm and leads him to adjoining seats along the side. He wonders whether she can smell the beer on his breath. Although he only had two, he's light-headed. It must have to do with how fast he chugged them.

Because they're late, there's barely time to talk. Just as Toni begins to update Brian on the twins' activities, the lights dim and

"Land of Hope and Glory" is piped into the room through loudspeakers, marking the entrance of the graduates, who in their black gowns and tasseled mortarboards file into the room and take their places in the front rows. Brian looks for his brother, but it's impossible to locate Rory in the crowd of identically gowned students. Giving up, he opens his program and scans the pages. The metamorphosis from student to physician will occur at the very end, after the awards and speeches.

Halfway through the fifth speech, given by a wizened female doctor who Brian sincerely hopes has retired, Toni looks at her watch and nudges him. "I need to leave right at the end," she whispers in his ear. "Anna has a birthday party, and Frank has to meet a client."

"That's okay."

Another hour passes before the diplomas are distributed. Brian longs for another beer—or a cigarette. Ideally, both. Finally, the roll call begins, as each student—and there are over two hundred—mounts the stage. When it's Rory's turn, Brian's eyes fill with tears. *That's my brother,* he thinks, as Rory almost bounces up the steps for his diploma, quickly shaking the presenter's hand. *That young guy there, that physician, is my little brother.*

He remembers what Rory said about wanting his father here. Brian, too, wishes there were someone who could share the moment. Someone other than Toni, that is. His father, or mother—or even a friend, if he had one. *That's my brother,* he'd say, pointing to the broadly grinning young man in the oversize black gown retracing his steps to his seat. *The reason he's on that stage is because he always completed his homework. He always studied for his exams. He always finished what he started, even when he was little. He's on that stage because he had plans and accomplished them. He's there because he walked toward the future without getting waylaid by circumstances, or drink, or his own, useless emotions.*

He reaches up to wipe his eyes, knowing as he does it that even though he's crying out of pride for his brother, he's also crying for himself.

"Whatever happened to the 'Do no harm'?" Toni asks. They're in front of the building, sharing a cigarette. Rory is still inside for the graduating class photographs. In a moment Toni will leave and Brian will go back in for Rory, who's riding with him back to the city.

"I guess the oath has changed. Along with everything else. I kind of liked this new version. 'I will not be ashamed to say I know not.'"

Toni passes him back his cigarette and says, "I'd have preferred 'I will not be ashamed to say I know not, but I promise to rack my brain until I can figure it out.'"

"Ha." He takes a long drag, then reaches to undo the top button of his shirt. Sweat is trickling down his neck.

Toni says, "I was wondering whether you ever tried to find your mother. Remember that day you came to the house?"

God, that had to be more than five years ago. "Yes. I do remember. But no, no I didn't."

"I figured I would have heard."

"Yes."

"If it was me, I think I'd go to the ends of the earth to find her." She stares hard at Brian. "No matter how pissed off I was."

"I'm not pissed off." He grinds the cigarette butt into the ground. Then he picks it up and jams it into the space between the packet and the wrapping. "I think about it from time to time. I'm just not sure I want to put myself in a position to—" He stops.

"—to be rejected again?" Toni finishes for him. She stands on tiptoe to plant a kiss on his forehead. A moment later she's gone, her Red Riding Hood coat swirling around her as she hurries down the pavement to the parking lot.

On the way to the party Brian manages to quell the urge to stop off for a beer, despite the fact that he's noticed at least one liquor store on every block on his way uptown. He will not get drunk at his brother's party. Maybe later, when he's home by himself, he'll have a beer. Just one, sitting on the fire escape, while his brother and Lily and their friends rock the night away.

He won't stay long. He always feels out of place with Rory's friends. He's sure they view him with pity—how can they not? *There's one in every family,* he imagines them saying. *That one's the bad one.*

Lily's apartment is on the sixth floor. The door is open when Brian steps out of the elevator. In the kitchen a man in a leather jacket is pouring a supersize bag of potato chips into a bowl, and a young woman is sitting, almost obscured from sight, behind a towering ficus. Votive candles have been placed on the windowsill and on every available surface. There must be twenty or thirty of them, flickering wildly in the disturbance of air as people pass through the room.

On the table are empty glasses and coolers of ice and cases of beer and bottles of wine and vodka. He scans the selection, then, taking a breath, moves into the living room, which is packed solid with people—doctors—all writhing to the Chili Peppers' "Suck My Kiss." He spots his brother and Lily in the middle of the room, jerking in time to the music. He waves at them, but their eyes are closed.

How old he feels, in this crowd of twentysomethings. They're children, really. In the corner he sees Rory's friend Clay, soon to be a hand surgeon, tossing down a beer in four seconds flat, then reaching into his overcoat pocket for another can.

Brian elbows his way back into the kitchen, where the young woman behind the plant has emerged to pour herself a drink.

"Want some Sprite?" She holds up the bottle.

"Thanks. I'm a Coke kind of a guy," he says, and to prove it he reaches for a can lying on a bed of ice. Flipping the tab, he takes a long swallow.

When the music stops, a few of the dancers stream in to replenish their drinks. Brian catches a conversation between two of them about the relative merits of physiatry and orthopedics.

"It's more money," the girl says. "Orthopedics is *way* more money."

"Oh, I don't know," the man says. "Physiatrists don't do too badly. They don't call it PM&R for nothing."

"I know, I know. Plenty of money and relaxation. If I have to hear that joke one more time, I'll puke."

"Still."

When they've left, Brian turns to the girl, who's now peering into a cabinet.

"Food," she says, inspecting the label on a packet of crackers. "I need food."

He takes another swallow of Coke. "What's *your* specialty?"

She turns and faces him. "Oh, I'm not a doctor. At least, not the medical kind. I'm a friend of Lily's sister."

There's something about her that reminds him of his first girlfriend. She is, he thinks, the prettiest girl he's seen since Louise.

"Anyhow," she says. She opens the fridge and pulls out a stick of butter, then grabs a knife and, shaking some crackers from the packet onto a plate, begins to butter them. When she's finished, she pops a cracker into her mouth, whole. She looks over at Brian. "Sorry, but I'm starving." She offers the plate and Brian takes a cracker.

"I teach math," she finally says. "At Columbia."

Her green eyes are flecked with brown, setting off her long dark hair. As far as he can tell, she's wearing no makeup, and although he doesn't know her, he can see from the way the corners of her mouth tilt up that she's easily amused.

"My name's Brian," he says.

"I'm Edith. But I answer only to Edie. What's your specialty?"

"I'm not a doctor either. I'm a real estate agent. I'm just here for my brother, who's been a physician now for all of"—he consults his watch—"three and a half hours. Rory Somerville."

"Rory!" she says. "I've met him." The door to the living room opens again, and her voice is nearly drowned out by the words "Conversations kill! Conversations kill!"

"STP," Edie says and, seeing the blank expression on Brian's face, laughs. "Stone Temple Pilots. Not, as you might have thought, a sexually transmitted disease."

He would like to ask her to dance but doesn't, because he's not sure whether it's still done, asking someone to dance. It seems to him that people just sort of slowly ooze from wherever they are onto the dance floor and ooze back off when the music stops.

He *is* an old man.

Two women enter the room from outside, bearing cheese cubes stuck with toothpicks and more bags of chips. Edie dives for the cheese. The music stops, and Lily comes in and pours herself a hefty glass of red wine. Then she catches sight of Brian and Edie in the corner, and, joining them, gives Brian a sloppy kiss on the cheek.

"My soon-to-be bro," she says, slurring her words slightly.

More people throng into the room. Corks pop. Bottles are opened. Beer is poured into glasses.

"What kind of real estate do you sell?" Edie asks after much of the crowd has drifted away, leaving Lily in the corner talking with a few friends.

"Oh, you know—the usual. Apartments. Condos. I did go to Princeton, but I dropped out..."

Now, why did I mention that? But, of course, he knows why: to get it right out there at the start before he's asked, which he's sure will eventually happen in this apartment full of doctors.

But she's listening to Lily, who's telling a story to the few people left in the room.

It was during an anatomy class in their first week of med school, Lily says, when someone put a body part in her pocket.

"What was it?" a girl in a purple tunic and floppy hat asks. "A finger?"

But Lily doesn't answer, instead going on to describe how it felt to discover it when she got home that night and checked in her pockets for her scarf.

"From a corpse, one would hope," the man with the cheese cubes says, and everyone laughs.

"What was it?" the floppy-hatted girl asks again. "Was it—" She breaks off, and Brian, looking around the room, can see that every male there is wondering the same thing.

When it's clear that Lily will not be divulging, Brian asks, "Who put it there?"

"Who do you think?" Lily says, holding her finger up to the light, to show the room her new ruby engagement ring.

"And you're marrying the guy?" someone else says, and everyone laughs again, including Rory, who, having come back into the room, has caught the tail end of the story.

Finally Brian asks Edie to dance. He leads her into the living room, where Rage Against the Machine is drowning out the noise of the couples dancing, the shrieks of the woman in the corner whose boyfriend has put ice down her front, the scrape of the sofa being pushed further to the side. The room is dark, except for the lamp that someone keeps switching on and off to emulate a strobe light. Brian knows he is meant to stand alone, moving along with—but not touching—Edie. But he puts his hands on her shoulders anyway and pulls her toward him. She smiles, and twisting her long hair around the back, rests her head lightly on his shoulder.

After a while they go outside. The sun has set, but the night is still warm. Brian takes Edie's hand and they stroll toward the river. The city is quiet; all you can hear is the water lapping against its bank, the odd tugboat horn and the distant, muffled sound of traffic.

"Look," Edie whispers, nodding at an older lady with a feather boa wrapped around her neck, clicking across the street in red high-heeled shoes. A few steps behind her is a man in a suit and tie. "Wait for me, Lulu," he pleads. "Please. I didn't mean it. Please!"

"You hear that?" Brian says. "Sadness. All over the city. Sadness."

"But we don't know what he didn't mean, do we?" Edie says. "He might have called her a fat slob. Or maybe he admitted to poisoning her husband." She bends to remove a pebble from her shoe, holding on to Brian's arm and hopping on her other foot while she shakes it out. When the shoe is back on her foot, she says, "Maybe he told her he'd gone to Princeton but didn't bother to mention that he'd dropped out." She looks at Brian. "Maybe he just wasn't that honest a person."

The woman grabs one end of her boa, which has been dragging along the ground, and stops, allowing the man to catch up. The two disappear around the corner. Edie takes Brian's arm and they walk back toward Lily's. A few of the party guests are drifting past them. When he sees them, Brian realizes he has no desire to return to the party.

"Where's your place?" he asks, barely believing his own boldness.

"Just a few blocks from here, actually."

"Do you think—?"

"Yes."

Past the Italian *grocerias*, past the huge hospital complex, past a couple of drunks weaving together along the sidewalk, past the puddles of vomit, past a small white dog yipping for its owner. Edie's is on the top floor of a brownstone. Her apartment is small and uncluttered and smells of lavender. In the bedroom she removes his shirt and runs her fingertips over his chest before pulling her dress over her head. They kiss and lie together on the bed, and after, Brian watches her, asleep and curled toward him and naked. And again he is struck by her resemblance to Louise, not only physically but also by the way she speaks, as if it's important for her to tell only the truth.

He lies awake until morning, smiling and thinking that so much of his life has felt like an ending, but this here, this right now, feels different. It feels the opposite.

PART FOUR

fourteen

2001

It's a cloudless late-summer morning. Sun is pouring through the bedroom window as Rory dresses for work. Lily's been gone for ages; she always delivers Tess to daycare on the way to the hospital before her shift begins, but Rory's schedule, less rigid but with longer hours, has more to do with when his patients are scheduled—or at what stage of labor they're in.

An early morning call had informed him that although Mrs. Brezinski was already at the hospital, she was only two centimeters dilated. *Plenty of time,* he thinks, especially given the fact that his patient is twenty-two and a primipara. Not much that could go wrong there. Grabbing a fresh lab coat from his closet, he leaves the bedroom. As he passes the living room door, he notices that Lily had failed to open the drapes, which, coupled with the series of snorts being emitted from the direction of the couch, reminds him that his brother has spent the night.

Drunk? he thinks automatically, recalling past times when

Brian had crashed on the sofa. But then he remembers that his brother had phoned the night before, when Rory was putting Tess to bed, asking to stay for a few days. The painters were taking their bloody time, he'd said, referring to the fact that his tiny apartment was being redecorated, his kitchen redone, in preparation for his being allowed to have Chloe for the odd weekend. Finally.

Almost a year has passed since Ava turned up at Brian's door with her news: he had a six-year-old daughter. The existence of the child put Rory in mind of that "Good News, Bad News, Who Knows?" story. If his brother hadn't fathered a child (*bad news?*) he never would have gone on the wagon (*good news!*). And a month ago he'd celebrated his first year of sobriety with Rory and Lily and Ava and his Chloe, who sat on his lap and kept sitting on it until Ava had to haul her off and take her home because of school the next morning.

In the kitchen, he pours coffee beans into the grinder, then, realizing the noise it will make, abandons the idea and reaches for the instant. He looks out the window. One fire truck is screaming by, followed by another, and then another. He'd been planning to drive to the hospital today, but if there's a big fire somewhere nearby, it might be safer to take the subway—or even walk.

He pours boiling water into a mug and applies butter and jam to one of the croissants Lily had picked up before she left. Then he loads his breakfast onto a tray and takes it into his study, where he turns on *Good Morning America*. There's a British veterinarian chatting about DNA damage and pets, and the benefits of providing them with antioxidants. Rory, amused, hears her out until the commercial, when he goes back to the kitchen for more coffee. When he returns, the Duchess of York is, sadly, recounting the details of her horrific life (*how awful, to be a princess,* Rory thinks, reaching for his napkin) and how she had gained weight because of it, but then, because of Weight Watchers...

Blah, blah, blah, and then more ads, including one, actually, from Weight Watchers—a coincidence? Rory points the remote at the TV as the camera pans to Diane Sawyer, who is speaking, in measured tones, about an explosion that had been reported at the World Trade Center: "...A plane may have hit one of the two towers," Sawyer is saying, and the screen is filled with an image of a building engulfed in smoke.

He places the half-eaten croissant back on his plate, leans forward, and squints. *Wow.* How could a pilot miss seeing a whole building? He can only imagine what it must be like inside the tower. Thousands work there; his friend Joel works at Cantor Fitzgerald. Hopefully, CF is in the other tower, or at least on a lower floor.

Wasn't there a helicopter crash on the top of the Pan Am Building when he was little? He can recall sitting with his father and Brian in the family room, watching a picture of a chopper flipped onto its side. He remembers his brother pointing out a picture of a body, covered in a white cloth, and his father saying, "Turn that off, Bri. Rory doesn't need to see this."

And then there was that Trade Center bombing back in the early 1990s. But of course, that was a terrorist attack, not an accident, like this.

Well, it's sad about the plane and the building, sad about those people who might be wounded or worse, but it probably won't affect him today, since the hospital is uptown and the fire engines were heading downtown. He'll walk, after all. It's a beautiful morning and he has the time. He licks the jam off his fingers, and after, he rinses his plate, grabs his black bag, and quietly, so as not to awaken his brother, lets himself out the door.

In the elevator, his mind turns to the baby he's about to deliver. He's only been in the game a couple of years, not long enough to have become jaded. He hasn't even been sued for malpractice yet—what you can pretty much expect with a "bad" baby every few years, which is, unfortunately, how the members of his profession refer to it. Even though he doesn't have a religious bone in his body, each child he delivers feels like the work of a divine agent. Hopefully, it will be the same with this one.

Outside, Fifth Avenue is busier than usual, and not just with the usual well-dressed matrons hailing cabs to take them uptown for their coffee dates or to Bloomingdale's, but with young men as well, gathering in groups on the sidewalk. Two young women running up from the direction of Twentieth Street nearly plow into Rory. As he steps down from the curb, an ambulance speeding by startles him, and he steps back up again. Glancing down Fifth, he notices the smoke rising from the Twin Towers. Both of them. Which must be a trick of light. How could both towers be on fire? Unless…

Banishing the thought, he breaks into a run, crossing Twenty-First Street and continuing past the Flatiron Building, past Lord

& Taylor, past Saks and Henri Bendel (the clothing stores reflecting the increasing wealth of the populace the farther north you go), keeping up a steady pace until he reaches Central Park, where the tops of the trees are beginning to turn. Nearly fall, his favorite season. He stops to absorb the scene.

The light is milky, almost hazy. It's a beautiful day, and the sight of the park—the perfection of it—makes him shiver, slightly, at his good fortune. He stretches out his calves and takes a deep breath. If he were given the choice, there isn't a thing he would change about his life. Both he and Lily, who works in Emergency, like their jobs. Tess is an easygoing three-year-old who loves her day-care center. They live in a lovely apartment with a large kitchen and a real fireplace, a rarity in the area and something Lily had always dreamed of. To top it off, they have enough money and very little debt.

He glances at his watch. He should be at the hospital in ten minutes. And soon—perhaps later this morning—he will deliver into the world a new soul, and present it to its mother, who will, hopefully, fall in love with it. He considers that to be part of his job, an important part—making someone love the child she has just given birth to. It doesn't always happen, but mostly it does.

Brian wakes from a deep sleep. The phone is ringing. He lets it go—he's not ready to talk to anyone yet—and it stops. Then it rings again. He sits up and attempts to dispel the fog that has engulfed him. *What the hell?* And then, seeing the stylized wood sculpture on the mantelpiece, he realizes he's in his brother's apartment. It's quiet; everyone has obviously left for the day. Of course, Lily leaves early with Tess, and Rory not that long after. But it's late—Brian can tell that from the clarity of the light that's crept around the edges of the drapes, which are still drawn. The telephone rings again, and he wraps the pillow around his head.

He's hungry and needs to eat, plus he needs, mostly terribly, a large cup of strong black coffee. Then he will face the day, which consists of a noontime client—a woman who's been wavering, and all bets are off on whether she will show up to view the elegant brownstone on Sutton Place that is Brian's exclusive. Then he has a late-afternoon meeting with the painters at his own apartment, to choose the color for his bedroom (any color but that bilious green they suggested, he wanted to tell them but didn't, not wanting to come across as elitist). This evening he'll attend an art exhibit at Chloe's school. Before Chloe, he would have scoffed at the idea of "art" exhibited by seven- and eight-year-olds, but today it's the only thing he's looking forward to.

He stretches and yawns, tempted to close his eyes for just another few minutes, but hunger wins out, and he hauls himself off the sofa and reaches for his jeans. When he pads into the kitchen and opens the fridge, he's pleased to see that the shelves are full—eggs, bacon, milk, yogurt, raspberry jam, anything he needs. And—as he knew there would be—a packet of croissants in the bread bin, fresh from Mahoney's. Lily must have gone across for them before she left for work. (*Thanks, Lily.*) Everyone's comfort is constantly on her mind, even Brian's, although he's not sure she likes him terribly well—and no surprise there, given his earlier history of turning up in the middle of too many nights, stinking of cigarettes and beer and—sometimes—puke.

He tries hard not to be jealous of Rory's marriage. His brother has worked hard for it, which is far more than Brian's done, on the whole. Sometimes he feels like a voyeur, watching his brother and Lily and Tess: the perfect family. At least, that's how he thinks of them.

What, precisely, is the magic ingredient that guarantees a successful relationship—and why has he never been able to get some of it for himself? He almost had it with Louise, his first, but not with Ava. And certainly never with Edie, who stuck with him and kept sticking with him, long after anyone with any sense of self-preservation would have left. She's the only woman who's ever made him cry. God, what a dick he was to her.

He places a croissant in the toaster oven and pours water into the coffee machine. The phone rings again. Who is it, and why do they keep calling? It can't be for Rory or Lily; their friends don't expect them to be home during the day. After twenty or more rings, he picks up. Dead air. Something must be wrong with the phone; he'll mention it to Rory tonight.

Chloe! he thinks, almost smiling as he applies jam to his croissant. Of all the things that could have—that *should* have—made him give up alcohol, including the fact that he'd more than once woken in a puddle of vomit on the stoop of an apartment belonging to a woman who had tossed him out of it, it was

Chloe—her mere existence—that had made him turn up in the dank room of a church basement, stand before a disparate group of people—from a kindergarten teacher to the head of a Boy Scout troop to the star of a popular TV series to the priest of that very same church—and announce, "Hi, my name is Brian, and I'm an alcoholic."

He'd tried AA several times before, but this time it had stuck. He had no choice, not if he wanted to be part of Chloe's life; Ava had made that clear from the beginning. She'd come alone the first time, arriving at his apartment late one evening. When he opened the door and saw her standing there, he almost didn't recognize her. She was wearing makeup, which she never did when they were together, and in her navy pleated skirt and white blouse she appeared as if she were trying out for the part of lawyer or accountant.

When he asked her in, she shook her head, and for a moment he wondered whether she was there as the bearer of bad news, even though as far as he knew she had no connection to anyone or anything in his life.

"You have a daughter," she finally said. She waited, watching him take in the news.

For a long while—although it was probably under a minute—he was stunned. When he did speak, his mouth was dry, and what came out was a croak.

"I thought you had an abortion." Meanwhile he thought, with a surge of joy, *I have a daughter!* He looked behind Ava and down the hall. Where was she, this child of his?

"I didn't bring her," Ava said. "I thought it best..." She paused, then said, "I came for two reasons. Because I thought you should know about Chloe, and because I wanted to know whether you'd given up alcohol. Do you still drink?"

Wordlessly, Brian met her eyes. "I do," he answered honestly.

Ava paused for a moment and then said, in a firm voice, "When you stop, let me know."

When you stop. Not if.

She pulled a card from her pocket, handed it to him, and turned to go. At the elevator she turned back around. "She's six years old," she called to Brian. "She likes sticker books and ponies and Barbie dolls, and she loves wearing dresses with sparkles sewn on. I sew them on myself. She plays the piano beautifully. I don't know anything about music, but I think she's a prodigy. And, oh, yes, she has black hair. Straight black hair. Just like you."

Brian took a breath. His mind was a jumble. Where once there had been nothing, now there was something.

"And Brian. One more thing."

He waited.

"This was her idea, not mine. She wants to meet you."

That night he went to his first meeting.

A month later, a month of sobriety, Brian called the number on the card Ava had given him. The plan was for her to bring Chloe to his apartment after school. When they were ten minutes late,

Brian was nearly frantic. Ava had planned the whole thing as revenge, assuring him that he would meet his little girl, when in fact she had no plans to allow such a meeting. Or perhaps the whole thing was made up. Maybe he had no daughter. *No Chloe,* he thought, almost in tears, grieving someone he had never seen, a person who might not even exist.

But the buzzer finally sounded, and when Brian opened the door, mother and daughter were standing there, hand in hand. For a moment, he just stared. She—Chloe—was wearing jeans and a green sweater. Ava was right. With her pale complexion, her prominent cheekbones, and deep blue eyes, she did resemble Brian.

He finally collected himself and, saying hello, led them into the tiny living room. When they were seated, Ava said, unnecessarily, "So. This is Chloe."

The little girl, whose head had been down, looked up and briefly met her father's eyes. "Hi."

What do you say to a child you never knew you had? Was there a right way and a wrong way to behave? If there was a wrong way, Brian was sure he'd find it.

"Hi, Chloe. I'm so happy to meet you."

Ava said, "Chloe had a piano lesson after school. She was late getting out." She mouthed the words: *She's amazing.*

Grateful for the opening, Brian said, "I used to play piano. Do you like music, Chloe?"

The little girl nodded, then lowered her head again.

Ava, to Brian's relief, began talking about her recently

acquired job, counseling Spanish-speaking prisoners at Rikers Island. After she and Brian broke up, she had gotten a teaching degree at NYU, then a master's in social work. This was her first job in nearly seven years, she said, her first job since Chloe. And all that time, all those years—the pregnancy, the birth, the little girl's infancy and early childhood—how he would have loved to have been a part of it. Instead, he had blown it big-time.

Ava seemed to guess what he was thinking. She reached into her bag and pulled out a small album, which she passed to Brian.

The first pages were of the infant Chloe—a newborn—wrapped in a pink blanket. You could barely see her face. He turned the page. There she was, age about one and a half or two, in denim overalls, sitting on some unknown man's lap.

"My brother," Ava said. "Her uncle."

He leafed through: Chloe in front of a pink frosted cake with the words *Happy Birthday Two-Year-Old!* emblazoned on top. Chloe sitting cross-legged in a sunlit garden somewhere in the world, grasping in her little fingers a wilting bouquet of flowers. Chloe and another child on a teeter-totter. Chloe at the beach, in shorts and a yellow T-shirt, wading in the shallows, age about five. Chloe sitting at the top of a waterslide, a huge smile on her face.

"Do you like waterslides?" Brian asked, holding out the album so Chloe could see the picture of herself.

The child looked up, then took the album from him. "That was the day we got Prince, wasn't it, Mommy? On our way home from the waterslide, we stopped at the shelter and bought Prince."

Ava glanced at Brian. "Prince is Chloe's dachshund. We didn't really buy him, Chloe. We *selected* him."

"I love dogs. Tell me about him," Brian said to Chloe, and that broke the ice. Chloe described him (*he has a long, long back and tiny little paws*) and told Brian about the time she thought he was lost, when he was really hiding under her bed.

When it was time to go, Ava said, "Maybe next time you can come to our place. You could meet Prince—couldn't he, Chloe?"

As Brian walked them to the door, Chloe grabbed his hand and said, "You could meet Prince, and I could show you my Halloween costume!"

He's been to their apartment many times since that first one, when he met Prince and saw Chloe's Halloween costume. He's spent a Thanksgiving there and a Christmas, and on Chloe's birthday he took her to a puppet show in Hastings-on-Hudson, with a boat ride after. And now, finally, she'll be spending the whole weekend with him. He must stock up on all her favorite foods. What do seven-year-olds like to eat, besides ice cream? When he was that age it was bologna sandwiches and cream soda. He remembers the arguments he had with Olivia about that—the ones she lost every time.

The clock above the refrigerator says 11:21. *Eye on the ball, Bri,* he thinks, patting his pocket for his glasses and casting about for his jacket, which he thought he had dropped on the floor beside the door last night, so where is it? There's just enough time to catch a taxi uptown, on the presumption that his client will turn up. By the time he's found his jacket and sorted through his briefcase for the comps the client requested, it's nearly 11:28. Rather than waiting for the elevator, he bounds down the steps two at a time and hits the pavement almost running.

Outside, a crowd of people have gathered, for no other reason he can fathom except to prove the validity of Murphy's Law and the fact that if he isn't on time for his client, he stands to lose thousands of dollars. He weaves his way through the crowd until he reaches the curb, where he waits. Minutes go by, but there are no cabs in sight. In fact, the traffic is much sparser than it usually is. If he walks fast he might make it in time, but the air is terrible—there's a weird haze that seems to have settled over the city, smelling like a mixture of concrete and burning metal. The notion of breathing that for the next twenty minutes sends him running for the subway station at Twenty-Third and Fourth.

But when he gets there, the entrance is blocked with people. He sidles his way through the crowd to see what is happening, when someone barks in his ear, "Can't you read? 'Service suspended until further notice.'"

He stands helplessly by the barrier, holding tight to his briefcase. His client must be waiting now, in front of that beautiful, expensive Sixty-Third Street brownstone. It's 11:53. Even if he runs the whole way, he won't make it. Arrivederci $100,000. Then, turning back, he sees, for the first time, the twin columns of smoke rising in the air, notices the crowds continuing to gather, and hear the sirens screaming, it seems, from one end of the city to the other.

Finally, it hits him. Something has happened, something terrible and something downtown. Chloe and Ava live in Chelsea, and it's all Brian can do, on this beautiful September morning, to stop himself from crying out.

Chloe!

"I wonder why," Rory says, echoing what everyone in America is saying to one another. The brothers are seated in front of the TV at one in the morning, watching people jump from the towers. And keep jumping. The station keeps replaying the reel, over and over, as if, viewed a sufficient number of times, the question will be answered—*Why?*—after which everyone will be able to brush their teeth and go to bed.

Brian isn't sure what his brother means. Why did the attacks occur? Or, why did the victims, knowing they faced certain death, fling themselves off the buildings? He can't pull his eyes from the screen as the bodies drop, little black specks; you can barely make them out.

"There's too much suffering," he says, of this and of the world in general. The horror of it makes him want to run screaming from the room, but he can't, he just can't. He's incapable of pulling himself away, because somewhere inside he feels that the longer he sits there, the longer he watches, he will eventually achieve some level of understanding—yet at the same time knowing in his heart that no one will ever be able to understand what has happened in New York City today.

"Don't you think it's time to pack it in?"

The voice startles both brothers, although Lily has come into the living room innumerable times during the course of the evening, with coffee, with buttered toast, with extra blankets. Because she works in emergency, Brian had assumed she would be kept on duty until morning, but Rory said that although extra emergency personnel had been summoned, there really wasn't much action. In fact, a colleague of his over at St. Vincent's mentioned that although the hospital had prepared for a flood of people, the day was remarkably quiet. By five barely anyone had shown up.

"I guess they all died," he'd said.

"Soon," Rory says to Lily, who's now staring at the screen. "Five minutes."

"I don't know how you can keep watching," Lily says. "All those poor souls, gone in a flash." She collects the cups and spoons and leaves the room.

"Don't you wonder," Brian says, when she's gone, "whether *she's* watching this?"

Rory asks, "Who?"

Brian turns from the screen to look at his brother. "Our mother. If she's still alive."

"She'd be, what—in her sixties? Right?"

"Sixty-three. She turned sixty-three last week."

"I suppose," Rory says, "that if she's watching this, she's probably wondering the same thing about us. Whether we're alive."

"She must have been wondering that for the past thirty years."

"I meant—"

"I know." Brian pulls one of the spare blankets Lily had provided around his shoulders and says, "Isn't it weird, that when you don't know where someone is, and you don't know who they are or what they look like, they could be anyone. Anyone you see, out there in the world."

"Yes."

"I was at the movies the other night, and before I went in, I noticed this woman in a wheelchair in the lobby buying popcorn, and I actually thought, 'That might be her!' Can you believe I almost went over and said something? Or there was that time last summer when I was walking through the park, and there was this older lady sitting on a blanket, eating a sandwich. I thought to myself, *'It's her.'*"

"Or that creased and disgustingly fat, drunken slattern, ordering another drink at the bar," Rory says.

"Very funny."

After a few moments, Rory says, "You know, don't you, that you're not the only one who suffered from her leaving."

"You mean Dad?"

"You always acted like she was just your mother. Not mine."

Rory has never hinted at anything like this before. Brian catches himself before he says, *But you were so young. And besides, you had Toni.* Instead, he says, "Dad told me once that you got teased about it."

"Yes. I got teased for not having a mother, and I always pretended not to care—although I always did." Rory straightens the cushion behind his back and squints at the TV. "But, that thing about seeing her places—I've actually thought the same thing myself. Tess has a friend at daycare whose grandmother comes to pick her up every afternoon, and she looks like—well, she looks just like someone from our family. You know, hair color—and those dark blue eyes, and thin build. That kind of pale look we all have." He pauses. Someone on the TV is screaming at someone else. "And sometimes," he goes on, "when I'm waiting, I catch that grandmother's eye and wonder—just what you were saying a moment ago. It's like, when you don't know who someone is, you don't know who they aren't." He stands up and goes to the door. "I'll be right back. There's something I want to show you."

Brian turns back to the TV, but now he can't make sense of what he's seeing: the angle of a building appears to be leaning to one side of the screen, stacks of ladders look as if they're propped up against thin air, white plastic sheeting is spread here and there, exhausted-looking emergency workers in their orange jackets are milling aimlessly around, and the debris—*the debris*—layers and layers of it, everywhere you look.

Rory comes back in and hands his brother a single sheet of paper. At the top, in large black type, are the words Women Missing in the 1970s. Beneath that is the name Olivia Somerville, along with her description and the details of her disappearance. To the side is a small, faded black-and-white photo.

"'Hair: black, long, straight,'" Brian reads out. "'Eye color: blue.'"

"What did I tell you? That lady at the day care—"

There's only a sentence or two about her; the rest of the page is devoted to three coeds who disappeared on a train trip to Denver in 1978.

Brian keeps reading. "On the day of her son's death." He looks up from the paper. "Dad told me about this a long time ago. I think it was when I came back for his wedding. It does make it kind of real, doesn't it? After all this time. *Her son's death*." He puts the page down on the coffee table. "Andrew."

"That photo," Rory says. "Dad must have given it to whoever filed the report."

"She looks exactly as I remember. So young. Younger than I am now."

"And me." Rory reaches for the remote and turns off the TV. "Lily found it recently. Every so often, she does a search. This time, *bingo*."

The room is silent. Even the sirens have ceased their incessant wailing. You'd be forgiven, Brian thinks, for believing that it was a normal evening, on a normal September day.

"I can't imagine doing what she did," Rory says. "I could never leave Tess." He slides open the drapes and peers out the window. Brian joins him.

The street is empty now, of people and of traffic. Across the way are more apartments—hundreds of them—and most of their windows are dark. It's as if everyone has finally had enough, has decided that since they are powerless to stop the evil that has been set into motion, the least they can do is sleep—all the while aware that when they wake, it will be to a different, scarier world, requiring a whole new set of rules. A whole new way of being.

Down the hall, Tess cries out in her sleep.

"I wonder if she's ever been tempted to come back," Rory says. "Or at least to contact us. If she's even still alive, that is."

"I imagine the guilt would be too much to bear."

"Yes. Guilt that she left. And guilt that she never returned."

"Probably guilt that Andrew died in the first place."

"But it wasn't her fault, right?" Rory says. "Andrew was being babysat. *We* were being babysat!"

Brian turns to face his brother. "That doesn't matter. Just think about it. If Tess died when she was being babysat, wouldn't you feel responsible?"

Without skipping a beat, Rory says, "I would." And he turns out the remaining lamp and makes for the door.

But Brian, wanting to hang on to the moment, muses, "You were always so perfect."

Rory turns. "Well, *someone* had to be." And then he does something that surprises Brian. Something he's never done before. He walks back over to Brian and plants a kiss on the top of his head.

Brian goes to the bathroom to shower. The room is strewn with the detritus of family life: a potty seat in one corner, wooden puzzle pieces spilled across the floor, a half-eaten banana on the side of the sink, rotting in its skin. In the bathtub, along with the requisite yellow duck, is a chain of multicolored tugboats, in graduated sizes, hooked one to the other. He smiles. He's about to experience this disorder himself, when Chloe comes for her overnights. He's already bought a camp bed—not for Chloe, but for himself. He'll roll it into the living room whenever she comes. She'll get the king-sized bed. The toys in the bathroom remind him to buy some items—a doll? some crayons? He's already purchased new sheets, printed with big purple butterflies.

Back in the living room, he pulls the sofa out into a bed, undresses, and slides beneath the sheets. After a moment he begins to shiver, even though it's a warm night. He reaches to the floor for one of the blankets Lily had brought in and spreads it up around his shoulders.

But sleep doesn't come easily. His mind keeps wanting to review the day, in scenes, one after the other. If he is to get any sleep at all, he has to find a way to wrench it back from that very first moment, at the subway station, when he'd been terrified that he'd lost Chloe. Olivia must have felt this, too, magnified a million times, when she came back from her hike that day, to discover that she'd lost a child. She would never have done what she'd done if she hadn't been in intolerable pain.

"There's too much suffering," he had said to his brother, and beginning to feel drowsy, he knows this to be true.

I'll find her, he thinks, not for the first time in his life, but for the first time, meaning it.

fifteen

2001

Olivia doesn't find out about the attacks until early afternoon. Because it's a beautiful day, she's planned to go to the organic market on its closing day, the last before next spring. She needs a dozen leeks for the freezer, and some acorn squash and red potatoes, to be wrapped in newspaper and stashed in the crawl space below the kitchen.

She contemplates walking to the market but decides that the trip back with bags of groceries might be too challenging. In town, she parks and walks around the back of the library to the courtyard. The large, tented area where the market is held is nearly empty, most of its stalls closed—or removed entirely. She looks up and down the street. Odd, to be so deserted on a weekday. Her watch says it's nearly two. Where are the high school students who, during their free periods, hang around the front doors of the library? Where are the mothers who are out shopping before their young children come home from school?

But the cheese stall is open, and so is the bread stall, its baskets filled with baguettes and ciabatta. Olivia walks over. Not many loaves have sold.

"Slow day?" she says to the young man behind the barrier. He nods. She selects a loaf, then opens her purse and takes out two crumpled dollar bills.

He doesn't take them. Instead, he says, in a gruff voice, "You can have it." Then he reaches for a second loaf and thrusts both into her bag.

"I don't need two," she says, but he's already turned away and begun to pack up his stall.

With her bread bag dangling from one arm and her purse in the other, she stands in the middle of the square, confused. The cheese lady has now gone, and the bread guy is packing to go.

She walks slowly back to the parking lot and puts the bread in her car. Then she goes around the building to the library entrance.

The main room is practically empty, the two librarians behind the front desk speaking in low tones. Three teenage girls, at a table under the window, are patting a fourth girl on the back as she sobs quietly.

Then Olivia catches sight of the large TV screen at the back of the room. A few people are standing in front of it, watching a building being made almost invisible by the black smoke that surrounds it. She walks over to join them.

That night she takes the quilt from her bed into the living room and turns on the small black-and -white TV Elaine convinced her to buy years before. Wrapping herself in the quilt, she takes a seat. She's been watching, on and off, since she got back from the library. The reel keeps repeating itself: the first building, then the second, the flames, the smoke, the jumpers.

This is a horror film. And it's taking place close to where her family lived.

Or lives.

The commentator says that all over America, people are thinking about their loved ones who aren't there beside them.

They must be watching, along with the rest of the world, Olivia thinks. Perhaps they are even thinking about her.

The phone rings.

"Are you watching?"

For a moment she thinks it's Harry, but of course, it isn't. It's Jude.

"Of course. I can't make myself stop. Can you?"

A beat, and then, "Can I come over?"

She almost says no. She has so many feelings, all jumbled up together—fear, sadness, yearning. Feelings she can't possibly share with anyone. She might have shared them with Elaine—at least some of them—but Elaine's death last February has forced Olivia back into her previous solitary exile.

But of course, Jude must come. Since Elaine died, he too has become solitary, having no one left in his family but his daughter, Marcy, who lives in Australia. The events that have happened today in New York, in D.C., in Pennsylvania aren't meant for solitary viewing.

A few minutes later he opens the door and calls out *hello*. Olivia makes tea, and they sit with their mugs, glued to the set.

After a while, Olivia says, "Do you really want to keep watching?" but Jude is too intent on the screen to hear her. Two young men are giving a whoop and a high five as a body—a live body, thank God—is lifted from the rubble.

Jude says, "I wonder what Elaine would say."

"Do you want me to turn it off?"

"Even if we stop, it'll be all we can think about."

"Well, it's over, anyway," she says.

"I don't know. Do you really think this will be the end of it? Four planes, and all those people. For what?" He pauses, then says, "Whatever it is, it's far from over."

She studies his face. It's a perfect oval, and his white hair, straight and still thick, flops to one side, nearly covering his eye. When he speaks, he often sounds as if he's on the verge of laughter. But not tonight.

He says, "I've barely seen you since Elaine died."

"Oh, you know how it is," she says too quickly, too casually, regretting that she hadn't called him, hadn't sought him out. "My lessons started up again last week. Plus, there's the garden to be put to bed. All those eggplants I planted, and not one did I get. Beautiful flowers and leaves, though."

Lame. But he's turned back to the TV, and when she looks again, the North Tower is collapsing, in what must be the hundredth replay since she got back home from the library. Both of them stare as the building appears not to fall so much as to settle, in slow motion. Pieces of iridescent cladding break away and flash across the screen before they hit the pavement. And then smoke, black smoke in the place where the building stood, is replaced by what appears to be a white mushroom cloud billowing up from the ground. When it dissipates they can see the steeple of a church.

"See that there?" Jude says, pointing to the church, which is suddenly thrust into the spotlight.

"Hmm." She hopes he doesn't say anything about God. She has a feeling that He has played a starring role in the reason for what happened today.

"My first job was there. At Trinity. Before the Towers were even built."

He reaches over and takes Olivia's hand, and they tighten their grip on each other as they watch. After a few minutes, he says quietly, "Does this make you wonder about your family?"

For a moment she's stunned. *Her family!* Was that an innocent comment? She has never told anyone, not even Elaine. She meets his eyes.

"Peter," Jude says. "It was Peter who told me."

"Ah." Of course. She remembers Peter's difficult, angry daughter who'd discovered the missing person report and wasted no time in informing her father. She did it to break up the two of them, and it worked, clever girl. "Yes," Olivia says. "I do wonder about them. Every single day, as a matter of fact. Not just today."

"I'm sorry," Jude says. "I didn't mean to—"

"It's okay. It's just, I've had years of practice not talking about them. Not ever telling anyone." She pauses, then tries to smile. "I'm not used to sharing."

"I mentioned it because I was thinking how much worse it must be for you, watching this. And not knowing."

A car goes by, its radio blaring, someone inside it screaming out, "Yo," followed by loud male laughter.

Talk to this good man, Olivia thinks. *You can do it. Tell him what's in your heart.*

She meets his eyes. "I chose this," she says, at the same time wondering what, exactly, she had chosen. It was such a long time ago. She's gotten too old to even believe in the concept of choice.

"Would you like to find them?"

A moment goes by before she says, "They must be so angry. Anyway, it was a long time ago."

A long time ago—nearly a lifetime. She used to deliberately not think about them; she used to try not to remember. In recent years, though—and especially since Elaine's death—she's found her mind circling back. Sometimes, now, they do seem real: Harry, Brian, Andrew, Rory. But, of course, they're not. They're not real; they're shadow people. She wants them, oh, how she wants them—but she knows they exist only in the dark places of her mind. The people who have replaced them are strangers.

"Most people don't hold on to their anger forever," Jude says.

He can't possibly know that—how could he? The families of today's victims, she is certain, will be angry for the rest of their lives. But: of course she would like to find her family. They are the part of her life that's missing.

There's so much space in life for despair.

The room is dark, except for the screen, with its flames and flashing lights. She doesn't want, any longer, to keep watching.

"Why don't we turn it off," Jude says, reading her mind. "Just turn it off. Like this," and he stands up and goes over to the TV and presses the button. The room is suddenly quiet. He returns to his place beside Olivia and puts his arm around her.

"Tell me about them," he says, and for a moment she's not sure what he's talking about. "Your family. Tell me about them. About your husband. And your children."

And in this dark, quiet room, she finally begins to speak.

"I had three children," she says, her voice strong and clear. There—she said it. The word "had."

And they begin slowly to come out, the memories that she has spent such a long time burying. She describes the day Brian was born, riding in the taxi with Harry as the urge to push overwhelmed her, and then, giving birth in the hospital elevator.

"Brian was always impatient," she says, remembering how he wanted to join Boy Scouts rather than Cubs, because he'd heard that Boy Scouts got to use real knives. But he had become a Cub and loved it. And how he had learned to read when he was four, by pointing to objects in his picture books and asking Olivia how they were spelled, and then committing the spelling to memory.

"He was good at piano," she says, wincing at the past tense, but how else, now, can she put it? "He learned Bach's F Major

Invention when he was only seven, and by the time he was nine he was learning pieces from *Children's Corner*."

Stopping for a moment, she settles her feet on the coffee table and leans back. It feels good to have a friendly arm around her.

"He was nervous, though. A nervous boy. He always seemed to be waiting for something bad to happen." Whatever she does, she mustn't let the tears come.

"He adored Rory. When I was pregnant, he would run his hand over my stomach. Sometimes he'd put his mouth against my stomach and whisper. He was talking to his brother." She repeats, "He loved Rory." And then, "I'm tired."

Jude gets up, but she says, "No, no. I didn't mean for you to go. I'll just go and lie down. Come with me, and we can keep talking."

He follows her to her bedroom, and when she's lain down, he pulls the covers up and takes a seat beside her on the bed. The lamp in the corner casts a faint glow in the room, but despite it Olivia can see, through the window, stars, millions of them. "You'd think, looking at that sky," she says, "that all was well with the world."

After a moment Jude asks, "What about Rory? Was he the youngest?"

"Yes, he was the baby. He had a sunny disposition, at least when things went his way. He was two when I left. He was spoiled, slightly—as youngest siblings often are. His brothers spoiled him. They carried him around the house like he was a doll. We had this little wagon, and they pulled him up and down the driveway in it. As soon as they stopped, he screamed bloody murder." She smiles, remembering. "He had this pig, this awful, pink, ugly cloth pig. He used to suck on its snout, instead of his thumb. It was soggy and disgusting. He sucked his pig, but Andrew sucked his thumb. I tried to get him to stop, but it was no use."

Before Jude has time to respond, she says, "Andrew. He was four when I left. Your classic middle child." She speaks of how he often got overlooked, remembering that first night at the lodge when she took the boys down to the dock. She had Rory on her lap while Andrew and Brian were skipping stones.

"Andrew wanted me to look at him; he wanted to show me that he could skip stones, too. Even though he couldn't, he thought that he could. He was so proud. But Rory was on my lap, straining to get off, and I was worried that he'd fall in the water."

Sitting up, she reaches into the drawer of her night table and pulls out a piece of purple cloth. "This was Andrew's. One of the many squares I cut his blanket into, so that when one got lost or destroyed, he'd still have others." She buries her nose in it for a moment, then replaces it in the drawer. She looks up at Jude. "Even now I think I can smell him."

Jude smiles. "And Harry? What about Harry? Did you have a good marriage?"

Without missing a beat, Olivia says, "We had a wonderful marriage." She pauses. "The best. But, of course, it was way too short." She turns to look at Jude, notices that he's shivering. "You're freezing!" she says. "It's late. Shouldn't you be on your way?"

He stands and looks down at her. "I don't really feel like being alone right now. Do you mind if I just curl up beside you?"

No one should be alone tonight, she thinks and then says as she moves over. Jude kicks off his Birkenstocks and climbs in beside her.

She remembers him at Elaine's funeral sitting in a front pew with his daughter and a few of Elaine's extended family members. It was at his own church, but of course another priest had been called in to take the service, someone who didn't even know Elaine. Has it really been that long since Olivia has seen him?

She feels ashamed. Tonight he sought her out, and all this time she's been speaking of her own family, her own tragedy. She should have called him. She should have invited him to dinner, or stopped by with food or flowers.

After a while his breathing becomes regular. The moon has risen in the sky, and Olivia can almost make out Jude's features in its faint light. She thinks back to their conversation, and all of a sudden a lightness—an old, recognizable feeling—touches her heart. She tries to catch hold of it, tries to keep it close, but as fast as it appears, it departs, and she is left only with her memories, and this kind, sleeping man beside her.

Not a small thing.

sixteen

2001

Late summer becomes early autumn, and suddenly it's nearly Christmas, and to Brian, who thought the world was close to ending on September 11, each day—which is filled with thoughts of his daughter, his future plans with her, and memories of her past visits—seems a miracle.

One day he calls Ava to ask if he can have Chloe the coming Saturday, even though the past weekend he took her to see *The Grinch* and isn't scheduled to see her again until Christmas Eve. He'd like to take her to the Met. It's one of his favorite places in Manhattan, and even though she's young and unlikely to appreciate much of what the place has to offer, he can show her what he liked when he was her age.

No problem, Ava says. When he arrives at their apartment just after lunch on Saturday, Chloe opens the door and throws her arms around his waist in a tight hug.

Ava appears from behind. "If you could have her back by six, her friend Juliet is having some kind of birthday clown thing." She pauses. "Not sure whether we'll go, though. Chloe seems awfully tired. Tired for Chloe, that is."

"I'm not tired!"

They drive slowly along Park, which is plugged solid. Brian points out the Christmas trees up and down the avenue. "At night, they're all lit up. Every Christmas they do it. If it's dark enough on the way home, we might be able to see it happen."

"I remember," Chloe says. "Last year Juliet's mom took us."

"I was there!" Brian says, wondering whether his daughter, a stranger to him then, passed by him as he stood in the dark among the people gathered on the pavement, waiting for that magical moment when the lights flickered on, as far down Park as they could see.

He manages to find parking on Eighty-Sixth Street, and they walk over to the museum and proceed up the steps and into the Great Hall, which with its stone arches and marble columns has always reminded him of a cathedral—or a Victorian-era train station. In the middle of the information booth in the center of the room is a towering display of Christmas greenery.

Chloe's eyes are huge as she takes in the enormity of the place. There are people everywhere: standing in line, consulting their brochures, walking to and from the various galleries, meeting friends. She looks up at her father and says, "I thought there were pictures."

"Wait," Brian says. "We're going to see pictures, but first I have something to show you."

They pass through the Egyptology exhibits until they reach a small alcove lined with cases filled with ancient wall and floor tiles. Off to one side is a high, narrow table and, on top of that, a tiny blue clay hippopotamus. Brian lifts Chloe in the air so she can see it better.

"This is William," he says. "William the hippo. He's the mascot here."

Chloe laughs in delight. "Can I touch?" she asks, reaching out her hand. Brian grabs it and notices how warm it is. Ava mentioned Chloe was tired, but he wonders whether the child is well.

"They don't let you touch anything here. Everything is old. Even William is old—he was made almost four thousand years ago. Isn't that incredible? We'll come and say goodbye on our way out."

He guides Chloe past the tombs and back to the Great Hall, where he picks up a brochure with a map. *What would a child love here?* he wonders, thinking that the day may have been a mistake. What he had loved as a child were the mummies, and in fact he's itching to see them now. But in the brochure, there's no sign of them. Anyway, tombs and mummies might not appeal to seven-year-old girls. Perhaps instead they would visit the sculptures in the European section, or the decorative arts. Jewels—little girls love jewels, don't they? Chloe plays endlessly with the set of beads he gave her for her birthday.

On the way to the decorative arts they pass through the rooms of paintings done by the European masters. They proceed past a line of English oils, mostly landscapes that would hold no interest for Chloe, so Brian doesn't stop. Chloe lets go of his hand and skips on ahead, and as he moves to catch up, he almost misses it.

But there—it's unmistakable. The picture that hung in his mother's bedroom all those years ago. The Constable. The painting she took and presumably sold—for a price that could still sustain her.

He stands before it. The boy with his pole, leaning over the brick wall of the tree-lined canal—such a familiar sight. The man in the boat with his punt. The red-roofed houses. The gray sky. It's all there, just as he remembers.

Chloe tugs on his arm. "What about the beads?"

If Brian believed in God, or predestination, or even some unholy plan untethered from religion, he might conclude that he was meant to see that painting on this particular December afternoon, in this particular gallery, in this particular museum in New York City, with the granddaughter his mother would never know.

"What are you looking at?"

"It's just a painting. A picture of—" He stops and points. "It's a boy—see, he's leaning over the water fishing? And the man in the boat?" He turns to his daughter. "It was my mother's a very long time ago. It hung in her bedroom when I was little."

"Is that the grandmother I'm not supposed to talk about?"

"Is that what your mother told you? You can talk about her, Chloe. It's just that I don't know very much about her. She went away when I was nine..." *Oh, God,* he thinks. *Don't ask me any questions.* He doesn't want to have to tell a little girl that she lives in a world where a mother can just vanish and never come back.

But she's already at the end of the room. Brian catches up with her, and they enter a corridor and then a room filled with quilts and jewels and wooden carvings. A few minutes later, in front of a stained-glass window depicting purple irises, he notices that Chloe is drooping. This was not a good idea. How could he expect a child of seven to have the fortitude—not to mention the attention span—to withstand an afternoon-long museum visit?

"What about some food?" he says. "There's a café just through there. Let's go get something." He consults his watch. Nearly four thirty. He could have her back home by five thirty and she'd still make her clown party.

Inside the café he orders a chocolate milk and a coffee. Chloe isn't interested in the cookies or squares behind the glass cases, which surprises him. They take a seat at a little round table, and, as Brian tears open a packet of sugar, Chloe fixes her eyes on him with a look of panic, then proceeds to vomit the contents of her stomach into her lap.

Ten minutes later, after a quick, embarrassed apology to the lady at the cash register—and after taking Chloe to the men's room for a mostly futile clean-up job—they walk back to Eighty-Sixth Street to pick up the car. It's grown dark. Chloe seems better, and as he drives, she talks about the upcoming party. A real magician is coming, she says.

Clowns and magicians, Brian thinks, turning onto Park Avenue. His childhood parties weren't nearly as exciting, pizza and ice cream cake being the main attractions. He remembers one in particular, when his mother placed a plastic sheet on the kitchen floor. You had to twist yourself into a pretzel, while around you others were doing the same, and if you fell, you were out. Twister, that's what it was called, and just then the lights on Park Avenue blink on.

"Look, Chloe!" he says. "The Christmas lights." And he points to a majestic pine, wreathed in blue and topped with a white star.

"My neck hurts," Chloe says in a small voice. She places her hand on her father's knee. "It hurts to move my head."

Brian brakes at the light on Park and Sixty-Third and glances over at his daughter. Her eyes are closed, her cheeks bright red.

When he reaches Sixteenth Street he parks and hurries around to open the passenger door. Gathering Chloe in his arms, he carries her up the steps and into the elevator. He pushes the buzzer and, when no one answers, bangs on the door. Finally, Ava opens it.

"What's all this?" she says, and when she sees Chloe, the color leaves her face.

Chloe says, holding her palms in front of her eyes, "My head hurts."

Brian lays her down on the couch, and Ava goes for a blanket and pillow and the thermometer. Moments later, they're on the way to the hospital.

At one in the morning Brian is in the hospital waiting room, standing beside the window, looking at—but not seeing—the traffic speeding down FDR Drive. After at least five physicians examined Chloe, after a tube of oxygen was fitted over her head, after a saline drip was placed in the crook of her arm, after numerous vials of blood were taken and an X-ray and a painful lumbar puncture were performed, the diagnosis was confirmed: bacterial meningitis.

She's been delirious since they arrived at the hospital, and even now, six hours later, she keeps going in and out, wailing for Ava when Ava is right there beside her, sponging her forehead with a cool cloth. And then, moments later, asking about the clown party she missed. And then, crying about the monster she can see in the window beside her bed. An hour or so ago, a young man wheeled a small fold-out bed into the room so Ava could sleep beside her daughter.

Brian is afraid to leave, although as Ava pointed out, he might as well go home since there is nothing he can do. He can come first thing in the morning, she says. Maybe he can stay with Chloe while Ava goes home to shower and change.

But what if something happens in the night? Hadn't someone once told him that dawn is the critical time? That if you make it past dawn, chances are you'll live to see another day?

He didn't mention this to Ava, though. He knew that although she seemed calm, inside she must be panicking. The doctor had said that even though Chloe was in the safest place possible, bacterial meningitis is dangerous. Brian knows that himself; he's read that one out of ten people don't make it. He tried to pose a question about this to the doctor without Ava understanding the terrible implication underlying it, but the doctor pretended not to understand, merely repeating, "Healthy young people generally recover."

Generally? What kind of answer is that? He reaches for his jacket. He only recently became aware of his daughter's existence, and now she owns a large corner of his heart. He couldn't bear to lose her now.

He leaves the waiting room and walks through the ward and then through the doors that lead to the elevator. The lights have been dimmed, and most of the medical personnel on duty—doctors, nurses, aides—are sitting quietly behind their banks of computers observing the vital signs of their small charges who are tucked away in their beds, unseen, in their rooms up and down the hallway.

What a miracle modern medicine is, or so he hopes. At the same time, though, he knows that little girls are not immune from assaults on their fragile bodies. Even little girls can die.

He rides the elevator down to the lobby. Outside it's snowing—the first snow of the season, falling thickly, coating the sides of the streetlights and the sidewalks. Ordinarily he would be thrilled at the sight, but tonight he can't enjoy it because Chloe isn't with him to see it.

In his apartment, finally, he casts off his clothes and climbs into bed. He closes his eyes—he'll be good for nothing tomorrow if he doesn't sleep. But images of his little girl keep flashing through his mind. Chloe, in the museum, looking up at the Constable. Chloe, vomiting in the cafe. Chloe, red-cheeked in the car. And then, Chloe, lying quietly in her hospital bed, connected to monitors and tubes.

He would call first thing in the morning; her fever should have broken by then. In the morning they would know more, the doctor said. *Know more? Know more what? Whether she will live or die?*

Finally, he dozes off, but his sleep is fitful. He dreams of doing impossible things in impossible situations, and through them the voice of his daughter cries out his name. When his alarm clock goes off, he stumbles out of bed and, in the kitchen, pours himself a glass of cold water. It's just after seven. Ava said to wait until nine.

But at nine thirty he's sitting at the kitchen table beside the telephone, unable to pick it up and dial. What if something happened in the night, something terrible, and Ava was only now being told? What if she was screaming and crying, too upset to remember to call him?

He remains there for another hour, paralyzed, reasoning that if he doesn't call, he won't know. And if he doesn't know, he can still imagine that Chloe is fine.

"Dear Miss So-and-So," Brian writes with his pencil on a yellow legal pad a few weeks later. It's the first draft, but he wants to get it right. "I am writing to inquire about the person who sold your museum the painting by John Constable that I saw in Gallery #111 two weeks ago." He crosses out the word *saw* and exchanges it for *viewed*.

The name of the painting eludes him. Did he even know it? How silly, that he never made a note of it. Wasn't the word *lock* in the title? Or was it *loch*? And the word *boat*? He really must find that out before he sends the letter. He crumples the page into a ball and tosses it in the wastebasket, deciding, instead, to stop by the Met on his way back from visiting Chloe, who's at home now and nearly recovered.

But standing before the painting later that day, he decides that as long as he's there, he might as well try to find someone who has the information he needs. Person-to-person might be better than a letter—or at least, he hopes that it might. He approaches the uniformed guard beside the exit door and asks to be directed to Acquisitions.

A few minutes later he's seated in a small office, waiting to speak with a curator. Ten, twenty minutes pass and no one comes. Just as he's decided that a letter might be better after all, a young woman enters the room and, with her hand out, introduces herself as Nina Taylor. She takes a seat behind the room's only desk and, folding her hands in her lap, waits for him to speak. Which he does, briefly explaining that he would like to know where the museum acquired the painting.

There's a silence as she studies his face. "Just a moment," she tells him.

She walks over to a bank of file cabinets and, after scanning the labels, pulls a drawer open, then returns it and pulls out another. A moment later, she has a file in her hand, and standing beside the window, she opens it.

He waits quietly as she reads. Finally, she looks over at Brian and shakes her head. "I'm sorry. I'm afraid that information was flagged confidential."

"You mean—"

"I mean, we can't provide you with the information you need. The person who sold it to us requested anonymity."

"Forever?" Brian asks foolishly. "I believe that sale was almost thirty years ago. Are you saying—"

"Yes. Forever." She snaps the file shut. "I'm sorry." She waits, her face impassive, for him to leave.

But Brian is not so easily cowed. "The person we're talking about here," he says, "that person was—or is—my mother."

Ms. Taylor waits.

"She left when my brother and I were little. She just—disappeared. There were three of us—three brothers—" He stops. How futile is this? He should have known better, known not to come. Bureaucracies operate according to their own immutable non-human rules. This attempt to locate his mother was never going to be anything other than a failure. The only saving grace is that he hasn't put much time or effort into it. Nothing ventured…

He makes one last stab at it. "My little brother drowned. He was just four years old. And my mother, before she could find out who it was—" He stops speaking and holds up his hands, as if in surrender.

Ms. Taylor, still beside the door, blinks, then says, "Yes, well. We do have these rules, don't we? We have to have them. It wouldn't be fair to our clients if we just gave information out, willy-nilly. We need to offer—and honor—the confidentiality option." She stops and then, fixing her eyes on Brian, says, "Would you mind excusing me for a moment?"

She places the file on the desk and says, "I'll be back in a few minutes." Then she leaves the room.

For a moment, he's confused. Surely she didn't mean… He gathers himself together and, reaching over, pulls the file toward him. He glances through the glass window. No one is watching him. Then he opens the file. At the top of the first page is the name of the painting and the artist, along with the unfathomably large price the museum paid for it. Beneath that information is the date: *October 11, 1971*. And below that: *Olivia Enright. North Port, Vermont. Street address unknown. No contact number offered. Seller will call back with particulars. Confidentiality requested and approved.*

The rest of the page is devoted to the authentication details and, at the bottom, in blue ink, the scrawled signature: *Olivia Enright*. His mother's handwriting, very nearly illegible, as if dashed off as quickly as possible.

For a moment Brian sits, thinking. *North Port*. The name rings a bell. He reaches out and, with the tip of one finger, traces the faded ink of the looping signature. *Olivia Enright*. Closing his eyes, he summons up an image—a woman with long black hair, one strand of it caught in her smiling mouth as she's turning away from the camera.

He grabs a pen from the desk and hurriedly copies out the relevant information on his left arm. As he lets himself out the door, he catches sight of Ms. Taylor in the anteroom, leaning back against the opposite wall, her eyes on him. She's waiting for him to leave. He raises his hand in a brief wave, and although she doesn't return it, he's certain he can discern a tiny smile on her face.

North Port, he thinks, later that evening, as he washes up his dinner dishes. *North Port, Vermont.* Amazing that she lives there, right near the resort—or did.

It's a lot to take in. He pulls a map book from the bookcase and, taking it into the living room, opens it out on the coffee table. First he finds Montclair, New Jersey, and circles it with a red marker. Then he locates North Port and does the same, after which he follows, with his finger, the route north between the red marks. New Haven, Springfield, Northampton, and then, just east of the Green Mountains, North Port.

It's been a long while since he's thought about the details of that trip, but it's not because he's forgotten them; it's more that they never led to anything other than a dead end. Now he leans back on his sofa and allows himself to think.

He remembers arriving at the resort that first day, remembers jumping out of the car, glad to be outside instead of penned up with his family. He can even remember the bedroom he shared with Andrew. The bunk beds—they were painted shiny red, and he had the top, of course. Rory slept somewhere else, maybe in his own room—or with their parents?

The next morning they swam in the lake, and after lunch his father took him to the tennis courts to teach him how to play. After dinner in the café, his mother took the three of them down to the dock where he and Andrew skipped stones. When they came back, his father lit a fire, and he and Andrew sat on the floor in front of it, toasting marshmallows on the hangers his mother had discovered in the closet and untwisted. His mother held a sleeping Rory on her lap.

He can remember the cabin so well, each tiny detail: the clock on the mantelpiece that sounded like a bell, the children's books on the lower shelf in the living room, the little fridge that kept turning off and on as he was trying to get to sleep.

Then it was the next day, and here one memory follows another, staccato, like gunshots. Breakfast in the dining room. The walk with that girl—Carla was her name, and he can even remember the color of her scarf (turquoise). The swim with his brothers in The Shallows. Then to the barn where they kept the ponies, and Andrew riding the smallest one while Carla hung on to Rory. The return to the cabin, his mother nowhere to be seen. Lying on the top bunk looking up at the spider. Carla and the pony boy coming into his room to quiz him, and then his father, his face white, bursting through the door with his tennis racket in hand. The dock, where his brother lay. The police, in and out of the cabin several times that afternoon and into the evening, talking quietly to his father and taking notes before finally going away for good.

Today has been a long day, he thinks, turning out the kitchen light. Today he may have found his mother. Tomorrow is New Year's Eve, and he has no parties to attend, no friends to see. He wishes he had some place to go. Chloe and Ava will be with Ava's mother in the Bronx. But he can't very well complain. This Christmas was, by far, the best one of his adult life, even though it was spent in the hospital with Ava, himself, and Chloe, all together in the patient lounge with their plates of turkey and mashed potatoes, sent up from the hospital kitchen for the families of patients unlucky enough to be stuck there during the holiday.

When he got home from the Met this afternoon, he was filled with excitement, as if he had finally arrived at the place he'd spent his life longing for. Tonight, though, the feeling has faded with the realization of the enormity of the task he has set himself. If he finds Olivia—and after all, she could be living somewhere else now, or dead—what could she possibly say that would help him make sense of what happened to him all those years ago?

That's what he wants, isn't it? An explanation. That's what he's always wanted.

She can't change what happened. She can't mend the harm she caused by leaving. If he does manage to find her, isn't it possible that she might—by some method—taint the rest of his life as she tainted the first part of it?

He goes over to the window and gazes down at the empty

street. Maybe he'll go to Rory's tomorrow night, ring in the New Year with his brother and Lily and Tess if they don't have other plans. He wants to share his news with his brother, but not over the phone. He needs to see Rory's face when he tells him. He's fairly certain his brother will tell him to go to Vermont. *What have you got to lose?* he'll say, because of course, this is Brian's quest, in a way that it's never been Rory's.

Anyway, he's already decided. The real estate market is slow in January, even in Manhattan, and he has some time coming to him. He could sneak up to Vermont for a long weekend at the end of the month or even, perhaps, for a week.

How difficult can it be, tracking down someone in a town of 3,057 people? The obvious place to start is the library. You can't live in a small town without making your mark. Libraries have telephone books, and employees eager to share information. He isn't sure what he'll say to elicit the information, but it can't be any harder than it was at the Met. He'll figure it out. He'll ask his questions casually, as if he doesn't really care about the answers, one way or another. He doesn't want anyone to think he's a stalker.

When he finds out where she lives—if she's still there—well, he still has to think that one through. Maybe he'll approach her, or maybe he'll wait. He's good at waiting.

PART FIVE

seventeen

2002

In the frigid wind howling down Thirty-Second Street, he scrapes the ice from his windshield. A cold snap has enveloped the northeastern United States. When Brian woke this morning, icicles were hanging from the tops of the windows, partially obscuring the view. Outside, people were hurrying along the sidewalks, ducking in and out of shops as quickly as possible so they could get back home to the warmth.

On his way to the car he'd slipped and had to grab on to a lamppost, and, as he fit the key in the car door, the lock wouldn't turn. He'd had to rub the key in his palms and blow his hot breath on it before reinserting it.

Finally, the windshield is clear, and he tosses the scraper on the passenger seat. He might need it again. The tires of his car make a hissing noise as he pulls out of the lot and makes his way through Lower Manhattan until he reaches the entrance to the tunnel, where there's a backup of cars waiting to get through. An hour later, he's sailing up the highway.

He's headed to Vermont—North Port, Vermont—to find his mother. He both can and can't believe it. He thinks that he's ready to meet her, but that little voice in his head that advises caution has urged him to take it in small steps, and he's learned, more than once, that the little voice should be heeded. At the moment, he just wants to make sure North Port is where she is, and if he's lucky and is able to obtain her address, maybe he'll be able to see her coming out of her house—or apartment—or wherever it is that she now calls home.

He read a poem recently that began

They fuck you up, your mum and dad.
They may not mean to, but they do.
They fill you with the faults they had
And add some extra, just for you.

It made him wonder whether the poet was abandoned, too. Or perhaps everyone who escapes their childhood feels fucked up, not only those who were abandoned, or whose families were otherwise cleaved apart. How would he know?

He would have laughed if he'd read those lines before Chloe came into his life. Now he sees them as a warning. Whatever has been done to him, whatever violence has afflicted his soul, his goal is to not inflict the same on Chloe.

The small towns in New York State fly by. Newburgh, New

Paltz, Kingston, many of them—with their boarded-up buildings and cheap discount shops—appearing ragged and defeated. Even the people walking along the sidewalks appear beaten down. Or perhaps it's just the cold that's making them walk with their shoulders up and their eyes cast down.

He stops for lunch in Saugerties. It's larger than the places he's just driven through and doesn't appear as distressed. He cruises the main street for a pizza place, or a hamburger shack, anything that will keep him going for the next couple of hours. There's nothing. Then he spots, across the road, a Chinese restaurant with a yellowing Christmas wreath still fixed to its door. Its windows are filthy. He simply cannot. He's hungry, but not that hungry. He's heading back to his car, when he spots a deli.

Pulling over, he parks and goes in. Except for the two customers who are just leaving, the place is empty. Taking a seat at the counter, he opens the large, multipage menu. Eventually a young girl appears from the back, and in no time at all he has ordered and put away a huge plate of macaroni and cheese before he's back on the road, with North Port less than two hours away. He turns on the radio to a classical music station and minutes later is tapping his fingers on the steering wheel to one of the *Goldberg Variations*.

He recognizes it. The Aria. He used to play it, but that was a long time ago—possibly ten years. Rory had a piano in his first apartment; Lily played it a little, and Brian used it from time to time. But Rory sold the piano shortly after getting married and didn't acquire another until recently, when he bought a very expensive baby grand that now sits in his study, untouched. "I'm going to learn," Rory has told Brian more than once. "I'll be taking lessons, just as soon as I have a minute."

Although Rory has told his brother he's free to use it any time, Brian has hesitated. He's loath to become a fixture at his brother's family home—he's had too much of that, too much dependency in his life, especially during his drinking days. On the other hand, Rory always says what he means. Maybe Brian will take him up on his invitation. He could go over, between clients, when Lily and Rory are at work.

Hearing Glenn Gould now, Brian remembers the joy he felt when he used to play, remembers marveling that with ten fingers, a large instrument, and some musical sheets, a whole complicated emotional curve could be created. It was not only playful or romantic; it was sexual, even the names of the notations. Largo appassionato. Lento serioso. Allegretto. Vivace energico. And then, the climax: Crescendo.

He'll do it, he vows. His fingers will be rusty, but if he works at it every day, maybe he'll be able to tackle the Aria again. Gould plunges into the second variation as Brian enters the tiny village of Hoosick, just before the Vermont border. He's through it before he can blink, and moments later he's in Bennington. The contrast between Vermont and New York State is startling. Although both share the same climate and rural economy, Vermont with its shops, churches, homes, and barns is much better maintained than its western neighbor. It helps that decades ago, and for purely aesthetic reasons, Vermont banned billboards and roadside advertisements.

He drives through Bennington, then winds his way through the Green Mountains, reaching North Port by four. Driving down its main street, he has no memory of the town. Perhaps his family didn't drive through it to get to the resort.

He intends to explore before it gets dark; then he'll check into his hotel. He parks and makes his way along the street—past the pond in the middle of town, iced over now, past a Revolutionary War–era inn, with its prosperous-looking ground-floor restaurant, past a series of small stores—a leather shop, a bookshop, the inevitable pizza joint and hairdresser's—until he comes to the library. He'll be in there tomorrow with his questions. Right now, it's closed. He steps onto the porch and peers through the window. Tables, chairs, stacks of books, a fern in one corner, a set of armchairs beside a fireplace. He wonders whether his mother belongs, and if she does, whether she sits in one of those chairs, engrossed in a book on a winter afternoon.

He steps off the porch and walks down the street to the town green. The air is glacial, and only a few hardy souls—an elderly couple arm in arm in matching parkas and a young woman in a long black coat pushing a baby stroller—are out walking in the waning light. Wooden benches are positioned here and there, and Brian takes a seat on the one beside a footbridge that spans a frozen creek. He tightens the scarf around his neck.

He can't imagine the woman he once knew living in a place like this. Although it's quaint, and it's beautiful, it's also isolated. Brian hadn't even spotted a movie theater—or a bar—on his way through. There's nothing to it. And besides that, it's cold. Fucking cold.

As far as he can recall, his mother was a city person. She thrived on crowds and music and stores and lights. She loved going places and having lots to do. She could barely contain her enthusiasm about the move to New York City. He remembers her describing to him the place they'd bought, with built-in bookcases and a laundry chute and a real doorman.

Sure, the North Port library looks nice, and so does the inn. The town is immaculate. But it's a *toy* town—a place to vacation, perhaps, but not to spend a life in. How could she have survived it all these years? Assuming, of course, that she's still here.

But then, it's silly to surmise. What does he know? He was nine when she left.

He stands and stamps his feet. The cold has penetrated his sneakers and seeped through the crack between his scarf and his collar. He needs to find his hotel.

That night he barely sleeps. The room had looked fine when he first saw it—clean and bright, painted white, with blue drapes on its wall of windows, and with a wide-screen TV and a coffee machine—everything he could possibly need. But the only bedding provided was a heavy duvet, which was too hot for the room. Casting it off in the night, he soon became cold and had to get out of bed twice, once for a sweater and again for his coat.

The next morning, he has breakfast in the lobby, where small tables and chairs have been set out. By ten, he's in the car driving back into town. He parks in the lot behind the wine store, gets out of the car, and steps briskly aside as two skateboarders slam their boards onto the icy sidewalk in front of him.

The town appears more substantial than it did last night, perhaps because there are more people out. He walks over to the library. Inside, people are scanning the shelves or are seated at tables reading. On the floor at the back is a group of children listening to a story. There's a short line at the front desk, and Brian joins them. When it's his turn, he takes a deep breath, and then, screwing up his courage (*what's a sticking place?* he wonders), looks the librarian in the eye and says, "I'm trying to locate someone. Can you help?"

She waits patiently for him to explain, and when he doesn't, asks, "Do you have a name?"

"Olivia Enright."

The woman's face lights up. "You just missed her! She was here a few minutes ago! I think she was on her way to Lorna's. Or maybe that was later on today. I forget." She pauses, then says, "If you do see her, can you tell her the other book she ordered just got shelved? She knows we'll hold it until next Saturday, but still, if she wants it now before she goes home..."

As easy as that. He takes a step back. Through the window he sees a shop across the street with a sign that says Lorna's Cut-n-Curl. But can he really just burst into the place—where women are getting their hair cut and dried and tinted—with his questions and demands?

No, he decides. He will not embarrass her that way. But he

does need to know where she lives. He can't imagine spending a week here, waiting at the entrance to the library on the off chance that he'll run in to his mother while she's collecting her book.

He steps forward again and says, timidly, "Do you happen to have an address for her? I've just come up from New York, and I seem to have lost—"

His mind, she must think. *Lost his mind.* But meanwhile, the man behind Brian interrupts to tell the librarian about his new girlfriend, and she doesn't appear to have heard Brian's question. Saving the day, a woman dropping off her books steps forward and says, "I believe she's still living out in the schoolhouse by the church. On Armstrong Road. You know where that is, right?"

"That's right," a young girl volunteers. "Mrs. Enright is still out there. My sister takes piano from her every Wednesday."

He nods and smiles. Of course he knows that. It's just slipped his mind.

Back outside, he notices a coffee shop and, crossing the street, he goes inside. He orders a latte and takes it to a solitary booth in the corner and opens the map he has with him. Within a few moments he finds it, Armstrong Road, only a few miles from town. He'll drive out there this afternoon.

Back at the hotel he spends an hour responding to his phone messages. Then he grabs a bag of peanuts and a Coke from the snack machine in the lobby and gets in his car, following the route he plotted out until he's on Armstrong Road, which winds around the lake. After another half mile, the surface of the road gives way to gravel, crunching beneath his tires. He rounds another curve, and there, just ahead of him and bordering the water, is a clearing. He stops the car and looks across, and there it is. The lodge. The boathouse is on one side of it and the dock beside that. It's all so familiar.

His heart picks up its pace. His goal all along had been to find his mother; he's barely given a thought to his little brother. If it were summer, he'd pick a bouquet of wildflowers along the roadside and walk around to that part of the lake, the place where Andrew drowned. Then, if no one was around, he'd throw the flowers in the water.

Farther up the road is a small white church and, beside it, a smaller building in a similar style. There's no car in the driveway. This has to be it. He puts the car in park and looks across. The house is small, neat, with flower boxes at every window. There's a vestibule in front, and the windows on either side of it are large. In the middle of the peaked roof is a chimney. The house is white, but it could use a coat of paint. The gravel driveway is deeply rutted.

He continues to sit for a while, waiting. No one comes. An hour passes before he gives up and drives back to the hotel, but later in the afternoon he returns. This time a car is in the driveway and smoke is coming out of the chimney. It's growing dark, and inside the lights have been turned on. He pulls over and waits, watching the windows, but he doesn't see her. Maybe she's beside the fire reading the library book she checked out this morning.

That evening in the hotel café he has dinner and then returns to his room to pack his suitcase. He'll get an early start in the morning. Before getting into bed, he places his coat beside him, to throw over him in the night, should he get cold. Hopefully then he'll be able to sleep.

In the morning after he checks out, he decides to try one more time. He tosses his suitcase into the back seat and heads out to Armstrong Road, driving slowly as he rounds the final turn, then pulling over to the side of the road. He's in luck. She's there, just coming out of her front door, a white-haired woman in a blue jacket. As she turns to lock the door, he can see how slight she is, a mere wisp of a woman. Strange, he'd always thought of her as being tall. He keeps the car running and watches as she turns from the door, and as she pushes her hair out of her face, their eyes meet.

He's always imagined this moment. He's always thought that at their first meeting, each would instantly recognize the other.

It's not like that. She's an old lady. If he saw her on the street, he wouldn't give her a second glance. He'd walk right on by. And the same is obviously true for her.

She steps down off her porch and begins to walk up the road. He pulls ahead of her. Through the rearview mirror he continues to observe her figure as it becomes smaller and smaller, until his car rounds the bend and she's gone.

eighteen

2002

At the end of June, Brian and Chloe drive to North Port, where Brian has rented a house for the summer.

He has been wanting to return since his trip in January, but he'd had several weekend closings, two of them expensive apartments on Park Avenue, and after that he had come down with the flu, which seemed to go on forever. Then, in early March, Ava called to say that her boyfriend had taken a summer teaching job in England and she'd been granted a leave of absence from her job, and could he have Chloe for the summer?

Brian quickly said yes. He would love to have Chloe, even though her presence would potentially complicate matters. He was sure he'd be able to find the two of them a small house in North Port, but he wasn't certain about what he would be doing during the day, other than the fact that it would hopefully involve his mother. Whatever it was, an eight-year-old girl would be bound to put a dent in it. Perhaps there was a summer camp in or near North Port that she could attend during the day.

The other agents in his office didn't seem annoyed that he would be away. His coworkers were probably jumping for joy as he passed on his exclusives to them. After all, the hard work in sales occurs at the beginning of the process, from that first visit to view the property until the deal is struck and signed, or—as often happens—the client backs out, signing on with some other agent her sister's daughter-in-law's hairdresser had once used.

Ava left it to Brian to tell Chloe about the summer plan, and when he did, she wasn't thrilled. She wanted to stay in the city with her friends—and her piano.

"It's too far away," she told Brian, on the verge of tears. "I don't want to go."

"It's not that far," Brian said. And to sweeten the deal: "Maybe you could invite some of your friends up."

"As if. Nobody would come all that way just to see me."

"Wouldn't you drive four hours to see your friends?"

"Not if they were in Vermont, I wouldn't!"

"Well," Brian responded mildly, "I'm sure you'll make some new friends at camp." He had finally found a day camp and enrolled her in it for four days a week, to begin the week after they arrived.

The piano was another matter. Easily solved—or so he thought. But when he told Chloe he'd bought a keyboard for the trip, she wasn't enthused.

"It's not the same as a piano," she said. "A keyboard only has seventy-six keys."

"But the twelve keys a keyboard *doesn't* have are at the very bottom and top of the register. I'm sure you've never even played those keys. I know I never have. I don't even know if they make music for those keys."

"So why do they have them, then?" Chloe said. "I like knowing I can use them if I want." She paused. "Anyway, the touch is totally different. I don't like the feel of a keyboard."

He thinks about this conversation as he's outside his apartment loading the car. When she said that about a touch, he was amazed that a child her age could discern the difference.

She's been working on one of the French suites, plugging away at it every day, a few measures at a time. He himself had recently begun playing again on Rory's baby grand, and he envisions the two of them learning some four-hand pieces—a father-daughter duo.

In the car on the way up, Chloe says, "Why did you grow a beard?"

"Don't you like it?"

Silence for a moment, and then a small voice. "Not really."

They've just crossed over into Vermont, and already things look different. Greener. No billboards.

Before they left, he'd examined himself in the mirror. In the three months he'd been letting them grow, his beard and mustache had morphed into one of those shrubs that seem to reach out to ensnare you as you pass by. An azalea? No, something like a rose, but not a rose. Prickly, but lacking the actual flower.

Would *she* recognize him? It's doubtful. As much hair as he'd grown on his face, he'd lost, over the past year, from his scalp. Last week Rory had done a double take when Brian stopped by for the family photo albums to bring with him just in case.

He switches on the headlights, although dusk is hours away. With all that green, and the mountains that now surround them, it's harder to see.

"Every man in Vermont has a beard," he says to his daughter. "I think it's the law." He feels Chloe's eyes on him.

"Really?"

"You'll see."

A moment goes by before she finally says, "You don't look like you."

Exactly the point.

They are nearly there. Chloe is tapping on her lap with her fingers, her eyes closed. When he was her age, he did the same thing on his place mat while he was waiting for his mother to serve dinner.

"What's that lovely piece?" she'd say. "I didn't quite catch that." Or, "I believe you missed a key, young man. That was a B-flat. And it's staccato, not legato."

"What's that lovely piece?" he says to Chloe now. "I didn't quite catch that."

She doesn't crack a smile. "'Doctor Gradus ad Parnassum.' The first part of it."

"I used to play that."

"I know. You told me." She stops tapping and looks out the window. "Sometimes it makes me cry."

He'd like to tell her that he knows exactly how she feels; it makes him cry, too, but he's afraid she'll shy away. Things are fragile now between them. After the turnoff he begins counting the streets out loud: seven, six, five, four, three, two... "And he-e-e-ere it is!" He pulls the car up to the garage, then gets out and goes around back for their luggage.

But Chloe bolts out of the car and says, "Can't we go in first?" It's the first bit of enthusiasm she's shown.

It's a white clapboard one-story bungalow. They go around the back and let themselves into a small kitchen. Fridge, stove, sink, he counts off. And a narrow counter. Good. They walk through the house, Chloe skipping on ahead. The living room is not much bigger than the kitchen, but it's brighter, with a floor-to-ceiling window. Down a narrow hallway are the two bedrooms, and as he steps into the smaller one, which will be his, he hears Chloe squeal. He finds her at the back in a screened-in porch. There's a small bed set against the wall and a blanket chest—and not much else. Through the screen is a garden filled with cosmos and roses and nasturtiums, all in riotous bloom.

"Can this be my room?"

"It's a *porch*," he says, but of course she must have it if she wants.

After he brings in the luggage, he removes the keyboard from its case, takes it into Chloe's porch, and sets it up while his daughter watches from her bed. When he's finished, he brings a kitchen chair in and places it in front of the keyboard. Then he turns on the machine, sits down, and plays, by memory, one of the easier Chopin preludes. Amazing how easily it's come back to him. A couple of months on Rory's piano, and his musical muscles are almost back to where they were before his mother left.

When he's finished, he turns around. Chloe is pulling clothes from her suitcase and placing them, neatly folded, in the blanket chest. Had she even noticed his playing? Was she still upset about not having a piano? Perhaps the keyboard was a mistake; he probably could have bought an old upright, second-hand, for next to nothing somewhere near here.

But later, when he's in the kitchen heating the microwave dinners he'd stuck into the cooler to tide them over until he was able to go shopping, he hears a few tentative notes being plunked out.

The next day they explore the town. At lunchtime they share a pizza at a local shop and, afterward, go for ice cream at the mom-and-pop place that advertises a hundred flavors. Chloe chooses bacon, which she gags on, and then requests that Brian buy her another cone, but vanilla this time.

She wants to check out every gift shop in town, and there are a lot. Brian is happy to go along with whatever she wants, standing by the entrance of one kitschy place after the other as his daughter inspects every single embroidered cushion, every piece of cheap silver jewelry, every ceramic vase. For the moment, she seems to have forgotten the friends she thought she'd miss. That night they eat late—later even than her usual bedtime—grilling their meal on the hibachi beside the garage.

Early Monday morning, before it's completely light, Brian hears a noise. He gets out of bed and goes down the hall. Chloe is sitting cross-legged on her bed, fully clothed.

"I want to go home," she says when she sees him. Tears stream down her cheeks. "I don't want to go to camp."

Taking a seat beside her, he puts his arm around her and says, "I know it's hard, going into a new situation. But I bet a lot of the girls at camp don't know each other either. They'll be nervous, just like you! If you promise to try it, if you go for just this one day, sweetheart, I promise that you won't have to go back."

He hands her a tissue. When she's wiped her eyes and blown her nose, she says, in a small voice, "Okay."

"Okay? Did I hear that right?" He's making a joke.

"I *said* okay."

The camp is situated a half mile up the lake. Not the resort side, and Brian is glad of it. He's not superstitious, but he doesn't want his daughter anywhere near the place. The brick building that houses the camp is large and modern, with a lobby, a changing room, a small gym, and a lunchroom. Inside, a young woman greets them, introducing herself as Saskia. She points them to the registration desk, where another young woman hands Brian a sheet of paper.

When's he finished filling it out, he turns around. Chloe is standing stiffly beside the door. Noticing this, Saskia grabs a red T-shirt off the top of a stack and, taking Chloe's hand says, "And now the fun begins, Chloe! Here's a camp shirt. You can put it on over your own shirt. Then come with me and I'll introduce you to the other girls."

Chloe slowly pulls the shirt over her head and follows Saskia out of the building. The door swings shut behind her.

Brian goes back to the car, but instead of leaving right away, he sits behind the wheel and waits. What if she's crying? What if she comes looking for him and he's not there? He gets back out and walks around the side of the building. On the dock beside the water are ten or twelve girls in red T-shirts, talking furiously to one another and laughing. It takes him a moment to identify Chloe. She's saying something to two girls, and when she's done, the three of them dissolve into laughter.

He returns to the house. He washes the breakfast dishes, then goes into his room and stands in front of the full-length mirror.

He's gray at the temples, his hair a little too long to be deemed fashionable. He's a slightly overweight middle-aged man, and his beard and mustache do little to hide that fact.

It's time.

He lets himself out of the house and locks the door. Then he drives out to Armstrong Road. When he reaches his mother's house, he pulls over. Her car is gone. The little patch of lawn in the front is mown, the path to the vestibule neatly trimmed. On one side of the house is a small vegetable garden. She's planted red and yellow pansies in her flower boxes.

Perhaps she's shopping, or gone away. But the state of her garden—with its squash hills, divided rows of lettuce, and neatly tied pole beans—suggests that she hasn't gone on a lengthy trip. Why plant a garden if you aren't going to be around to weed or enjoy it?

He waits half an hour, then decides he'll return early the next day after he's dropped Chloe off. It's almost a relief to leave, to buy himself another day of tranquility he's sure won't last after he comes face to face with the woman who is his mother.

Back at the house he has a quick lunch, then lies down on his bed and falls asleep. When he wakes, it's nearly three, half an hour before he has to pick up Chloe. He goes into her room. On the shelf over her bed she's placed the books she's brought with her and, beside them, a acrylic box for her favorite necklaces, a diary with a tiny brass key dangling from a blue ribbon, and a selection of sheet music.

He thumbs through. There's Chopin, Tchaikovsky,

Beethoven, and that book of Bach suites she's working on. There's Debussy's *Children's Corner,* which, despite its name, isn't the least bit easy. There's Schubert's first Impromptu; he used to play that, but he can't imagine he'd be up to it anymore. Maybe he'll try it this summer. He takes a seat by the keyboard and sounds out the first few measures. Before he knows it, the half hour has passed.

When he pulls up to the camp, he notices his daughter standing beside a parked van, talking through the window to a girl who's seated beside a woman who is probably her mother. When Chloe sees Brian, she calls out, "I'll be there in a sec!"

After the van has driven off, Chloe slides in beside him and says, "That was Violet. Can she come over on Saturday? Can she, Dad? Can she?"

After dropping Chloe off the next morning, he drives straight to Olivia's. When he rounds the corner, he sees a car is parked in the driveway. He slows to a crawl. When he's just past the house, he glances over at the garden and there she is, bent over her plants.

She doesn't look up, and he takes the opportunity to observe her without her knowing. Her hair is done in a white braid that hangs to the middle of her back. She's wearing faded jeans, just like a teenager's, and a sleeveless plaid shirt. Every few moments she raises a hand to wipe the sweat from her brow.

He gets out of the car.

At the sound of the door, she turns and lifts her hand above her forehead to block out the sun as she observes him.

"Hello?"

He crosses the road. When he's a few feet away, he registers her pale, unmade-up face, her deeply grooved forehead. Although he can't exactly claim recognition, there's something about the erect way she holds herself, with her shoulders straight back, that seems familiar. The expression on her face is watchful as she waits for him to speak.

His mother.

"Hi," he responds, aiming for a casual tone. "I hope I'm not disturbing you."

"And I know you from—?" she says, but without making it sound rude.

He takes a deep breath. "I'm just sort of…passing through."

The corners of her mouth are turned down. Is she willing him to get back in his car and drive away but too polite to say so?

"Actually, I'm looking for work," he says finally and then kicks himself for saying it. That wasn't the plan. The plan was for him to introduce himself—but it somehow doesn't seem quite the right moment. If he goes too fast it might scare her off. The whole thing could backfire; he can see that now, just looking at her face. She appears slightly fragile. He clears his throat. He'll give himself time. He'll give them both time.

She raises her eyebrows but doesn't respond.

He shrugs, and, saying "Sorry," he turns to go. He's officially out of courage. He'll come back again. Soon.

But then he hears her voice—and recognizes it. It's as clear as a girl's. "What's your name?"

He turns back and, naming one of his coworkers, says, "Alex. Alex Washburn."

"Can you paint?" she asks, nodding toward the house.

They arrange for him to come the following Wednesday, when she will have purchased the primer and top coat. "I'll leave it to you to pick up the rollers and brushes," she says.

They're still standing in the garden. Looking around, he sees the tomatoes she's staked with strips of gray cloth. The lettuces, red and green ones, bursting from the soil. The asparagus, already bolted. The lines of marigolds planted, like soldiers, between each row to deter the pests.

"I can't keep up with it all," she says. "It's just me here. Help me out—take one." She stoops and twists a head of red romaine from its stem.

"I pay cash," she says, handing him the lettuce and walking him to his car. "I presume you're all right with that?" She sets a price. Brian nods.

"Well then, Alex." She holds out her hand.

He switches the lettuce to his other hand and takes hers. It's small and dry. There's earth beneath her fingernails. After they shake, she turns back to her plants.

On the way home he remembers the expression on her face

when his father came in the door after work, how she would pour them both a glass of wine and they would then shut themselves in the study while he and his brothers played upstairs. He remembers how she used to play the piano after they were in bed. Even though she wasn't fond of Broadway tunes, she played them for Harry, who liked to sing along.

When he was little, he used to believe that as long as he kept his eyes shut, as long as he remained in that dark, private place, time wouldn't pass. The world wouldn't change and he was safe. Then when she left, he knew how wrong he'd been, and he felt betrayed. He still does. But seeing her today—her black hair gone white, her slight figure, the lines around her eyes and mouth, *her elderliness*—it occurs to him how young she'd been when she left. Just a girl, really, a girl with demons of her own, demons she wasn't strong enough to face.

He knows all about that.

nineteen

2002

He's never painted a thing in his life, Olivia thinks, watching him through the window as he struggles with the lid on a can of primer. He pulls something from his pocket and uses whatever it is to pry the lid off, but that doesn't work either. Finally, he gives up, and for a moment she loses sight of him as he walks to her back door.

This is his first day. She actually surprised herself the other day by giving the job to a stranger, but there was something about the man that made her want to help. He had a way about him that seemed, somehow—*lost,* that was the word. A victim of lost causes. Which is something she can certainly understand.

She reaches in the drawer for a screwdriver. Meeting him at the door, she holds it out. "Are you looking for this?"

He flushes and she's sorry. She's embarrassed him. But he's a puzzle. His beard and mustache may be out of control, but he's wearing a clean brown T-shirt and a pair of khaki pants—hardly painting clothes. Also, he speaks in an educated voice. His car is well maintained, and it has New York plates, so she knows he's not local. He appears to be in his forties, yet here he is, in rural Vermont, roaming the countryside, looking for work from strangers.

What could have brought him to this, whatever *this* is? Hard times, probably. A lot of people move to Vermont when they've fallen on hard times. It's cheap, and employment is readily available if you're willing to work hard. The hippies knew this, but most of them have gone now, back to their cities and the jobs they were destined to take, before they veered briefly and unsuccessfully off course.

She'd like to know his background, but she won't ask him; she'll let him have his secrets. If there is one thing she understands, it's allowing people their secrets.

Anyway, he's not her problem. She will bring him iced tea in a little while and maybe offer him something at noon. There's egg salad from yesterday in the fridge.

A few hours later she brings out a tray of sandwiches. It's hot, hotter than usual for a late-June afternoon in the Green Mountains. He's standing on the second-to-top rung of a ladder, with a paintbrush in one hand and a can of primer on the rung above. Just looking up at him makes her dizzy. For a moment she stands there foolishly, not wanting to call to him for fear he'll startle and fall, but unwilling to go back inside with the sandwiches. Thankfully he notices her below with her tray, and seconds later he's back on the ground.

"I thought you might like these."

"Thanks, but I brought my lunch. It's in the car." He nods across the road at his Subaru.

"They'll go to waste," she says briefly and, leaving the tray on the grass, turns back to the house.

"Did you make some for yourself?" he calls after her, but she pretends she hasn't heard him. It's enough that she's brought him something. There's no need for them to socialize.

When she goes back out for the tray, he's pouring turpentine over a rag. He looks up and says, "Have you lived here a long time?"

"Long enough," she says shortly, noticing that despite the lunch he'd allegedly brought, there are only crumbs left on her tray.

When she checks later, he's gone.

For the next couple of days the scene is repeated. Olivia brings him a drink in the middle of the morning and sandwiches at noon. She never sits with him, purposely providing only the one folding chair for him to sit on while he eats.

The following Monday morning she looks out to see his car pull up. He's early. She's surprised he's come at all. The western sky is black, and severe storms are forecast for the area. Nonetheless, she hears the ladder jingle as it's propped up on the side of the house, and for a while the only sound she notices is when he descends it to replenish the paint.

Mid-morning, as she's pouring his coffee, she hears a dull rumble. A few moments pass, and then the sky opens up. A deluge. She looks out to see Alex hurriedly descending the ladder, the can of paint in his hand.

She opens the back door and shouts, "Inside! Quick!" And a moment later he's standing in the kitchen dripping water onto the floor.

"Sorry," he says.

She fetches a towel. As he's drying his head, there's a streak of lightning and an almost simultaneous crack of thunder. The overhead light flickers and goes out.

"Here," she says, handing him his mug of coffee. "That'll be it for you today, I think. And just when you were about to start the top coat. These storms are supposed to keep up, off and on, for the next couple of days."

He hands her back the towel, and she says, surprising herself, "Why don't you sit down, until the worst is over?" She leads him to the opposite corner of the room and, taking a seat on the sofa, indicates the armchair opposite.

"Don't you have to call somebody about the electricity?" he asks.

"That never does any good. I learned that long ago. It could take a day, or a couple of weeks. There's no way of knowing." She glances out the window. The rain is still driving, but it's slowing down. "This isn't New York." There, she's given him the bait to explain who he is.

He doesn't take her up on it. Instead he drains his mug and nods at the piano. "Do you play?"

"I used to. I give lessons. So, yes. I play."

"So do you teach?"

He seems surprised. Does he think that because she lives by herself on this lonely road, she must be a country bumpkin?

"Yes, children. I teach children." *Okay, Alex. You've had your drink.*

He must sense this, because he gets to his feet. "Thank you for the coffee. And the towel."

He says it like a schoolboy at the end of a birthday party, whose mother, before dropping him off, had overzealously coached him on the correct behavior. Olivia has rarely met anyone so socially awkward. Not that she's any great conversationalist herself.

As he follows her into the kitchen, he says, "I have a little girl."

"Do you?"

"She plays piano, too. She's only eight, and she plays really well."

"Really?" A surprising number of parents think their child is a musical genius. Very few actually are.

"She's with me now, for the summer. She goes to day camp."

"Ah. That girls' camp on the lake, just outside of town?"

He nods. "I brought a keyboard with us. She's not crazy about it, but she's playing it. Do you think maybe you could give her a few lessons while we're here, to sort of keep her hand in?"

She reaches for the door. "I'm sorry," she says. "I don't teach during the summer."

He continues, as if he hasn't heard, "She been practicing the Fourth Suite."

If she were a comic book character, Olivia's mouth would have dropped open. "Bach?" she asks, startled, obviously surprised that an eight-year-old would even think of attempting the Fourth. She wonders whether there's a version of it that was created expressly for children. If there is, she's never heard of it. "His Fourth *French* Suite?"

Brian nods. "Well, the Allemande, anyway. To start with."

"Well…I might be willing to give your little girl a lesson or two."

They agree on Saturday. He'll bring her by, then do a little shopping before he returns for her.

"What do you charge?" he asks before he goes.

She considers for a moment, then says, "Never mind that. We'll do a trade. An hour of painting for an hour's lesson. How does that sound?"

He's walking down the path when she remembers and calls out to him, "What's your daughter's name?"

"Chloe," he says, reaching for the car door. "Her name is Chloe."

twenty

2002

It's threatening rain, but she never minds about the weather. Mostly she walks just before dinner, but today, because Alex is bringing his daughter for her lesson, Olivia decides to go earlier. Grabbing an umbrella, she lets herself out the door and sets off as she usually does—walking, walking—faster and faster.

I have three children, she says out loud. *Three children.* She repeats the phrase over and over, the beat taken up by her feet pounding the hard earth—one, two, three. The woods are silent, as they often are on hot summer afternoons. All she can hear are her footsteps and the murmur of waves lapping against the rocky shore. She rounds one bend, then another until the path narrows and she reaches *the* bend, where she stops, gazing across the lake to the resort on the opposite shore. Today there's no one in sight.

The rumble of thunder that began when she left home is getting louder. A bird along the shoreline gives a plaintive cry. Olivia doesn't linger; she never stays long. It's enough that she comes every day, as she has for years. It's enough. After a final look at the deserted dock, the motionless trees and dark water, she turns back.

At home she pours herself a glass of water and takes it across to the cemetery behind the church next door. When she reaches the marker of the seven Ward children, she sets her glass on the grass and sits with her back against the stone, watching as bolts of lightning streak the sky. It begins to rain.

Sometimes when she sits here, Olivia thinks that Mary Ward was the luckier woman. She lies over by the fence, carried away seventeen months after burying the last of her children. The insertion of a mosquito's proboscis into her flesh had taken her. "Ague," her stone reads. And beneath that: "She delighted in the Lord."

Here in the graveyard, Mary's children are more real to Olivia than her own three. It seems that proximity is everything. She can almost see Mabel, in her white lawn dress, playing with a lump of dough while her mother rolls out a pie crust. She can hear the twins, John and Ezra, as they careen down a snow-covered embankment, shrieking as their sled picks up momentum until it's virtually flying through the thin, cold air. And she can imagine, in their turn, Frances and Tom and Matthew and baby Nancy, scattering chicken feed in the pen beside the barn or, after a hot summer's day, dancing barefoot in the rain.

Occasionally in the night she's awakened by a giggle, or a scream, or by someone calling out *Mommy*. It used to distress her. Now she just smiles. She doesn't know whether it's Brian or

Andrew or Rory, or one of the Wards. Perhaps it is none of them. Perhaps it's some other child—a lost child or a former child. A present child or a future one.

Because the call is never repeated, she believes that the child, whoever it is, has found its way home. Or she assumes that it has. There's no proof, one way or another.

The lightning flashes again, and the spatter becomes a deluge. *I have three children,* Olivia says as she walks back to the house through the pouring rain.

They're late—it's nearly five o'clock. It could be because of the storm, but perhaps he's just forgotten.

She stands beside the front window, where she can see Alex's car if he comes. Why in the world had she agreed so readily to teach his child? She has been asking herself that question all week. She'd been looking forward to a much-needed break, and here some stranger arrives and she finds herself succumbing to his demands at the drop of a hat.

But truthfully, she's intrigued. Any child who can actually play the Fourth deserves to have all the summer lessons she wants. It's for that reason Olivia's stationed herself by the window. She's eager to meet this child. She wants to hear her play.

Not to overlook the fact that there is something about her father.

A few days before, after he left her kitchen during that first violent thunderstorm, she removed the towel—his towel—from the back of the chair where she'd draped it and ran her fingers over its nap. Although it was already dry, it still bore the smell she had noticed as he passed her in the doorway—the turpentine he'd been using to clean his paintbrushes, and the paint itself. But there was another smell she couldn't put her finger on that reminded her of the time—could it really have been thirty-five years ago?—when she and Brian went on a picnic, all by themselves.

When they were finishing their lunch it began to rain, and as they scurried for their plates and cups and the shower became a torrent, Brian had thrown himself in his mother's lap and wrapped his arms around her neck. And as she carried him to the car, she smelled it: a combination of the wet wool of his sweater, the orange drink he'd just had, and something else she couldn't quite put her finger on but what she'd always thought of as his little boy smell.

"This is Chloe," Alex says. They're standing in the kitchen after their mad dash to the house. "I'll be back in an hour, sweetheart." He turns and goes back out to his car.

The child is small, Olivia notes. Small even for eight. And she looks nervous, standing there clutching a stack of sheet music to her chest and looking warily around the room.

To put her at ease, Olivia keeps up a steady flow of talk. She asks the girl whether she'd prefer a stool or a bench ("A bench, please" is the faint response), and when they are seated on it side by side, she asks to see the music Chloe is holding.

There are some Chopin waltzes and a piece by Debussy that Olivia can't imagine a child of her age even attempting, no matter how talented she is. But then she sees the book of French suites, *not* a child's version after all, and knowing that Chloe is working on the Fourth, asks her to start at the beginning.

"I'm just learning. I can play the Sixth, though."

"Why don't we start with the Sixth then, and after that we'll move on to the Fourth."

She's a pretty child, slight, with pale skin and a nose dusted lightly with freckles. Her face is a perfect oval, with a small pointed chin. Her straight black hair is tied back with a ribbon, and her eyes are dark blue, almost turquoise—which with her pale skin, Olivia recalls being told as a child, is an Irish combination.

As she plays, she keeps her mouth slightly open. Olivia can remember doing just that as a child and being told that she looked stupid. "Close your mouth," her teacher would say, placing his fist under her jaw and pushing upward with a bang, so that her tongue would be caught between her teeth.

At the end of the piece, Olivia says, simply, "That was perfect."

The child is quiet.

"But the Fourth. Do you want me to play it, to show you how it goes?"

"I know how it goes. My father played the top line for me last night."

Strange. When they were talking about the piano, he never

mentioned that *he* played. She turns some pages. "Play the first few bars to—here." She points.

Chloe's back is straight, her elbows slightly elevated as she lifts her hands to the keys. Olivia notices that her fingers are long and slender, and—oh, how strange—her left pinky finger is crooked at the first joint. Just like Olivia's and Olivia's mother's.

She swallows, then breathes once, twice, three times, to keep from exclaiming.

When the girl has reached the end of the second line, Olivia interrupts. "What happened to your pinky finger, Chloe?"

The girl stops playing and raises her finger in the air. "It's always been like that," she says. "I was born with it like that." She turns back to the music and repeats the sequence. "I can't—" she says, still playing.

"Slowly, slowly. No need to race; you're just learning."

"It says here—"

"Don't worry about that trill yet. That's right, it's an A-flat. Although I don't know why they saw fit to note it. It's not like it isn't in the key signature."

The lesson proceeds. When it's nearly time for Alex to come back, Olivia places her fingers on Chloe's hands and says that now *she* is going to play something. Perhaps it's something that Chloe has heard it before?

Chloe stands so Olivia can take her place. From memory Olivia plays, very slowly, the first few bars of "Doctor Gradus ad Parnassum." After a few measures she stops and says, "Do you recognize it?"

"I can play it, but I play it slower," the child says. "My daddy plays it, too."

Breathe, Olivia tells herself. Through the window she can hear the call of a mourning dove, signaling the end of the rain. She used to think they were called morning doves, until someone told her it was their plaintive call—cooooo, cooooo—that gave the birds their name. Whenever Olivia hears it, she feels sad.

"Where does your daddy come from?" she asks.

"He lives in New York. But he grew up in New Jersey."

"And what does he do?"

"He sells people houses. And apartments."

"Where?"

"In New York City."

"What's his name?" she asks in a light, matter-of-fact voice, fearing she may have taken it too far.

The child looks up at her. "*You* know that!" she says. "It's Brian!"

"Of course." She falls silent as the child taps her fingers lightly on the keys. Tap, tap. Tap, tap, tap.

She can't stop now, even if she wants to. "Do you have any aunts or uncles, Chloe?"

"I have an uncle."

"What's his name?"

"Uncle Rory. He's a doctor in a hospital. And I have a cousin. Her name is Tess. She's only little. She's almost four. When I'm twelve, I'll get to babysit her."

Andrew. Somewhere, deep inside, she's always known it. She's tried to call him to mind so many times, tried to imagine what he might look like now, as an adult, but she's never been able to do it. Somehow he's always been frozen in place, as she remembered him that day at the lake.

She slides off the bench and says, "Let me hear you do the Sixth again." And after Chloe has taken her place, Olivia sits quietly, her hands in her lap, listening as the child performs her magic. She's heard child prodigies before and has always felt that their technical ability exceeded their ability to express. That comes later in life, she has always assumed. Until now.

A car draws up the driveway, and there's a honk.

Leaving Chloe at the piano, she goes to the window. A man is at the wheel of the car. The man who's been painting her house. The man who told her proudly that his child was talented. The man who, in their very short acquaintance, has seemed to her to be troubled, or lonely—or both. She watches him now as he gets out of the car. His hair is graying. He's wearing a blue shirt.

He's always worn a blue shirt.

Chloe finishes the piece and, joining Olivia at the window, sees her father coming up the path. She opens the door and runs to greet him. Olivia can hear her laughter as he picks her up. Then he opens the car door, places her on the seat, and for a moment, as he bends to fasten her seat belt, he moves out of Olivia's line of vision.

Then he closes the door and, looking up at the house, sees her watching him. He stoops to say something to Chloe, and before Olivia can turn away, their eyes meet. Ten, twenty seconds pass, while neither of them pulls away, and then he's coming back up the path.

Olivia closes her eyes, the way she did as a child on her birthday when the candlelit cake was brought to the table. After a moment her mother would say, *Open your eyes, Liv,* and there it would be, with her name emblazoned in blue—her favorite color—across its top.

Open your eyes, Liv. She can almost hear her mother's voice, as if it's not a memory but something happening right here, right now—along with the voices of the others, past and present. Harry's deep voice, never raised but a little impatient, urging her to hurry, they'll be late; Rory's voice, wailing for his bear; Andrew, now forever four, calling for her in the night; and then, joining in, Chloe, as she talks about her uncle and her little cousin, Tess.

And now, Brian, his voice so tentative she can barely hear it as he opens the door.

"Hello?"

Olivia opens her eyes.

reading group guide

1. How would you have reacted to Eleanor's gift of a famous, expensive painting? Would you be offended by the gesture or appreciate your mother's willingness to offer you a "ticket out"?

2. Olivia was on a solo hike, enjoying a rare moment of alone time, when her son drowned. If you were in her shoes, would you feel guilty or responsible for what happened to your child?

3. How would you react to the news of your child's death if you were in Olivia's situation? Would you be tempted to run from the truth and never turn back?

4. Do you sympathize with Olivia's choice to run, or do you condemn her for leaving?

5. Do you think that if Olivia's grief eventually led her to return home, she would be welcomed by her family?

6. Harry never seemed to be angry at Olivia for leaving. Instead, he quietly mourned her absence. How do you think you would feel in his situation?

7. Why couldn't Toni's maternal presence fill the void left in Brian's life? What does the concept of "abandoned child syndrome" look like in both Brian and Rory?

8. Why do you think Olivia chose to live so close to the resort where her son drowned? What was the significance of her proximity to the lake?

9. The Ward family held special significance for Olivia. After living near their graves for so long, she reflected that "Mary's children are more real to Olivia than her own three. It seems that proximity is everything." What do you think she meant by this?

10. What motivated Brian to find his mother? What do you think the turning point was?

11. What was the significance of Debussy's *Children's Corner*, and what meaning did it hold for Olivia, Brian, and Chloe?

12. What do you think the future holds for Olivia's relationship with Brian and Rory? Do you think they will grow together as a happy family, or are the wounds too deep to heal?

a conversation with the author

What inspired you to write *The Ones We Keep*?

The starting point for *The Ones We Keep* was a solo walk that I took at a resort. I was staying there with my husband and (then young) four sons, and on the way back from the walk, I thought: What if someone told me that one of my sons had died but not which one? I decided that I would be tempted to run. If I didn't know which child had died, it would have been my way of keeping all of them alive.

Many years later, I turned the idea—the walk, the death, and Olivia's flight—into a short story. I had by then published other stories, but this one stalled and had no takers, in part because it was already too long. The story ended up in a drawer. Looking at it again many years later, I realized that the more interesting aspect of the story was the unknown life that followed Olivia's flight. So, what began as an unpublished short story grew into a novel.

Olivia makes an impossible decision when faced with the death of her child. How do you hope readers will react to her choice?

Some readers challenged me in earlier drafts by suggesting that no mother would abandon her surviving children in the way that Olivia did. So I kept re-drawing Olivia's character to try to make her actions at least understandable in the context of who she is and who she becomes after the tragedy.

I think a novel has to challenge readers to understand characters who may be, in some sense, odd. I wanted readers to understand this woman, whose whole life is essentially a tragedy.

The characters in your book go through some truly emotional and sometimes traumatic situations. Did you find these scenes difficult to write?

Not at all. I found them fun to write! I was just super glad that what was happening to them wasn't happening to me.

Music plays an important role in this story. Are you a musician?

All the pieces of music Brian and Olivia and Chloe play in the novel are pieces I've played and loved. I started the piano at the age of five. Until I was fourteen, my dream was to become a concert pianist, but then I had an accident that severed a tendon in my left hand. The surgeon wasn't able to connect it back to the tip of my forefinger, which I was never again able to curve. I was devastated. I mean, for starters, forget all of Bach.

But I still played. Later in life, I learned the organ. I remember vividly the day when some part of my brain opened for the first time, allowing me to play that third, extra line of notes with my feet that the piano lacks. I played professionally in churches, in funeral homes, and for weddings. I don't play piano or organ often these days, although I still feel there's music in my future. I keep the pieces I'd like to learn stacked up on my piano. However, these days, writing tempts me more than music. It seems I am only able to practice one art form at a time.

What's the most important thing you hope readers take away from your book?

That my first novel was published when I was 76!

What does your writing process look like?

My process has evolved over time. I have another novel ready to go, and the way I wrote it differed from my approach to *The Ones We Keep*. In my current writing, I, of course, have a basic plot, but I now plan out each chapter as a series of scenes. I sit in my armchair with my notebook, asking myself what I want to accomplish in each scene. I then make notes (for example, my character thinks her mother doesn't love her anymore, and she decides to run away from home). When I rough out the scene's mini plot points, I take the notebook to my laptop and start. After I've finished each scene, I edit. I'm painstaking: I examine every word—is it the right one? Does the scene flow? Does it get me where I want to go? Sometimes in bed at night, I'll re-read what I've written that day on my phone, and because there are so few words on the screen, I feel I'm better able to spot when a paragraph or word is not quite right and should be replaced with something better—or expunged.

When you aren't writing, how do you like to spend your time?

I read, of course, and I listen to or watch far too much news. I volunteered as a patient advocate when I lived in Canada, and I'm still fascinated with the field of medicine and spend quite a lot of time reading about new medicines, studies, clinical trials, etc.

I have four sons and four wonderful daughters-in-law and numerous grandchildren (also wonderful, btw) who live nearby, and I spend quite a lot of time with them, especially on weekends.

acknowledgments

I would like to thank the following people:

My brother-in-law Alex Huff, who, when I asked him for his account of 9/11, wrote a profoundly moving piece about that awful event, which he watched, in terror, through the window of his New York office.

Blanca del Castillo and her colleagues in the curatorial department of the Frick museum, for kindly sharing with me the normal acquisition process for works of art.

Rick Crootof, now-retired ob/gyn, who, after vetting some scenes, told me how they *really* would have gone down.

Stacey Miller-Smith, daughter-in-law and doctor extraordinaire, who told me the story of the male body part removed from the corpse in her first-year anatomy course. (For fear of implicating someone, I won't mention exactly which body part it was.)

My sister Jessica Huff, who acquainted me with the habits and practices of the inhabitants of certain New York State towns.

Dr. Joseph Rochford, who explained to me the ins and outs of PTSD and guilt and abandoned child syndrome.

The Pennington New Jersey Police Department for providing me with information about past missing-person procedures.

The Literary Consultancy in the UK: Aki Schilz, Joe Sedgewick, and, especially, incredible editor Anna South, whose enthusiasm for my writing made me persevere at times when I was almost ready to give up.

Diane Schoemperlen, novelist and short story writer, who was the first person to read the novel and, even though it was barely out of the cradle, was an indomitable cheerleader.

Editor Allyson Latta, who taught me all kinds of techniques and tricks I never would have thought of (such as: You don't have to keep repeating *He says, She says*. Your readers will get the picture!). But also, it was Allyson who taught me the meaning of the phrase *Save the cat*. I hope I've successfully saved it!

My agent, Natanya Wheeler, for her wonderful advice and support and perseverance, not to mention her willingness to take a chance on an "older" newbie novelist.

Kate Roddy at Sourcebooks, who possesses The Eye.

My early readers for their patience and enthusiasm: Linda Crootof (my first bestie), Ellen Goodman, Mary Elizabeth James, Jim Higginson, Lynn Nimmo. I'm sure there were others I've missed, and for that I apologize.

Story Huff-Miller, my niece, who, whenever I had a question about whether something or other worked, always responded instantly and wisely.

My brother Cameron Huff, who must have been bored by the time I sent him the tenth draft but would never admit it—and was unfailing in his honesty.

David Allen, without whose life-improving time-management techniques I might have begun the book, but I'm certain I wouldn't have finished it.

I would also like to thank my children, Jesse, Abel, Zachary, and Tobias, for their willingness to always listen (now that they're adults, that is) and for their sick jokes, especially the constant repetition of the question Stewie in *Family Guy* poses to Brian ("Still working on that little novel?")—not to mention their remarks about the potentially posthumous publication of this book.

Most of all, the hugest thank-you to Tony Smith, my amazing husband and hero, who never failed to cry by the time he reached—for the hundredth time—the last page of the novel. This is for you.

credits

Quote on page 201: "The Spacious Firmament on High," by Joseph Addison, first published in *The Spectator* in 1712.

Quote on page 209: L.P. Hartley, from *The Go-Between*, published in the UK in 1953.

Quote on page 290: Philip Larkin, "This Be the Verse," from the 1974 collection *High Windows*.

about the author

Photo © Zach Smith

Bobbie Jean Huff is a Canadian American now living in the U.S. Her fiction, poetry, and essays have appeared in the Canadian journals *Quarry*, *Queen's Quarterly*, *Queen's Alumni Review*, *Room of One's Own*, *Event*, and in the *Globe and Mail*. One of her poems, published in the *New Ohio Review*, was nominated for the 2019 Pushcart Prize. An earlier version of this novel, titled *The Children's Corner*, was long-listed for the Faulkner Fiction Prize and short-listed for the Dzanc Prize for Fiction. She lives with her husband in Pennington, New Jersey.